M000311872

KERI ARTHUR

Wraith's Revenge

A LIZZIE GRACE NOVEL

Copyright © 2023 by Keri Arthur

Published by KA Publishing PTY LTD

All rights reserved.

No part of this book may be reproduced in any form or by any electronic or mechanical means, including information storage and retrieval systems, without written permission from the author, except for the use of brief quotations in a book review.

Cover Art by Lori Grundy from Cover Reveal Designs

All characters and events in this book are fictitious. Any resemblance to real people, alive or dead, is entirely coincidental.

ISBN: 978-0-6453031-7-9

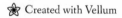 Created with Vellum

With thanks to:

The Lulus
Skyla / Indigo Chick Designs
Hot Tree Editing
Debbie from DP+
Robyn E.
The lovely ladies from Indie Gals
Lori Grundy / Cover Reveal Designs for the amazing cover

CHAPTER ONE

I leaned back and stared at the four men sitting on the opposite side of the table. They were all tall and thin, with silver eyes and the crimson hair of royal witches.

They all wore the same type of expensive-looking suit—though three were in gray and one in blue—and the same holier-than-thou expression that graced the faces of so many royal witches up here in Canberra when confronted by someone they considered below their station.

In my case, *far* below.

That they wanted to be anywhere but here was obvious —and something I could totally understand. I mean, I *did* have bigger problems in my life right now—a relationship with an ornery werewolf hanging in the balance, a court case against my father to testify at, and a reevaluation of my magical powers to attend, the result of which could cause me major fucking problems with the High Witch Council.

But here we were, staring at each other across the vast sea of polished wood in a room that wasn't only sound-proofed but also warded against magic.

The latter was definitely a good thing.

1

I didn't want them attempting to spell me, because that might lead to a reaction from my inner wild magic and more questions than I wanted to answer right now.

The only reason we were here in the first place was their refusal to accept Clayton Marlowe's will. To say they were seriously annoyed by the fact that I'd inherited a good portion of his estate would be the understatement of the year. It was also understandable, given said estate was worth tens of millions and that was just the property portfolio.

Of course, it was never meant to come to me. At *all*. My father, who'd magically forced me into the marriage with Clayton when I was below the legal age, had always intended the so-called "bride price" inheritance to be transferred to him. Then I'd gone and upset everything by not only running away on my wedding night but basically disappearing for well over ten years, sending Clayton into a destabilized mental state and ensuring my father never got his hands on the estate he'd always coveted.

An estate he *still* coveted.

Problem was, he'd done too good a job of tying down the will's legalities, and there was nothing he or anyone in this room could now do to stop me inheriting. Not without challenging the will in court.

"Ms. Grace," Ryland said, in a tone that managed to be both condescending and pitying. He was the oldest of Clayton's two brothers and the one that looked the least like him. "Surely you must understand that if this goes to court, you *will* lose. One hundred thousand is more than enough compensation—"

"In what century?" I cut in coldly. "I was on the fucking run for ten years—"

"It's hardly the fault of anyone in this room that

wedding night jitters got the better of you," another man said. Francis, a cousin, if I remembered right.

I met his gaze evenly. "You just added another million to the end cost."

"Don't be fucking—"

"Francis, quiet," Ryland snapped, then gave me what I presumed was supposed to be a soothing smile but instead looked predatory.

But that was okay. After all the goddamn supernatural entities I'd fought over the last year, a human predator was something of a welcome relief.

"We'll double the offer," he continued. "It is more than fair given the marriage was recently annulled and there was no son produced, as stipulated—"

"Actually," my lawyer cut in smoothly, "the require-ment of a son was not tied to Ms. Grace's inheritance on Mr. Marlowe's death but rather the bride price. It was a bonus to be paid to her father, Mr. Lawrence Marlowe, if a male child was produced."

Because we daughters were *not* valued at *all* in the Marlowe world. Or, at least, unpowered daughters like me weren't.

Of course, my father's attitude had done something of a backflip recently after discovering my ability to manipulate wild magic. Royal witches had been attempting to control it for eons, simply because the wild magic—and the well-springs it formed—were a source of untapped but poten-tially unimaginable power.

But it was a power that called as easily to darkness as to the light, and if left unprotected, could cause great harm to the people and areas around the wellsprings.

It was Mom's attempts to protect one such wellspring that had formed my connection to the wild magic. I'd been little more than a bean in her stomach, and the force that had almost killed her had fused to my DNA, forever changing me.

Not that anyone had been aware of this until Belle—my best friend and familiar—and I had set up a café in the Faelan Werewolf Reservation and subsequently come into contact with an unprotected and very old wellspring.

My link with it was now so strong I could feel its furious pulsing even though I was hundreds of kilometers away. It felt like all I had to do was metaphysically reach out, and it would answer.

Which was ridiculous, of course. While all wellsprings came from the same source deep within the earth's outer core and *were* theoretically linked, there were no wellsprings within Canberra itself and therefore no means for it to answer.

"That does not discount the fact that two hundred thousand is a very reasonable offer in these circumstances," Ryland commented.

"In these circumstances?" I echoed. Anthony Fitzgerald —my lawyer—placed a warning hand on my arm, but I shook it off. "And what circumstances would you be talking about? The magical manipulation of a minor? The attempted rape of a minor? The kidnapping and torture of my familiar? Threats to kill her if I didn't give your brother his conjugal rights and produce the heir my father promised him?"

Ryland had the grace to look uncomfortable. "Well, no, but Clayton did pay a high price for those deeds—"

"A price *you* had a hand in" came a soft comment.

I wasn't sure who said it and didn't really care. I slammed my palms on the table and thrust to my feet. "You know what? The price is five million for me, and another five for Belle. That is my one and only offer. If you don't like it, well then, I'll see you in court." I gave them a cold, hard smile. "Let's see how well your precious reputation holds up once the details of Clayton's actions are brought into the open."

I grabbed my coat from the back of the chair and marched out of the room, slamming the door behind me. As the sound echoed through the empty corridor, I stopped and pressed back against the wood paneling to the right of the door, closing my eyes and drawing in deep breaths to calm the anger and inner shaking.

It probably hadn't been a good idea to lose my temper like that, but fuck them. I was sick of people taking me for granted and looking down on me. Sick of being considered less than worthy just because I hadn't been born as magically strong as my brother or my long-dead sister.

In fact, it had been Catherine's death—and my father's need to get rid of the magically challenged daughter who'd had the audacity to survive what his precious heir apparent had not—that had led to the whole Clayton mess in the first place.

The fact that Cat might still be alive if they'd trusted the strength of my psi powers was a point they continued to ignore.

The door to my right opened, and Anthony stepped through. He was tall, blond haired, and blue eyed, with a mild manner that belied a razor-sharp mind. He worked for the Black Lantern Society—a privately funded organization whose charter was to right wrongs and bring justice to those who escaped it, by whatever means necessary—and was representing me in the court case against my father. He was assisting me here as a favor to Ira Ashworth, an investigator with the Regional Witch Association, and a man who'd become a grandfather to me in all ways except blood.

"Sorry," I said. "But those bastards—"

"Are rattled." Amusement danced around the corners of his pale eyes. "They're unused to a mere slip of a woman talking back to them."

I laughed, as he'd no doubt intended. "If they think I'm a 'mere slip,' they need their eyes checked."

"I was of course speaking in magical terms. They're unaware you're no longer the underpowered child you once were, and that plays to our advantage."

Anthony had been given full access to the reports compiled by the Black Lantern Society's auditors and truth seekers on the events surrounding my marriage to Clayton, but I'd also made him aware of my ability to manipulate wild magic. While that was something I'd much rather have kept secret, if things went bad for my father, he *would* use that juicy bit of news to his own advantage. The last thing I needed was for Anthony and the Society to be caught unawares, especially given they were representing me pro bono.

I pushed away from the wall and fell in step beside him. "Why would them uncovering my power boost make any difference to mediation?"

He cast me a wry look. "Have you been away so long that you've forgotten the importance of magical strength?"

"Well, no, but I can't see why it should make any difference in this matter."

He made an odd sort of sound in the back of his throat. "You're inheriting a good portion of Clayton's estate, and that currently ties you to them. Were they to uncover the truth about your magic, they might well make settlement conditional on the fulfilment of certain conditions in the marriage contract."

Though he didn't say it, I knew he was referring to the production of an heir. I stopped and stared at him in horror. "Surely a clause like *that* would be considered illegal."

"There are varying degrees of legal up here."

"Yes, but my father is being hauled in front of the High Witch Council for what basically amounts to coercion. Why would they risk a similar charge?"

He cast another amused glance over his shoulder but didn't stop moving toward the exit. "Clayton's line might currently be one of the lesser Marlowes here in Canberra, but don't for a moment think they're not working behind the scenes to rectify that matter."

"Well, yeah, because backstabbing and undermining everyone to gain even the smallest advantage is part of the game up here." I hurried after him. "But I can't see how they can make the payout conditional on the production of a child."

"They legally can't, but that won't stop an attempt to tie it to a payout. Remember, had you produced an heir, your share would have been greater."

"I don't need greater."

"They don't know that. Again, you have to remember the mindset of everyone up here—more is always better."

I snorted. "God, I'm so glad I escaped this place."

"You were lucky. Many aren't."

There was an edge in his voice that had me looking sharply his way. "Are you one of them?"

"No, because I did escape. I came back to represent those who can't." His brief but bright smile was delightfully wicked. "There is great joy to be found in being an under-powered and very definitely underrated Fitzgerald who

7

constantly sticks it to those who think they are above the law."

A smile tugged at my lips. "My father being chief amongst *that* lot."

"Indeed, but even he will have a reckoning. Whether it be this case or a future one remains to be seen."

"Knowing my father, it'll be sometime far, *far* in the future," I muttered. "He has too many friends in high places right now."

"Perhaps, but the mere fact charges have been laid and the high council is hearing evidence will deter other, less-connected families from basically selling off their underage children to the highest bidder."

"The mere fact it is illegal should be deterrent enough."

"Again, we both know legalities matter not to royal witches when there's money and power to be had. Besides, I personally believe your father will face a greater penalty than a metaphorical slap on the wrist. There are too many on the council who wish him taken down a peg or two, however temporary it might be."

One of the two guards up ahead keyed open the door for us. I pulled on my coat and waited until we were well past them before saying, "I guess we'll find out who's right tomorrow."

"There are as many for your father as against on the panel, and the adjudicator is neutral. We made sure of that."

I hoped he was right, but I had no doubt my father was beavering away behind the scenes to ensure an "appropriate" outcome.

But before I could make a comment, Anthony's phone rang. He pulled it out of his pocket and then grimaced. "Sorry, it's the office—I need to take this."

I nodded, well aware that he was juggling over a dozen cases at the moment. "I'll meet you at the car."

I kept walking. The mediation center was part of the new High Witch Council Complex, which was situated to one side of the Supreme Court, in what had once been a parking area. It overlooked both City Hill and the revamped grasslands situated within the looping off-ramp that swept from Commonwealth Avenue onto London Circuit. The fully fenced park could only be accessed from the complex itself, though I had no doubt there were locked gates at ground level, as the grass areas were pin neat. The gardens were a respite for all those who worked within the complex. Of course, that only meant witches who'd reached a certain level of authority and did not include humans or even any of the three lower-ranking witch families.

I came out of the building's shadow, and the wind whipped around me, holding the bite of winter despite the fact we were now into spring. I drew in a deeper breath but couldn't scent any rain, despite the foreboding darkness of the clouds.

I zipped up my jacket and shoved my hands into my pockets. But as I walked down the ramp that led down into the underground parking area, energy touched my skin, a gentle caress that was both electric and ethereal.

It wasn't magic. It wasn't even wild magic. It was something else.

I stopped and looked around, but there was no hint of anything untoward. No shimmer to suggest a ghostly presence, and certainly nothing to indicate some kind of supernatural creature had just slipped past. Nor was there anything tweaking my psi radar.

And yet... unease stirred.

I frowned and forced my feet on. I'd obviously become

so used to battling demonic and supernatural entities over the last year that I was now sensing their presence every-damn-where.

As I stepped off the ramp and entered the parking area, it happened again. This time, it definitely felt as if some-thing—some*one*—was tugging at my arm.

I shivered and reached for Belle. While telepathy wasn't one of my psi skill sets, there was a natural mind link between a witch and their familiar, and ours had deepened drastically since my connection to the old wellspring in the Faelan Reservation had formed. Of course, our ability to mind speak wasn't the only thing that was altering—there was a definite combining and strengthening in both of our talents.

But while I could now sense ghosts and the like, Belle was one of the strongest spirit talkers in Australia. If it *was* a ghost I was feeling, she'd be able to see what I currently couldn't.

How did the session with the dinosaurs go? she immedi-ately said.

You weren't following along?

No. I had a feeling the process would just enrage me, and I'm mad enough at the bastards. Did they offer the expected pittance?

Yes, they did. They also pissed me off, so I demanded they pay us five million each or I'd see the bastards in court.

She laughed, the sound like a warm summer breeze flowing through my mind. *Wish I could have seen their faces when you said that.*

According to Anthony, they were expecting a mouse.

And when the mouse roared, it blew their tiny little minds.

Apparently. I stormed out, so missed it all.

She laughed again. *Are you coming home now?*

Home in this case being the residence of Henrietta—or Hattie, as she preferred to be known—Marlowe. While she was no relation to me by blood or marriage, she was the middle sister—and a high-profile judge—of Eli's, who was Ashworth's husband and a retired RWA witch. We were staying at her compound for the duration of the court case, mainly because—according to Ashworth—even my father wouldn't fuck with her.

I was, I said, *but something odd just happened.*

Of course it did. I mean, it's been days *since you last felt something supernatural.*

Her tone was dry, and I chuckled. *I think there's a ghost or some sort of entity trying to get my attention, but I can't see or sense anything and I was wondering—*

If I could jump in and check things out for you, she finished.

It might be nothing but—

Your track record for these things would suggest it's actually something. Give me a sec to say goodbye to Monty—

He's called again? Didn't you talk for hours last night?

Well, yes, but in his words, he's missing my "before morning coffee" snarkiness, and just had to ring.

I laughed. Monty Ashworth—who was a cousin of mine —had been in love with Belle since we were all teenagers and had been trying to convince her he was utterly serious about his desire to marry her from the moment he'd been assigned the reservation witch position almost a year ago.

More like he's missing your "before morning coffee" sexing.

Oh, that's definite. She laughed, and the line muted as she said her goodbyes to Monty. *Righto, let's get this party started.*

Her being flowed into mine, fusing us as one but not so deeply that I lost physical control or that her soul left her body and became a part of mine. It not only meant she could see and hear everything I did but could also use her talents through me if necessary, and vice versa.

I'm not seeing anything untoward, she said, after a few seconds. *There're definitely no ghosts lurking in the shadows. Where did the event happen?*

Here, and at the top of the ramp.

Maybe if you moved back up?

I did, then glanced around the corner of the building to check that Anthony was still on the phone. He was pacing, his expression intent, so something bad had obviously happened.

Again, instinct twinged, but as usual, it wasn't coming forward with any details and that was damnably frustrating.

I scanned the immediate area and then the park on the other side of the road. It was almost ten, so the traffic was nowhere near as frantic as it had been an hour ago— although what most Canberrans called "traffic" would be considered laughable in either Sydney or Melbourne.

I'm still not seeing anything, Belle commented.

Neither was I, but instinct still insisted there was something here.

I stepped away from the path and moved down the grassed slope toward the off-ramp. I was about halfway down when the caress of energy happened again.

It really did feel like a hand tugging at mine.

Belle?

I felt it, but I'm not seeing anything.

Does that mean it's not a ghost or a spirit, but something else?

To be honest, I don't know.

What about your spirit guides? They got anything useful to say?

While many believed spirit guides were simply ghosts or spirits who had nothing better to do, they were in fact powerful, knowledgeable witches who'd either decided to dedicate their afterlife to the counsel of other witches, or who were always destined to become a guide. They were also generally the province of royal witches; it was extremely rare for a Sarr witch to be gifted with one, let alone a number of them.

According to you, they never do. There was amusement in her tone. *However, they're suggesting that our inability to see the spirit stems from the fact it is daylight.*

I frowned. *Why would that make any difference?*

If we're dealing with a younger spirit, they might not have the presence or power to fully form during the day.

That made sense. The otherworldly touch ran across my fingers again, a little more urgently this time. *It seems to be pulling me toward the high council's private park.*

Then you'd better get across there.

I glanced around at the sound of footsteps. Anthony approached, and his expression was grim. "A case I was handling has just gone south—will you be okay to head back to Mrs. Marlowe's alone?"

"Sure." I hesitated. "I need to get across to that park—I don't suppose you'd be able to pull some strings and get me in there, do you?"

He frowned. "Yes, but it'll take a few hours. How urgent is it?"

I wanted to say very, but he was obviously in a hurry, and it wasn't like I could justify the urgency. I waved a dismissive hand. "Don't worry about it. Go."

He gave me a look that suggested he saw through the lie,

then glanced down at his watch. "Fine. I'll meet you in the chamber at three. Don't be late."

"I won't."

He hurried off. I returned my gaze to the park. The decorative metal fencing was six or seven feet high and designed to keep all but the most athletic human out. It wasn't, however, so high that a werewolf couldn't leap it.

I wasn't a werewolf, and even though the wild magic had been altering my DNA to give me some wolfy characteristics—sharper hearing and sight, faster healing, more strength—I was a long way from wolf lean. I had serious doubts about my ability to haul my ass up and over that fence.

But the covered walkway that arched across the road from the first floor of the Council's building was the only other means of entry. I wasn't getting back in that building until my allotted time this afternoon, so I really had no other option but to try.

I stopped on the footpath and zipped up my coat pockets to keep my phone and my wallet in place, then waited for a couple of cars to go past. After looking around to ensure no one was taking undue interest in my actions, I ran across the road, reaching for every bit of speed I had, my eyes on the top of the fence and the decorative metal spikes I had to avoid.

When I hit the opposite path, I leapt high, grabbed the top of the fence, and swung myself over the metal points. My sweater ballooned underneath me and caught the top of one spike, ripping lengthwise as I dropped down on the other side and almost choking me in the process. I swore, stripped off my coat, then pulled off the sweater and left it dangling on the fence.

As I tugged my coat back on, the touch that wasn't happened once more.

Whatever it wanted me to find, it was in the center of the park, hidden behind the ring of trees protecting what I presumed was a seating area.

I wrapped my coat around my body, well aware that it was a defensive gesture that wouldn't help if there was something nasty waiting beyond those trees.

But I still wasn't getting anything on the psychic radar, and that was rather odd. Generally, my nose for trouble and supernatural beasties was rather sharp, even if sometimes less-than-giving information-wise.

I cautiously moved on. Belle remained connected, her tension pulsing through me, adding to my own. The trees were a mix of silver birches and crab apples, all just coming into bud, as well as plenty of bottle brushes, and they formed an impenetrable screen. I had no sense of movement, and I couldn't smell anything untoward.

Of course, the wind was at my back, so I actually wouldn't. Not until I was much closer, anyway.

There was no entry point into the center from this section of the garden, so I walked around to the left and eventually found a path. The shadows grew thicker the closer I got to the entrance of the center circle, and a frisson of fear ran through me

Those shadows weren't a product of the darkening day and the storm that was growing ever closer.

They were a product of magic. *Dark* magic.

I'm not liking the feel of that, Belle commented. *Maybe you'd better call someone.*

Ashworth and Eli are the only ones in this city who'd take any notice of me, and they're not close enough to get here quickly.

What about that high council investigator? The one who came to investigate Clayton's murder?

Samuel Kang?

Yeah, him. You still have his number, don't you?

No. I never put his number into my phone, and I tossed his business card into the junk drawer, I said. *Besides, what am I going to tell him? That I've got a bad feeling? What if it amounts to nothing?*

She snorted. *Your bad feelings usually lead to either trouble or a trap rather than nothing. Besides, those shadows hardly feel like "nothing."*

I eyed the shadows warily. There was no movement in them, despite the stirring wind. They hung like a blanket, thick and ugly looking, and yet I could sense no threat within them. Nothing to indicate it was, in any way, some sort of snare.

I could be wrong, of course. It wouldn't be the first time.

I flexed my fingers. Tiny threads of light danced around them, moon-bright against the shroud ahead. They were a manifestation of my inner wild magic, and an instinctive reaction connected to the rise of fear.

I edged closer to the central seating area. The shadows fell around me, a thick, foul blanket that made my skin crawl.

Then the wind sharpened, and that's when I smelled it.

Blood.

Death.

I stopped, but that unearthly presence tugged at my fingers again, urging me on. The tiny threads of wild magic crawled up my arm, and just for an instant, illuminated a hand.

A *woman's* hand.

Belle, do you think our ghost is the soul of whoever has died here?

She hesitated. *It would be extremely unusual for someone freshly passed to be so aware of their surroundings and situation, let alone be able to travel so far from the site of their death. I guess it would depend on who lies here, though. If it's a royal witch of some strength, it might be possible.*

She wants me to follow her through that shroud.

If she intended you harm, you would have felt it through her touch.

Unless she's an unwilling participant in the trap.

You'd sense that, too.

Belle was undoubtedly right, but the notion that these shadows were something other than a mere cover for whatever lay beyond them remained.

I created a light sphere, then cast it into the foul blanket. The shadows briefly peeled away from its presence, then returned to their original position. It left me with little choice but to enter the shrouded circle if I wanted to see what was going on.

I drew in a deeper breath to shore up my courage, then warily pressed into the shadows. Sensory input disappeared, and it briefly felt like I was walking through a void—one unconnected to this world.

But I wasn't alone here. Aside from the ghostly presence, there was something else, something that was almost predatory even if I wasn't feeling an immediate sense of threat.

I shivered and resisted the urge to turn and run. There was something here my ghost needed me to find, and it didn't matter if it was her body or something else. I simply couldn't let someone else deal with it.

Besides, after everything we'd gone through over the last

year, I was probably the most experienced demon hunter currently in Canberra.

Whether we were dealing with an *actual* demon was something we'd uncover soon enough.

But I personally doubted it. This shroud might feel otherworldly, but I had no sense that it was created by anything other than a human hand.

After several more seconds of pushing through what felt like treacle, I came out of the shadows and into the light.

That's when I saw the pentagram, the black candles, and the body of a woman.

A woman who'd been ritually murdered.

My stomach twisted and bile rose. I bolted for the nearby bushes and was completely and violently ill.

Not because of the brutality of the death but rather, the memories it evoked.

My sister had died the same way.

Almost *exactly* the same way.

CHAPTER TWO

*W*ell, *fuck*, came Belle's comment. *This is not a good development.*

Understatement of the goddamn year, in a year that's had so many of them. I straightened and spotted a water fountain off to the right. I walked around the perimeter, keeping my gaze well away from the ritual murder dominating the seating area's center. My stomach needed more time to settle before I dared confront the collision of past and present.

We can't be dealing with the same sorcerer, Belle said. *He was declared dead after Cat's murder.*

Except his body was never found. They presumed he died because the souls of dark sorcerers are generally consumed by the demons they deal with when they get close to death.

His demons wouldn't have consumed his entire body as well, though. Granted, he wouldn't have had the magical strength left to fight them off given what we did to him in the end, but it's rare for soul-consuming demons to also have a taste for flesh.

If he was a grand master, he just might have had a

working relationship with a demon who did both. It would have made them a powerful combination.

If he was a grand master, there would have been a more concerted effort to find his body.

For all we know, there might have been. It wasn't like we'd been kept updated on the situation, despite the fact we were the ones who'd finally stopped him.

I still think the similarities are either a coincidence or a copycat, Belle said. *Besides, our dark sorcerer's demons consumed the souls of his victims, and that doesn't seem to have happened here.*

True, I replied. *And in all honesty, what are the odds of this happening at the same time I return to Canberra?*

I would have thought fairly low, but hey, maybe fate doesn't want you feeling bored up here.

I laughed, though it was a very halfhearted sound. *Boredom was never going to be a problem. Is Ashworth or Eli close by? It'll be quicker—and easier—if they report this to the High Council Investigators.*

Already onto it, she said. *I also asked them to request Samuel Kang. At least he's aware of your talents and is less likely to be hostile.*

Wouldn't be matchmaking again, would you?

No, because I'm fully aware it's a lost cause. But he's a familiar face, and in this place, that's always a bonus. She paused, then added, amusement in her mental tones, *Of course, he's also very easy on the eye. A bit of window-shopping never hurts, even if one's heart is already taken.*

I had a feeling she was talking about herself as much as me, but kept that thought well and truly to myself. Which, these days, was far easier than it used to be. Belle might be a little worried about the development, but in many respects, the separation was necessary, especially once she and

Monty got married. The last thing she needed was my intrusive mutterings hitting her twenty-four seven.

Ashworth just asked if you'd like them to come down there.

I hesitated. Ashworth and Eli had basically become my family, and leaning on them when this murder too closely resembled the past was tempting. But they were already doing a lot of emotional lifting these days, and they both had family to catch up with. Besides, I was up here to prove I could stand on my own two feet, and it was about time I started doing just that.

I'm good, I said.

No, you're not, but I understand the need to not lean too much.

And yet you complain when I refuse to do exactly that with you.

Yes, but being the support system for my witch is part of my job description.

And something that can't continue when you have a family of your own.

That is a long way off yet.

I smiled. *Not if Monty has any say in it.*

She mentally smacked me. I laughed and turned to confront death. It still hit like a punch in the gut, but at least this time my stomach stayed put.

There were odd threads of magic floating around the edges of the pentagram, and while they didn't look active, they nevertheless made my skin crawl. Every instinct said I simply didn't have the knowledge or the training to deal with the spell those lingering remnants represented.

That had never stopped me from trying before and probably wouldn't in the future, but for once, I was going to listen to inner reason and not move any closer.

I crossed my arms and leaned back against the water fountain's stand. The black candles that had been placed on the cardinal points no longer burned, and the wax had congealed, meaning this sacrifice had happened at least two hours ago, if not three. Time wise, that placed the ritual after dawn, and that was damn unusual. Sorcerer and dark witch ceremonies tended to be performed at night, particularly during the witching hour, when the moon was at the highest point in the sky and the night sang with her power.

Of course, there was nothing stopping them doing a ceremony at any other time—a point we'd discovered the hard way not so long ago. But if we *were* dealing with the same sorcerer who'd killed Cat, why would he change his timing? The little I'd learned about dark practitioners suggested deviating from norms was rare, simply because when dealing with darker forces and demons themselves, alterations could be deadly.

I forced my gaze to the woman who lay in the center of the pentagram.

She wasn't young—which was another difference from those long-ago murders—but she had the crimson hair and pale skin of a royal witch, suggesting she was either from Marlowe or Ashworth stock. She was naked, her arms and legs positioned so they pointed toward the elements of earth, air, water, and fire, while her head was close to spirit.

Her head *wasn't* attached to her body, though there wasn't much in the way of blood, suggesting the decapitation had happened after death. The top of her head had also been sliced off, and I rather suspected her brains had been sucked out of her skull. I wasn't going to check though, because my stomach wasn't up to it.

If my guess that we were dealing with the same sorcerer was correct, then that made two more points of difference.

There was obvious bruising on her wrists and her ankles, suggesting she'd been physically bound and possibly even drugged for at least a few days before she'd been killed."

Why would he do that, though? Belle said. *He didn't need to last time.*

Last time he attacked younger royal witches. He could overwhelm them magically.

Even at nineteen, your sister was far stronger than many here in Canberra, so that's not exactly true.

She might have been magically stronger, but she wasn't what anyone would term experienced. The last year has certainly proven that sheer magical strength isn't always the best weapon.

Besides, I'd bested Cat's killer when I was little more than fifteen. And okay, that had been due more to my psychic skills than magical, but it still rammed home the point that the latter wasn't everything.

A fact I wished my father would cotton on to.

I still believe there're too many variances in this murder for it to be Cat's killer, Belle said.

I hope you're right.

But fear I'm not?

Sadly, yes.

Her trepidation stirred through me, as sharp as my own. *But why would he bother to come back here?*

Revenge? If he did survive what we did to him, well, he'd be pretty pissed off.

How would he even know you're here? We've only been here a couple of days—the gossip lines in the spirit world don't work that fast.

I couldn't help smiling. *Your guides are certainly evidence enough of that.*

She snorted. *They heard that. They're not impressed.*

That's okay. It's not like I have to deal with them.

Did you touch wood when you said that? Because they're suggesting you might want to.

My smile grew, but I didn't reply because the gently stirring wind teased my nostrils with not only the smell of oncoming rain, but also a rich, woody scent that was vaguely familiar.

Before I could place it, Samuel Kang pushed through the shroud and then stopped. He was the picture of classic male perfection—an oval-shaped face, chiseled cheekbones, and somewhat shaggy, shoulder-length hair that was a slightly deeper shade of crimson than usual for a royal witch. His shoulders were lovely and wide, his frame lean and yet muscular. But for me, it was his eyes that drew the attention. They were mono-lidded and the most glorious shade of emerald green. The same shade, in fact, that mine had once been, and that meant there was human blood in his background somewhere.

Of course, his less-than-pure bloodline was the reason behind my father's recent attempt to broker a marriage deal between our two families. He no doubt figured I'd be more inclined to accept the suit of someone who was not only closer to my own age, but who also came from stock that wasn't "perfect."

Meaning Mom's bloodline, of course, not my father's.

Although given what we'd recently learned about the Fenna and conception binding—which was the mating of a witch and a werewolf within a new wellspring, creating a hybrid forever bound to the wild magic—maybe my green eyes were actually the legacy of a distant werewolf bloodline. And given the sole purpose of the Fenna was to protect and control the wild magic, it would certainly explain why both Mom and I had survived immersion in it.

Samuel's gaze swept across the pentagram and the body within, then moved to mine. He did something of a double take, and the hint of a smile tugged at his rather lovely lips. I hadn't spent all that much time in this man's orbit, but I'd gotten the impression smiling was something he did quite often. It made him rather a rare man up here in Canberra—especially considering he was the lead investigator for the high council and had to deal with all three royal lines on a regular basis.

Pleasant, they generally were *not*.

"It's lovely to see you again, Lizzie Grace," he said, his voice deep and warm. "You've gained a couple of impressive white streaks in your hair since we last met."

"They're the result of a confrontation with a rusalka that almost went very wrong."

"They suit you—and I'm thinking they serve as a good warning to all that they're dealing with a very different witch." His gaze returned to the pentagram. "How did you know it was here? It's invisible from the flyover and the main section of the park."

I wrinkled my nose. "A ghost led me here."

He didn't laugh. As Belle had said, he was familiar with the strength of my psi gifts. "Was it the soul of the sacrificed?"

"Unknown at this point."

"Have you been anywhere near the pentagram? Touched anything, or tried to counter the spells that remain?"

"No, though I did lose my breakfast in the bushes over there." I waved a hand in that direction. "Do you know who the victim is?"

"No, and we've had no missing persons reported in the last few days."

"I take it that means there *was* one placed earlier this week?"

He nodded. "Celia Ashworth was reported missing on Monday, but this isn't her."

I mentally crossed all things that she wasn't related to *our* Ashworth. "How can you be sure of that?"

"Celia is in her early twenties. This woman looks to be at least two decades older."

My gaze went unbidden to the woman's severed head. My stomach twisted, but I swallowed heavily and tried to view her remains clinically rather than emotionally—a rather hard task given my emotions were all over the place of late.

She definitely *did* look older—her face was drawn, her cheeks hollow, and there were white streaks in her somewhat dull-looking crimson hair. But the little creases that crept in around the forehead, eyes, and mouth with age were missing. That could have been a product of plastic surgery, of course, but something within doubted it.

And while there were demons who sucked the life force from people, a process that not only aged them in seconds but killed them in the most horrendous manner, I doubted this was what had happened here. No matter what the classification of demon, they all had one thing in common—they avoided pentagrams and certainly never used them in their own magic.

Of course, that *didn't* preclude the possibility of the dark witch or sorcerer behind this murder commanding such a demon to do his dirty work for him, but sharing breathing space with said demon would have been a risky business.

"There's deep bruising on her wrists but no rope burns," I said, "and that suggests that while she hasn't resisted, her arms have taken the brunt of her weight at some point, either when she was being hauled upright or dropped down."

Amusement lurked around his lips. "Hanging around a ranger has given you a sharper eye for details."

"It's not so much the ranger as the supernatural entities that keep rolling through the reservation." My voice was dry, and he smiled.

"There're very few hunters here in Canberra that would recognize such a specific detail."

Hunters no doubt referring to those who worked for the Heretic Investigations Center hunting down rogue witches. "If they're not aware of those sorts of details, then it's no wonder they don't always catch their man."

He laughed. "It's not physical tells they hunt, but rather metaphysical and magical."

Neither of which had helped them catch the man responsible for Cat's murder. "Does that mean they'll be called in here?"

He nodded and glanced at his watch. "Should be here in ten, in fact."

Meaning I needed to be out of here in nine. The way fate was throwing shit our way, it would be the same overbearing bastard who'd ignored me all those years ago. "Do you recognize the symbols carved into her torso?"

"They represent a summoning of some kind, but I won't be certain who or what was called until I can do a bit more research."

Maybe my guess about the life stealer was wrong—but that would mean my gut was also wrong about this being the same sorcerer, and I doubted that was the case.

"Can you tell offhand if we're dealing with a sorcerer rather than a dark witch?"

"Why would you think this is the work of a sorcerer?" His voice was just a shade sharper. "There's little indication in the remaining magic that it is."

I hesitated. Every instinct might be screaming that the timing of this kill and the echoes it held to the past weren't a coincidence, but I wasn't about to color his investigations. We'd know soon enough if said instincts were right.

"No reason. Just curious."

Though his expression didn't change, a swirl of muddy red ran though his otherwise bright green aura—an indication of frustration. He knew the lie, but he didn't push, though I had no doubt he would at some point. Especially if this *was* just the first kill in a line of six—six being the number of women sacrificed last time before Belle and I had stopped him.

Samuel pulled out his phone. "I'd better take a formal statement before the coroner and the dissector get here."

I raised my eyebrows. "Dissector?"

"A non-technical term for a coroner assigned to defuse and dissect dark magic incursions such as this. Until that's done, we can't approach the body."

"I had no idea there was such a position." I hesitated. "Does that mean he's different to a hunter?"

"They both work for HIC, just different umbrellas. And there's good reason few have ever heard about them—don't want to alarm the public needlessly about their necessity."

HIC being the Heretic Investigations Center, though people often confused the acronym with the HCI. "Given a good percentage of the public here are witches of some variety, I'm thinking they'd be well aware dissectors are a necessary evil."

"Royal witches are notoriously renowned for ignoring everything that doesn't apply to or affect them."

I half smiled. "Do I sense a little hostility in your tone?"

"You do not." His lips twitched. "Though having to constantly deal with the convoluted machinations of the royal lines is enough to jade even the most committed soul."

"Oh, I totally understand that."

"I bet you do." He hit record and took my statement, basically making me repeat everything I'd already said. Once done, he added, "I've unlocked the maintenance gates if you want to head out that way. If I need any more information, I'll be in contact."

I was tempted to ask he keep me updated on the investigation's progress, but he wasn't Aiden, and he was already suspicious I wasn't telling him everything. "Well, you know where to find me."

He nodded. "Good luck with the trial today."

"Thanks. I'll probably need it."

His quick smile touched the corners of his bright eyes. "If you can face down Clayton in all his madness, you'll be perfectly fine against your father."

"It's not him I'm worried about. It's the high council itself."

"As few as they are, the Society has done a pretty good job of getting the so-called 'rising star' progressives onto the trial bench."

His voice held a note of contempt, and I raised my eyebrows. "If you have such a low opinion of the council, why do you work for them?"

"A question I often ask myself." He shrugged and

pulled a business card from his pocket. "Ring me if you find another ghost or get more insights."

I accepted the card and tucked it into my pocket. "Don't take this personally, but I'm hoping I won't have to."

He smiled and pointed to the path heading off to the left. "Follow that out. The shroud won't impede you, as it's designed to slow and catalogue entry."

Meaning it was collecting information on whoever went through it?

Meaning if this murder *was* connected to those past ones, in walking through it I'd handed the sorcerer a whole lot of information about myself?

God, I hoped not.

A chill ran through me, but there was nothing I could do about it now. I turned and walked away. This time around, the shroud held the consistency of shadows rather than treacle, and I was out in a matter of seconds. The day had gotten gloomier—which was definitely appropriate given not only what lay behind me, but what I had to face in only a few hours—and the scent of rain was stronger. I probably had ten minutes, if that, to find cover.

What I really wanted to do was call Aiden. I missed him something fierce. Missed his warmth, his caring, and his stubbornness. Missed the brush of his lips and the press of his body against mine. But most of all, I missed simply talking to him—not just about cases, but anything else that might take our fancy.

But the ball was well and truly in his court now, and where our relationship went from here was up to him. I might believe he was finally ready to fight for everything he wanted—to fight for *us* against the will and prejudice of his mother *and* his pack—but actions would definitely speak louder than words.

Of course, that didn't excuse the fact he hadn't yet called me, although technically that might be my fault. I did tell him at the airport that I didn't want to discuss anything until I returned home. The damn man didn't have to take that *literally*, though.

I tugged up my coat's hood and loped toward the exit gates. As I drew near, several cars pulled up, and three people climbed out. The woman—a Sarr with dark curly hair streaked with a silver as brilliant as her eyes—gave me a nod of acknowledgement. The other two—royal witches by their coloring—strode into the park without even looking my way. I nevertheless recognized the second man—he was thinner, older, and grayer, with a thick mustache and a combover, but he was definitely the man who'd ignored my warnings all those years ago.

I couldn't help but wonder if me being so right last time would make any difference to him this time... and then crossed all mental fingers that it didn't come down to that. That I was wrong about this kill, despite every instinct saying otherwise.

I called for an Uber and headed to Hattie's compound. It was situated on Mugga Way in Red Hill, a street that was known as the golden mile, though it did in fact run for three and a half kilometers rather than a mere mile.

The compound was situated on an expansive corner block and, like so many of the houses along this street, was a large and somewhat sprawling sixties-style building. The bricks had been rendered over in a fashionable gray, and the old cypress pines that ringed the entire property had been cut back to form a tall but thick hedge. The gardens were spectacular, and the house, despite its age, modern and pristine. I'd never envied anyone's home before now, but I'd felt a twinge when I'd first walked through the place.

Just think of all the cleaning a place this big would involve, Belle commented.

I grinned and climbed out of the Uber. *If I could afford a place like this, I could afford the staff to look after it.*

Hey, if the ogres bow to your demand, you'll be able to.

Five million is barely enough to buy a house in the neighboring suburbs, let alone along this street.

But it would certainly buy Monty and Belle a rather lovely property in the reservation in which to raise their kids. She deserved that. They *both* deserved that—although Monty wasn't poor. He might no longer be the favorite son, but he was still a very wealthy man in his own right.

As I keyed in the code and pushed open the security gate, thunder rumbled overhead, and fat drops of rain began to fall. I tugged up my hood again and raced for the main door. While the house looked single story from this angle, it had been built into the hill and actually had two levels. The living areas and master bedroom were all located on the upper level, while the guest suites were underneath, next to the three-car garage.

The front door—a double width, intricately carved wooden thing—opened as I approached, revealing Belle. At a smidge over six foot, she was a good four inches taller than me. She was also built like an Amazonian, with long, straight black hair and silvery eyes.

Her looks, rather surprisingly, were *not* the reason Monty had fallen in love with her. Instead, it was her treating him no differently to anyone else, despite the fact he'd been deemed a child prodigy, that had made him fall.

"Perfect timing," she said cheerfully. "Eli is just dishing up lunch."

"I hope he hasn't gone all out, because I don't think my stomach will handle anything too fancy."

"It's just toasted sandwiches. We've dinner with Mom tonight, remember, and Dad is barbequing. You know what that means."

I did indeed—mountains of meat and a ton of salad. Dinner with her parents had been the highlight of my teenage years, and the one place I'd always felt wanted and welcome. "Looking forward to it."

I stripped off my coat, hung it in the concealed cupboard, then followed Belle down the pristine white hall to the open-plan kitchen living area. There was a more formal living *and* dining room, of course, but apparently, they were only used for very special occasions.

Ashworth and Eli were both in the kitchen, the former making tea and coffee while the latter flipped toasties onto a plate. Ashworth glanced around as we entered, his gaze scanning me critically. He was short, thickset, and bald, with a heavily lined face and muddy silver eyes. He looked more like an old rocker than a witch, and I rather suspected that was a deliberate ploy on his part. He might love his old jeans and band T-shirts, but he also loved being underestimated. In a world where royal witches judged *everyone* on their appearance and their bloodline, being easily dismissed definitely worked in his favor.

"You're looking a little peaked, lass," he said, the brogue in his voice stronger than usual. Not surprising given the copious amounts of alcohol the three of them had consumed during their "just a few drinks" reunion. Hattie might be a confessed teetotaler when she was home, but that had definitely gone out the window last night. "How bad was the crime scene?"

I stopped in front of a kitchen counter large enough to seat ten people and pulled out one of the barstools. "I've seen worse. It was more the memories it evoked that caused the problem."

"Meaning your sister's murder." Eli placed a platter of sandwiches on the counter and motioned me to help myself. He was a tall, well-built, and very handsome man in his late sixties, with neatly cut salt-and-pepper hair and bright blue eyes.

"Yes." I grabbed one of the chicken, avocado, and cheese sandwiches and bit into it. "The thing I'm wondering is, are my memories coloring my perception of today's crime scene?"

"Don't you be doubting or second-guessing your instincts," Eli said. "They've proven their reliability over and over again."

"I know, it's just—" I stopped and grimaced. "We never saw the official reports about the sorcerer who took Cat's life, and maybe there's something in them that could confirm whether I'm right in thinking we're dealing with the same one."

Eli and Ashworth exchanged a glance that tweaked my "something's off" radar, but I didn't bother questioning it. Whatever it was, they'd tell me eventually.

"They'll be in the archive, so Hattie could probably get hold of them for us." Eli slid a pot of tea and a mug my way. "But what's made you think it is the same man?"

I hesitated. "For a start, it struck me as odd that Samuel made no mention of the similarities and seemed taken aback when I asked if we could be dealing with a sorcerer."

Eli flipped several more toasties onto the platter. "Your sister's death was over thirteen years ago now. It's hardly surprising it's no longer a part of the general consciousness."

"Yes, but he's an investigator for the high council and we're talking about the worst serial killer Canberra has ever known." In fact, probably the *only* serial killer Canberra has known.

"Samuel's in his late thirties, isn't he?" At my nod, Ashworth continued, "that makes him a rookie at the time and eliminates any prospect of him playing any part in such an important case."

"But surely he'd have still heard rumors. If there's one thing the royal lines like, it's gossip."

"That depends entirely on the situation," Eli said. "In a case where the most promising elites are being murdered, there'd be a gag order well and truly placed on it."

Ashworth sat next to me and reached for several ham and cheese toasties. "I also think you'll find a carefully orchestrated erasure happened over the following few months. The council wouldn't want anyone believing a dark sorcerer had gotten the better of them."

"Especially when it was an unappreciated, underpowered witch who *did* stop him," Belle said. "With a little help from her underrated familiar, of course."

"Here's to being underrated." I picked up my mug and clicked it against hers. "May it win us the war in the end."

"Amen to that, sister."

I took a drink, then glanced at Ashworth. "Samuel said there was a missing person report out for a Celia Ashworth —I hope she's not one of your family."

"Not immediate family, as far as I'm aware, but I'll check with Sophie."

I nodded. All the witch lines were actually connected if you traced them back far enough; it was hard to be otherwise when there were only six branches overall. It was one of the reasons a close watch was kept on marriages, and why so many of them now involved overseas bloodlines. Like "real" royalty, witches had learned the hard way that interbreeding led to major physical—and in our case, magical —problems.

"Did Samuel give any indication that Celia might be our dead woman?"

"No. In fact, he said she was too old." I reached for another sandwich. My stomach, it seemed, had gotten over its tetchiness and was now rumbling hungrily. "But if the high council locks down information about these sorts of kills, how can we be sure this is actually the first of them?"

"We can't, but it *is* likely to be given what you've already said about Samuel's reactions."

"True." I thoughtfully munched on my sandwich for several seconds. "If this *is* the same killer, and he follows the same pattern, then it's likely he'll take his next victim tomorrow night."

"And there's little we can do about that, because it's not our problem. Not this time," Eli said.

I hoped that was true. I feared it was not.

"Do you think they'll at least put out an alert?" Belle asked.

"The high council is averse to causing undue stress to the upper echelons."

"They don't have to," I said. "Given he attacked the top half dozen university candidates last time, why can't they just discreetly warn next year's lot that they need to be cautious for the next week or so?"

Eli snorted. "Do young adults ever take any notice of such warnings? Do you?"

I grinned. "I'm hardly a young adult."

"By comparison to me, you certainly are, but the point remains. I mean, here we are discussing a murder, when for all intents and purposes, we should be concentrating on this afternoon's trial."

"I've been thinking about the trial for entirely too long now, and I just want it over and done with." I hesitated. "I *am* worried about my father using my ability with the wild magic against me if things don't go his way, though."

"If it's not confirmed by the tests, he won't," Ashworth said.

"I love the certainty in your tone, but you don't know my father."

"I know his type, and they never like being considered a fool."

Which would be a risk if he mentioned the wild magic only to have the null result of my initial test repeated. I just had to hope it *was* repeated and that the now activated inner wild magic didn't change my levels on the capacity indicator.

"All he has to do is direct them to the café," I said. "The proof is woven into the fabric of its protections."

"Which can be explained away by the fact that the well-spring was left unprotected for so long."

"They won't believe that." Neither my father nor Clayton had.

"Except the wild magic still roams the reservation, despite the protections placed around the older wellspring," Eli said.

"And if what Monty said this morning is anything to go by, it's worsened since you left." Belle wrinkled her nose and looked my way. "Sorry, I was going to mention it earlier, but the whole ghost and body thing got in the way."

I nodded, an odd sort of dread stirring. While I'd long had a feeling that I wouldn't be able to leave the reservation for any real length of time, I definitely *hadn't* expected the wild magic itself to react to my departure. I'd always thought the ties that now bound us would simply affect me physically.

"What does he mean by worse?"

"He just said the magic has become... wilder."

A smile twitched my lips, despite that growing sense of dread. "It *is* called *wild* magic for a reason."

"Yes, but he says there's a very different vibe to its energy this time."

I raised my eyebrows, even as my stomach did its knotting thing again. "What sort of vibe is he talking about?"

Her gaze met mine, her expression sober. "In his words, the wild magic is fucking angry, and it's lashing out at the reservation."

CHAPTER THREE

"Lashing out how?" I picked up my tea and half wished it was whiskey. Drowning my problems had definite appeal right now, even if I *did* need to have all my wits about me for this afternoon's trial.

Belle hesitated. "There's been nothing major yet, thankfully, but—"

"Define nothing major."

"Trees coming down, dams breaking banks, minor earth tremors causing damage to buildings. Stuff like that."

"Given the amount of rain we've had of late, the first two aren't particularly surprising." Nor was the third, really, considering there were hundreds of old volcanoes littered about Victoria and there were at least a couple of minor tremors every year.

"No, but the thing is, it's happening *solely* within the O'Connor compound."

"And Monty thinks the wild magic is somehow *targeting* them?" I couldn't help the incredulousness in my voice. "Is he forgetting Aiden's sister controls the other wellspring? She'd certainly put a damper on any such attack."

Hell, the ability to protect her pack was the reason *why* Katie had sacrificed her soul—and any possibility of reincarnation—to become one with the wild magic in the first place.

"Except she doesn't control the old wellspring, and it's all coming from there."

Because of my connection. Because of my absence. I took another gulp of tea. The hot liquid burned all the way down, but it didn't have all that much effect against the rising sense of guilt.

Of course, guilt was my thing. I did have a habit of wallowing in it, sometimes with good reason, sometimes not.

"Angry or not, the wild magic is a force—a power—that needs to be *directed*," I said. "It can't just randomly decide to attack things."

"Except this particular wellspring has gained some form of sentience through its connection to you," Ashworth said.

"And given how much we *don't* know about the Fenna and what they—and the wellsprings they were forged in—were capable of," Eli added, "it's not beyond the realm of possibility that it *could* physically react to your absence."

"And you *have* been saying for a while now that you don't think you'd ever be allowed to leave the reservation," Ashworth finished.

"I meant permanently, and we've only been gone two days. I hardly call that a long absence."

"It would appear the wellspring thinks otherwise."

I thrust a hand through my hair. "How bad do you think it will get?"

"*That* is the unanswerable question," Ashworth said. "One that depends entirely on just how much anger is gathering."

"There *is* another problem," Belle said. "And that's the noticeable amount of wild magic flitting about. Monty's worried that if it keeps increasing at the current rate, it's going to draw unwanted attention."

Which was the very last thing we needed. The echoes of its unprotected nature from a year ago were still washing through the outer reaches of the supernatural world, tantalizing all sorts of evil with the promise of unrestrained power. We didn't need fresh waves happening.

"How long does he think we have before that happens?" I asked.

"Maybe two or three days."

I glanced at Ashworth. "Is the trial likely to be over that quickly?"

"It would depend on what the council's aims are." He grimaced. "I suspect privately they want to see him squirm but publicly need to send a warning to all witch families still involved in the practice."

"Hard to send a public message when the trial is happening in a closed court."

He smiled. "They will still get the message. The council closed the court in order to not piss off your father too much. They do have to work with him in the future, remember."

"I take it that means you don't think he'll face any real consequences for his actions?"

"Many would say public humiliation and a slap on the wrist is more than enough punishment for a man like your father," Eli commented.

"And it *will* achieve what the council needs, without putting your father too offside," Ashworth said. "Those with less power and pull will know the consequences for *them* would be far worse."

Which was exactly what Anthony had said, though he continued to believe the punishment would be stronger. I wished I'd asked what that might be, because I doubted any of them had the courage to enforce prison time.

"I guess if it ends the practice of marrying off underage kids, then all the hassle will be worth it." Even if every angry part of me still wanted my father to fully pay for all the trauma he'd put me through. "That's presuming, of course, the wellspring situation doesn't throw a spanner in the works and force me to leave."

"You could fly down overnight if the escalation does become noticeable," Eli said. "Perhaps if you entered the wellspring and 'communed' with the magic, it might act more reasonably."

"It's hard to believe we're talking about a natural force from deep within the earth," Belle commented, "and not a toddler throwing a tantrum,"

"And yet, in some respects, that's precisely what we might be dealing with," Eli said. "Especially if the purpose of the Fenna wasn't only to protect and channel, but also, over the course of their lifetime, provide the means and the knowledge to enable self-protection."

I raised my eyebrows. "Is there anything in the book to back this theory?"

That book being *Earth Magic: Its Uses and Dangers.* Monty had found it in the Canberra archives, and it was basically a very early account of witches, including how they dealt with earth magic—the original name for wild magic. None of us were really sure how this book had managed to survive the many often-brutal centuries since it was written or why so much of the knowledge within it had been forgotten.

Eli hesitated. "I've got a lot of the book yet to read, but I did run a check on a couple of wellsprings mentioned, and rather interestingly, they're listed as unviable."

"How can a wellspring be unviable?" Belle asked. "They're either active, or they're gone. There's no middle ground."

Eli shrugged. "It could simply mean that those wellsprings are unable to be used."

"But they do *still* exist?" I asked.

"The two I checked did."

"Interesting." I drank a bit more coffee. "Perhaps it's not so much the wellspring gaining enough awareness to self-protect, but rather, the soul of the Fenna fusing with the wellspring on death. Remember, it was the references Gabe found to the Fenna that enabled him to fuse Katie's soul to the second wellspring, and she *can* control and protect it."

"But *his* magic is the reason no one knows it exists," Ashworth said. "It diverts anyone who tries to find it."

And he'd know, having done just that. "Because she's not a witch, so was naturally behind the eight ball when it came to getting a handle on things. That might well change in the future." I sighed and rubbed my face. Worrying about things beyond my control was starting to give me a headache. "Is there any chocolate in this house? I'm feeling the need."

Eli smiled. "Chocolate replaces alcohol when Hattie's home alone, so I'm sure there's plenty to be found in the pantry."

"I knew we were kindred spirits." I pushed to my feet and walked over. Like everything else in this house, the pantry was massive and probably bigger than the café's entire kitchen. Thankfully, there wasn't only a vast selection of chocolate blocks, but also a variety of bars and multiple packets of Minties and Fantales.

If things went ass-up at the trial today, I'd probably need them all.

I dug out a Black Forest block and happily retreated. "Has Monty said anything to Aiden?"

"Aiden's aware of the situation. I'm not sure about the pack, though."

"I'm betting they are," Ashworth said. "Monty will no doubt have made several very loud comments along the lines of, 'Well, you wanted her gone, and this is the result' by now."

"Oh, he definitely has." Amusement danced through Belle's expression. "We all know he's never backward when it comes to protecting those he loves."

It was one of the many things *she* loved about him. She didn't come out and say that, of course, but it hovered in her thoughts nonetheless.

I broke open the chocolate, snapped off two rows, and slid the rest across to her. "I take it he'll keep us updated via one of his many calls?"

She rolled her eyes. "Yes, and he only rings twice a day. That's hardly *many*."

I grinned, and the conversation moved on to other nonsense stuff. I enjoyed the banter and drew in the richness and comradery of it while I could. I had no doubt it would all wash away once I hit that goddamn courtroom.

The court was smaller than I'd expected and, like this morning's mediation room, lined with dark wood paneling. It gave the place a somewhat old-fashioned and forbidding air, which was no doubt the whole point. The ceiling was ornately plastered, which leaned into that "older" vibe, and the large windows to my left would have allowed in plenty of much-needed light if not for the heavy damask curtains that covered them.

The council of seven sat at a long wooden bench on the dais that dominated the far end of the room. There were five men and two women, and the woman in the middle wasn't only the youngest—maybe late thirties compared to the rest who had to be fifty or more—but also the adjudicator.

There was no jury box. In its place was the witness stand, which sat to the right of the dais, while the in-court clerk sat to the left. One table for the plaintiff and one for the accused filled the remaining space. There was no seating for members of the public or other interested parties, but this room had been designed as a closed court and probably never had them.

The entire room had a string of magical and psychic protections around it, but if anyone hoped that would stop Belle, they were sorely mistaken.

And I'll be more than happy to inform them all of that fact should this go ass up.

I somehow managed to hide my smile. *You need to hush up because I need to concentrate.*

It is my duty to provide snarky comments to ease your tension. Don't want you snapping at the wrong moment and either revealing too much or attacking your good-for-nothing father.

Which we both knew was totally possible. Just sitting in the same room as him was making my fingers twitch. Physical violence wasn't normally my thing, but punching my father's face in the café not so long ago had eased all sorts of anger, even if only briefly, and I had no doubt it would do so again.

My feelings toward my mother were more complicated. There was anger, sure, but it was mostly a deep sense of betrayal and disappointment. She hadn't supported me when I'd needed it most, and that had hurt.

Still hurt.

At least she wasn't here in the courtroom, supporting him, nor was she outside with other witnesses waiting to be called for the day's proceedings. I wasn't entirely sure how'd I'd react when I finally saw her. She was my mom, and I still loved her, despite the fact she'd never really been there for me.

Though I guess, in her own weird and distant way, she had at least tried. She'd never been outwardly hostile to Belle, after all, and that was something that could never be said about my father.

I dragged my attention back to the room as the recordings taken by the Black Lantern Society's truth seeker and auditor ended and the adjudicator said, "Please call your first witness to the stand, Mr. Fitzgerald."

He immediately called in Belle, who basically confirmed everything that had been said in the recordings about the events leading up to my marriage and the wedding night itself. She kept her gaze on my father the whole time, and if looks could have killed, he would have been coffin meat right now.

I rather suspected he found it amusing. That was the vibe I was getting, anyway.

"Mr. Moderno," the adjudicator said, once Anthony had finished, "do you wish to cross-examine the witness?"

"Yes." My father's attorney—a snappily dressed man in his mid-forties with a well-coiffed wave of silver hair and fierce blue eyes—moved around their table and stopped several meters away from the witness stand. "Tell me, Ms.

Sarr, what magical rating were you given during your evaluation?"

Annoyance briefly flickered through her expression, and her thoughts said it was more at the use of her birth surname rather than the bored tone of his voice. "Two point nine."

Which was actually a pretty high result for someone in the Sarr line, who very rarely registered any higher than two. Moderno nodded. "You also underwent a psi evaluation, did you not?"

"Yes."

"And that result?"

"I'm considered borderline gifted when it comes to spirit talking and telepathy."

I was betting she'd not only blow *that* result apart these days, but also her initial magical rating. My father hadn't insisted on her being retested however, and that was a definite mistake on his part. One that was no doubt due to the fact that he—and everyone else up here—wasn't used to dealing with a human familiar. The fact was, any power ramp-up in *me* was always going to be reflected through her, thanks to how closely witches and familiars were linked.

"Then it would be fair to say that while your magical range would be considered only slightly above average for a Sarr witch," Moderno said, "you are considered an extremely strong telepath."

"Yes, I guess it would."

Though her voice was even, her confusion flicked through me. She, like me, had no idea where this line of questioning was going.

Anthony's expression, however, suggested that he did. He rose and said, "Objection, Your Honor. The power rating of the witness plays no part in the accusations that stand before the court."

Moderno turned to face the dais. "It is our intention to prove that it does."

The adjudicator glanced at the other six then nodded. "We'll allow the line of questioning for the moment, but do get to the point, Counselor."

He nodded and returned his attention to Belle. "Does this mean you are, in fact, strong enough to rearrange memories?"

Belle stared at him for a heartbeat and then glanced toward my father. "Seriously? This is going to be your defense, you fucker?"

The adjudicator banged her gavel and said, "Ms. Sarr, please refrain from speaking directly to the defendant."

"The *defendant*," she said, contempt evident, "is obviously intending to victim blame, and that fucking sucks. As does he."

I swallowed a laugh and resisted the urge to stand up and cheer. *Belle, you need to be careful. They might be intent on stirring up an angry reaction so they can claim you're an unreliable witness.*

Both now *and* on that night long ago.

Hey, my response was utterly restrained. I mean, I could have given a demonstration of said telepathic strength and have him mewing the truth like a child... while making him shit his pants like one.

Appealing options one and all, although I would prefer the latter when we're not stuck in the same small room as him.

"Ms. Sarr," the adjudicator said, "please answer Mr. Moderno's question without side commentary."

"No, Mr. Moderno," she said, "I cannot totally

rearrange someone's memories and make it stick. Even if I could, any good telepath or auditor would see the tells and know what had been done."

"But theoretically, it *is* possible."

"Theoretically, yes, if you have had years and years of appropriate training. I have not."

Moderno shifted his stance. He looked pleased, and that worried me. "Let's talk about the night you rescued Ms. Grace."

"That's what I'm here for, babe."

"Ms. Sarr, please address the counselor correctly."

"Only if he—and this court—start addressing me correctly."

"Ms. *Kent*," Moderno all but drawled. "Is it your claim that you—a low-rated Sarr armed with nothing more than a very strong telepathic gift—were able to break through every protection Clayton Ashworth had around his building? Without help, and as a fifteen-year-old?"

"Your Honor," Anthony said, again rising to his feet, "the adjudicators' reports have been verified and found to be a correct reflection of memories. This line of questioning is out of line."

"I assure you, it is not," Moderno said.

"We'll allow it for the moment," the adjudicator said.

As Anthony sat back down, I leaned close and whispered, "Are you sure my father hasn't paid off those twats?"

Moderno shot me a glance, obviously having heard the comment, but there was no reaction from the dais, suggesting the seven councilors hadn't.

Because I threw a minor shield around them when I saw you lean sideways, Belle said. *Thought something less than polite might have been coming.*

49

Might want to keep it up. I suspect there'll be more impolite comments coming.

And they'll undoubtedly be warranted.

"Ms. Kent," Moderno was saying, "please answer the question."

"Yes, I expect the court and your good self to believe me because it *is* the truth."

Moderno smiled disdainfully. "So, you telepathically forced the guards, both at the gate and in the house, to give you entry and then you just strolled on through."

Belle's smile echoed his. "Tell me, Counselor, do you have a familiar?"

"Of course not—"

She turned to the councilors on the dais. "Do any of you?"

"Please, Ms. Kent, just answer the question and do not directly address the bench."

"I can't answer the question without addressing the bench, because neither the counselor nor his client have familiars and therefore no understanding of the complexity of the relationship."

"This has nothing to do with the question at hand, Ms. Kent."

"On the contrary, it has *everything* to do with the question at hand. Part of a familiar's job is to protect their witch's life, even if it results in the end of their own. My witch was in fear of her life, and I had no choice but to go in there and save her."

"That doesn't explain how you—a Sarr—got past magical protections raised by one of the strongest witches in Canberra."

She smiled benignly. "And *that* right there is how I got past."

Uncertainty flickered through Moderno's aura, though his expression didn't alter. "I'm unsure—"

"I'm talking about the disdain that literally oozes from your skin every time you look at me. It's that disdain that allowed me to get into Clayton's mansion. No royal family ever considers us a magical threat, so few ever write their protections to include us."

"Clayton's protection included protections against break-ins."

"By humans, yes. Not by a lowly old Sarr. But there's one other point you forgot—the link between a witch and her familiar goes two ways, and while my witch might be considered an underrated disappointment by her prick of a father, it was *her* magic that enabled me to defuse Clayton's spells. And let's not forget—though I'm sure every royal witch in this room would certainly prefer to—that it was Lizzie who finally stopped that sorcerer's killing spree, even if your client chose to blame Liz for the death of his precious heir, which is why he forced her into the marriage with Clayton. He wanted to get rid of her."

Fuck, Belle, tell it like it is, why don't you?

Someone has to.

"I have no idea what killing spree you're referring to," Moderno was saying, "but it is irrelevant—"

"No, it's *not*, because that fucker is alive and well, and there's a body in the high council's precious park to prove it." Her gaze cut to my father. "And you, fuckhead, are sitting right on the top of his 'unfinished business' list."

CHAPTER FOUR

To say this declaration was met with a fair amount of mayhem would be an understatement. There might only be ten other people in the room, but they sure as hell made plenty of noise. But then, the news of a sorcerer hunting for fresh blood amongst the royal ranks was always bound to raise a little alarm.

As the adjudicator used the gavel again in an attempt to regain order, I said to Belle, *Where the hell did that come from?*

Not from me, that was for sure.

She wrinkled her nose. *Got hit by a fragmented vision while you were coming back from the park.*

Precognition hadn't been one of Belle's original skill sets, but the day we'd done a deep merge to oust the White Lady trying to take over her body had changed that. She certainly didn't dream as clearly or even as often as I did, but the insights she did get were probably just as accurate.

Why didn't you mention it?

Because I didn't want to worry you any more than you already were. Ashworth and Eli concurred.

At least that explained the brief look I'd caught between the two men.

Why mention it now, then?

Because he's treating this whole trial as nothing more than an inconvenience at best, and a sheer waste of his time at worst. He doesn't believe anything more than a mild rebuke will come from it.

And with good reason.

Yes, but him sitting opposite me looking all smug and superior just got to me, and I needed to unsettle him. She mentally sniffed. *Sorry, but not sorry, you know?*

I certainly did. *Why on earth do you think the sorcerer will go after my father rather than me? I'm the one that stopped him.*

I think you'll be more the dessert after the main course that is your family.

Well, that would have to be the first time I've been described as dessert, I said, torn between amusement and trepidation.

Oh, I don't know, she said casually. *I'm pretty sure Aiden would consider you dessert. Not to mention entrée and main course.*

I mentally slapped her, and her laughter ran through my mind, fierce and bright. *Unfortunately, I think Cat's death gave the sorcerer a taste for your family's power. He may want revenge, but I think you're right in saying the timing is coincidental. If he does know you're here, then I don't think you'll be his highest priority.*

Because he tasted my magic last time and knows I'm not the strongest witch. Or, at least, I wasn't back then. *If that is true, then the woman in the park must be related to us somehow.*

Yes, but possibly on your father's side rather than your mother's.

I raised my eyebrows. *Was that part of the vision or just a guess?*

The latter. Cat was more your father's child in output and in looks rather than your mother's.

Doesn't mean he won't go after her.

No.

I drew in a breath and glanced up as the adjudicator's gavel bashing finally bought a halt to all the babbling.

"Ms. Kent, you will restrain any further such outbursts. They are not relevant to this case—"

"Actually," Anthony said, standing once again. "They are, because it was indeed the death of Ms. Grace's older sister that prompted the marriage to Clayton Marlowe."

The adjudicator hesitated, glanced at her fellow councilors, and then nodded. "I'll allow it to remain on record, then. Mr. Moderno, have you any further questions for this witness?"

"Just one, Your Honor." His gaze returned to Belle. "You said that you're unable to totally erase or rearrange someone's thoughts, did you not?"

"I did."

"And yet on that night, you not only froze Mr. Marlowe in place, but gave him a debilitating illness for which he could find no cure. Care to explain how a fifteen-year-old managed that?"

Ah fuck, Belle said. *He could only be bringing this up for one reason.*

He can't know about the wild magic enhancing the force of your spell, I said, more positively than I felt.

Why not? Belle said. *Both Clayton and your father were*

well aware wild magic kept the spell alive long after it should have logically faded.

Yes, but they'd have kept that to themselves. Clayton because he didn't want his impotence to become known, and my father because he didn't want the rest of the council knowing that his useless daughter maybe wasn't.

Doesn't mean he won't mention it here.

Until he gets confirmation from the test tomorrow, he'll keep it to himself. I think he's laying the groundwork just in case.

I can't see how it helps him, though. He remains guilty of unlawfully marrying off his underage daughter.

He's not worried about the case, I said. *Remember what Anthony said about the seven councilors being the rising stars? He no doubt intends to approach them later about a marriage alliance.*

God, he's a bastard.

Always has been, so I'm not sure why you sound so shocked.

She mentally snorted and then said, "Gifting Clayton the inability to get an erection was definitely an apt punishment considering he was about to rape his wife. Drugging someone into submission is illegal, you know, even in marriage."

"That does not answer the question at hand."

"No, but in truth, I can't, because I really don't understand how I managed such a complex and long-lasting spell myself."

Which wasn't a lie. Most incapacitation spells sat on the surface of the skin rather than under them; Belle's had been positioned near the base of Clayton's spine and thrust so far into his flesh that it was hard to see, let alone examine. It was generally only those spells designed to kill that went so deep, and few witches dared use them because of the whole threefold rule.

The other problem was the fact that the spell was a combination of both our magic *and* the wild, and we truly had no idea how the latter had gotten involved because, at the time, we'd had no clue it resided in my DNA.

Of course, the wild magic was not only the reason *why* the spell had lasted so long, but also why my father had joined forces with Clayton to look for me. It wasn't until his visit at the café that he'd realized I could manipulate it.

"And yet you were able to disentangle it, which belies your statement," Moderno said.

"No, it doesn't, because the spell was a combination of my magic and Liz's, and it took the two of us working in tandem to unpick it."

"Whose magic would you say was the stronger thread within that spell?"

"Your Honor," Anthony said, "this has no relevance to the charges."

"I tend to agree," the adjudicator said. "If you have a point, please say so. Otherwise, move on, Counselor."

"Very well, Your Honor," Moderno said. "But I reserve the right to come back to this point at a later junction."

The adjudicator nodded, and Belle was released from the stand. She blew me a kiss, scowled at my father, then headed out.

Anthony called his next witness, someone I didn't know and couldn't remember seeing when I had been living at home, and the questions rolled on. After another twenty minutes or so, the adjudicator called it a day and said we'd resume again at one tomorrow. Either they didn't like getting up early or they all had more important things to do in the morning.

I watched my father and Moderno leave and then said, "Do you think Belle's outburst has harmed our case?"

Anthony shook his head. "The adjudicator allowing it to stand on record means I can now bring in evidence to support the fact that your father agreed to the marriage as an act of revenge against you."

"*Is* there evidence, though? It's basically his word against mine now that Clayton is dead."

A smile touched Anthony's lips. "If there's one truth that can never be denied in any great house, be they witch or human, it's the fact that walls have ears and eyes."

"Staff are magically restricted from talking about private details of those they work for."

"And as with most restrictive spells of that kind, it's almost impossible to be truly specific about all the things that can and can't be discussed. Most spells are general in nature and include big tickets items like relationships and finances."

"A forced marriage would fall under those restrictions, surely."

"But an underage forced marriage would *not*, as it is illegal, and no royal family would risk a competitor seeing the inclusion in the spell and reporting it."

Which they would if it gave them an advantage over said competitor. "If there's a witness who can confirm this marriage is nothing more than an act of revenge, why wasn't he or she called first?"

"Because he's not back in Australia yet."

My eyebrows rose. "Where is he?"

"Touring Europe. It's taken us a while to track him down."

"Does that mean he's on the witness list?"

Anthony nodded. "With a question mark. The opposition will, of course, be hoping we'd be unsuccessful in getting him here in time."

"I take it that means my father had a hand in secreting him away?"

"It's a good bet, although we have no proof. The only reason I discovered his existence was because of the gossip brigade. He told a friend who told a friend."

"Got to love the power of gossips." We had a brigade in the reservation, and they rarely missed a morsel.

"Yes." He packed up his things and rose. "Do you and Belle need a lift back home?"

I shook my head. "Ashworth will be waiting in short-term parking for us."

"Then I will see you here tomorrow at one. Don't be late."

"Unless fate intervenes and tosses another dead body my way, I certainly won't."

He gave me an odd sort of look that suggested he wasn't sure if I was serious or not. I smiled and added, "Fate has a habit of doing shitty things like that. And Belle wasn't wrong when she said this sorcerer was coming after my family."

"He won't succeed. Your father is one of the strongest witches within the council."

"I'm sure Clayton thought exactly the same thing, and look where it got him—torn apart by a pissed-off vampire. Besides, we're talking about a dark sorcerer here—they're a whole different ball game."

I knew *that* from experience.

"I'm sure the council know what they're doing."

"I'm sure they think they do."

He smiled. "I know you have no reason to trust or believe them, but they are not all incompetent fools."

"Oh, I know, but let me ask you this—how many powerful supernatural entities have they had to deal with in the last thirteen years? I'm not talking psi bandits or rogue witches here, but fair dinkum demons and the like."

"None, of course, but that doesn't mean they can't pull in experienced people from elsewhere." He hesitated. "And even if they couldn't, there are elements within the Black Lantern that would be able to help them."

My eyebrows rose. "I thought the Society dealt with problematic witches and psychics rather than the supernatural world?"

"They do, but there is the occasional crossover."

Something Ashworth had once said. I rose and gathered my purse and coat. "I'll see you tomorrow, then."

He nodded. "Should be an interesting day—I'll be calling your mother."

"Color me unexcited."

He gave me a sideways glance. "I thought it was only your father you had a less-than-harmonious relationship with?"

"I think 'combative' would be a more apt word when it comes to my father. No matter what happens with the case, he still has every intention of trying to sell me off for the family's gain."

"You're an adult. He can't do or promise anything on your behalf now."

"Doesn't stop him from trying."

"I guess not." He opened the door and ushered me out of the room. "If that *is* the case, then I would be very cautious about getting too close to him. There're more sophisticated ways of drugging someone into submission these days."

"Trust me, when it comes to my father, I'm not getting

within ten feet of him." And I certainly wasn't going to accept any food, drink, or anything else from him or any other fucking member of my family.

"Good." He walked me down to the waiting area, nodded to Belle, and then continued on.

Belle picked up her coat and purse and slung them over her shoulder. "How'd the rest of the afternoon go after the fabulousness of my departure?"

I grinned and hooked my arm through hers as we headed for the elevators that would take us down to the parking area. "You weren't following it all through our connection?"

"Monty rang with another update."

My gut did its twisty thing. "What's happened now?"

"Rockfall. No one hurt, but several houses received minor damage. No prizes for guessing who owned one of them."

I wrinkled my nose. "Did you mention Eli's suggestion of me going back there?"

"I did, but Monty's not sure a flying visit will improve matters. He says the targeting is more refined than he originally thought, and maybe it isn't just the old wellspring."

My eyebrows rose. "It can't be the other one. Katie controls that, and there's no way she'd attack her family."

"Unless she's making a point."

"I doubt it. She knows why I'm up in Canberra."

"Yes, but that still leaves the possibility that she's gathering the older wellspring's anger and directing it to less harmful outcomes. It would certainly explain why no one has been injured as yet."

"If the old wellspring has gained some form of sentience from me, then I doubt it would actively set out to harm anyone. I mean, the do-no-harm rule is a governing mindset for all witches, so by rights that should leach over."

"Until we know far more about the interaction between the Fenna and wellsprings, we can't be sure of anything."

"True."

I unlinked my arm and pushed open the door into the parking area. The thick smell of exhaust fumes and petrol hit, and my already twisty stomach rose in protest. I stumbled to one side and threw up again.

"Fuck, Liz, are you all right?"

"Yeah." I took the water bottle she handed me and rinsed my mouth out. "I've been drinking their stale coffee all afternoon. I think the combination of it and the exhaust stench just got the better of me."

She sniffed. "Your stomach has been seriously tetchy of late—you sure you're not pregnant or something?"

I snorted. "I haven't skipped a period, and besides, I'm on protection."

"Accidents do happen. When are you due?"

"I'm a few days late, but that's nothing unusual given my period is often all over the place when I'm stressed." And stress had certainly been piled on over the last few months. I shrugged. "Fate is a bitch, but even she wouldn't do that to me."

Belle grinned. "I wouldn't be betting on it. Besides, with all the changes the wild magic is making to your body, there's an outside chance the pill will have stopped working."

"Very outside."

"Still worth checking. Besides, if you do the test up here, the gossip brigade can't report the event to anyone."

That was *definitely* a good point. I sighed. "Fine. Will

you be able to pick me up a pregnancy test kit tomorrow, while I'm in court?"

"Sure. And let's hope it is nothing more than a coincidence. Otherwise, it's going to throw a spanner in the relationship works."

"It won't change a goddamn thing," I said flatly. "There's no way on God's green earth that I'd ever use a pregnancy to retain a man."

She held up a hand. "I know, but Aiden may have other opinions on that. He *is* all about family, after all."

"His family, not *our* family." I sniffed. "And, right now, I just don't want to think about him or pregnancy or even the wild magic getting wilder. Let's just concentrate on the trial and getting the hell out of here."

"What are we going to do about the sorcerer?" she said.

I glanced at her. "I'm not sure we can do anything about him. We're not even involved in the hunt."

"You and I both know that's not going to stop you."

A smile tugged at my lips. "I think the bigger question is, can we trust my father not to use these kills to his advantage?"

"Hard to do that if he's been murdered." She paused. "Although, given he's such a determined bastard, he'd just come back from the dead and continue on as normal."

I laughed, as she'd no doubt intended.

"If we were home, I'd ask Aiden to let me view the victim's belongings and see if I could find something to trace him with. But we're not, so..." I trailed off and shrugged.

"You could talk to Samuel. He might be amenable."

"I guess, but they've no doubt a ton of stronger psi hunters they could turn to in this sort of situation."

"Stronger, maybe, but as experienced?" She wrinkled her nose. "Unlikely, given there hasn't been a 'this sort of situation' here for over a decade. We, on the other hand, have experienced said situations quite regularly."

"Let's hope the wild magic's new vigor doesn't mean we'll be facing more of them for years ahead."

"Amen to that." She tucked her arm back through mine. "Ready to move on? Mom will be annoyed if we're late for dinner."

I laughed again. "No, she won't. She'll just be happy to have us all the same city again."

We continued on through the parking area and found Ashworth and Eli parked in the short-term waiting zone near the exit gate.

"How'd things go today?" Eli asked, once we'd both climbed in.

"Aside from Belle informing my father the sorcerer had a body bag with his name on it, about as well as can be expected," I replied.

Ashworth laughed as he started the car and headed out into the traffic. "What happened to letting the authorities deal with that bit of news?"

"The bastard annoyed me," Belle said. "Couldn't help it."

"Understandable, I guess," Eli said. "How'd he take the news?"

"He was suitably unimpressed." I shrugged, though neither man would be able to see the movement. "Eli, did you contact Hattie about getting hold of the old files?"

"I did. She said she'd bring them home this evening." He turned around to look at me. "Are you sure you want to be viewing them? It might raise a few nasty memories."

"Can't get any nastier than unwittingly walking into an almost exact copy of my sister's death."

Or I hoped it couldn't. Precognition hadn't bothered me

much in the last couple of days, but the respite might not last if these kills ramped up.

Belle squeezed my hand, and I glanced at her, smiling. *I'm fine. Really.*

She didn't say anything, but she knew the lie.

As we crawled through the peak hour traffic, heading toward the Sarr family compound in Campbell, Eli regaled us with stories about their visit to Maya, his youngest sister, this afternoon. Apparently, her kids had managed to twist Ashworth around their little fingers and had even elicited a promise that they could come stay with him and Eli next school holidays.

"I am, of course, hoping that the RWA will call me out on a job during that period," Ashworth said dryly. "I'm not sure what madness had me agreeing, but as gorgeous as the three of them are, I doubt I can handle a week of them. Far too noisy and energetic for this old man."

"Says the old man who was down on the floor playing fairies with Monika for half the afternoon," Eli said.

I laughed. "Oh, please tell me you got photos."

"I surely did."

"And *I* threatened violence if he showed them to anyone but family," Ashworth grumbled.

"Just as well we're that then," I said.

"It's Monty I'm worried about. That lad would have a field day with such photos."

Belle grinned. "Since when has anything he's ever said worried you?"

Ashworth laughed. "True enough."

Belle's mom—Ava—was waiting on the balcony of their expansive home by the time we arrived. Like many of the witch compounds in this particular area, there were multiple generations in residence. Belle's parents lived in the main house—a long, sixties-style building that had been extended to add a second floor on one half of the building—while her grandparents on her dad's side lived in a granny flat behind the pool area, and her sister's family lived in the four-bedroom cottage that backed onto the Mount Ainslie Nature Reserve.

Belle climbed out the minute Ashworth stopped the car and ran up the steps to her mom, wrapping her in the biggest hug. The two of them were peas in a pod—so alike, in fact, that Ava really could have been mistaken for Belle's older sister.

I walked up the steps and said, "Lovely to see you again, Ava."

"Don't you be giving me any of that polite shit," she growled. "Get over here and give me a hug."

I did so, grinning like a loon. She'd always been a second mom to me, treating me no different than any of her own. In fact, if it hadn't been for Belle's family showing me what a loving relationship could and *should* be, who knows what sort of emotionally damaged mess I would have been.

She greeted Ashworth and Eli warmly and then said, "Edward's out in the courtyard, tending to the barbeque. We'd best get in before he starts burning things."

She led the way into the house. The screams of kids echoed through the wide halls, and I gave Ashworth a mischievous glance. "Sounds like there're more kids here for you to play dress-up with."

"You'll be appreciating my willingness to go the extra yard to entertain the littlies when you have them, lassie."

"Well, *these* littlies are into chasey at the moment," Ava said, "so if you're going to play with the lads, best borrow some running shoes."

Eli laughed. "Meaning my man will definitely sleep

well tonight."

We wound our way through the house—it might have been extended but it had retained its higgledy-piggledy nature—then walked through the dine-in kitchen with its sixties-style cupboards and colors out into the patio area. Everyone was there—Belle's sister Alison, her husband Dylan, and their kids Eddie and Beth; Belle's grandparents on her dad's side; and even her brother, Josh, who last we'd heard was working for the London PSI Unit—the biggest psi center in the world. While both he and Alison were strong telepaths, Josh's secondary talent was energy medicine—a rare and much sought-after ability that could heal using empathic, etheric, astral, mental, or spiritual energy.

We were introduced to Josh's partner, Jenny, who had two young kids the same age as Eddie—and then got down to the serious business of eating and catching up with what everyone had been doing. Needless to say, Belle also got the second degree from her grandparents over her current reluctance to permanently snare her man. Time was a-wasting, and they needed more grandkiddies, apparently.

It was close to ten when I felt the play of ghostly fingers down the length of my arm. Tension stirred through me, part of which seemed to be a transference from the ghost itself.

Belle, I said, not wanting to draw attention by speaking out loud and perhaps scaring away the apparition, *is there a spirit standing behind my left shoulder?*

Belle was sitting between her mom and sister but leaned past the latter on the pretext of grabbing some cheese. *Not that I can see.*

The caress came again, this time tugging lightly at my fingers. I looked around and, for the briefest of seconds, the air shimmered, revealing a humanoid form. It was definitely a spirit, so why wasn't Belle seeing her? She was the spirit talker, not me.

Maybe I'm not meant to, she said.

I frowned. *Meaning what?*

There are ghosts—and spirits—with the capacity to conceal their presence from spirit talkers. That's obviously what's happening here.

Why would she conceal her presence if she wants me to follow her?

I don't know. She paused. *You want me to try and talk to her?*

Do you think it'll work?

The only way we're going to find out is to try.

My spirit friend once again tugged at my hand. Her fingers were warm and almost real against mine, the touch filled with a sense of urgency. *I don't think we dare waste the time right now. Something is happening, and she needs me to follow.*

Well, you're not fucking going alone. Not with a sorcerer out there in the wild. For all we know, this could be some sort of trap.

It's not.

Why I was so sure of that, I couldn't say, other than the fact that I'd felt no malice or evil or anything that vaguely resembled deceit in that insubstantial touch. In fact, it had felt oddly... familiar?

Which was decidedly weird.

Belle waved her hands to catch everyone's attention. "Ladies and gents, we have a situation. It would appear Lizzie's friendly ghost has reappeared and once again wants us to follow her."

"Lizzie has a ghost?" Ava said, eyebrows rising. "This is a new development—do we know who it is?"

"Not yet," I said. "I only picked her up today. Belle hasn't had a chance to talk to her yet."

"Has she got anything to do with the murder this afternoon that you've all been studiously avoiding mentioning?" Edward said in a dry sort of tone.

"You know about that?" Belle said, surprised.

"Darling girl, have you forgotten we're still running the Psychic Advisory Commission? There's nothing psi related that happens in this town that we don't know about within an hour of it happening."

The PAC was a government-sponsored service designed to advise and help psychics on all matters, be they legal, personal, or talent related. Ghosts were part of their purview, and one they dealt with surprisingly often. Canberra might be one of Australia's youngest cities, but she hosted plenty of ghostly entities, thanks no doubt to the high number of witches living here. The two things often seemed related.

"The murder was sorcerer rather than psi related, though," I said.

"Perhaps, but the spirit world was abuzz with the news that a new player had risen," Edward said. Like Belle, he was a strong spirit talker.

"If she's only just risen, she wouldn't have the power to interact in any way with the physical world," Belle said.

My spirit tugged at my fingers again; this time, her demand I follow washed over me in a thick wave. Which shouldn't be happening and suggested that this ghost and I had a connection that went beyond the metaphysical. One that was strengthening with every interaction. "Um, guys, we haven't the time to debate what she should and shouldn't be able to do. She needs me to follow her right *now*."

Ashworth and Eli thrust to their feet. "Then let us be

going."

"This is not how I'd hoped the evening would go," Ava said with a soft sigh. "Do you wish us to accompany you? We know this city better than any of you—"

"And the four of *us* are better equipped to deal with this type of situation." Belle kissed her parents' cheeks. "I'll let you know the minute we uncover what is going on."

"Do, please," Edward said.

"And come back for dinner tomorrow," Ava said. "You can update us on the court case *and* the sorcerer hunt."

"If nothing else goes wrong, that would be lovely." I scooped up my purse and coat and followed the vaguely shimmering presence through the house.

"We taking the car?" Ashworth asked as we walked out onto the front patio.

When I hesitated, the spirit grabbed my hand and tugged me down the driveway.

"I guess not," Eli said, amusement evident. "You three go on—I'll grab our backpacks from the car."

"You came prepared?" Belle said, surprised.

"Lassie," Ashworth said, "with the habit you two have of landing us in strange and unusual situations, we concluded it's safer never to travel without all the necessary witch paraphernalia."

We were led to a path that took us from Cobby Street to the Mount Ainslie Reserve. Once we were through the bollards that signified the entrance, Eli handed out flashlights. I flicked mine on and swept it across the stone path that meandered through the white-trunked eucalypts. This area was well used during the day by walkers and runners alike—or had been, when Belle and I were kids—but there was something almost mystical about it on a still, foggy night.

We walked on and, all too quickly, the path began to climb. It soon intersected with another, and I paused, wondering whether we needed to go left or right. My ghost chose neither. Instead, she led us onto what looked to be little more than a roo track and went straight up the hill.

"We keep going this way," Belle said, her voice soft but nevertheless sharp on the still air, "we'll hit the outskirts of the old quarry."

"If the quarry is our end goal," I replied, a little more breathlessly than I liked. "Wouldn't it have been easier to approach it from the lookout? It's only a five-minute walk from there."

"Perhaps your ghost isn't aware of that," Eli said. "Maybe she's not from around these parts."

"Everyone in Canberra knows the lookout and the quarry," I said. "Most kids have played in the damn thing at one point or another."

"Not most kids," Belle said. "Royal lines wouldn't be caught dead around this area. I mean, *Sarrs* live here."

I snorted, though it was nothing more than a rather sad truth. Such was the disconnect between the upper and lower classes of witch that they did tend to stick to their "own" areas and school precincts. Belle had been the only Sarr in our school, and while the board would definitely have preferred she not be there, they couldn't do anything because of who I was.

We continued on through the ghostly gums, the fog getting thicker the farther up the hill we moved.

Then I smelled it.

I stopped so abruptly that Belle had to do a quick side-step to avoid me.

"Is there a problem?" Ashworth said.

"Yeah. There's blood up ahead."

"Fresh or otherwise?" Eli asked.

"Fresh." I swept the light across the trees, but I wasn't seeing a body and I certainly wasn't sensing anything resembling magic.

"And is your ghost still here?" Belle asked.

"Not only here, but insisting we hurry."

"Easy for her to say," Ashworth muttered. "She hasn't got old legs."

"Or indeed any legs," Eli said.

A smile tugged at my lips but faded all too quickly. I might not be able to sense any magic, but there was something here. Something unpleasant and *wrong*. Trepidation once again skittered across my skin, but I forced the concern aside and trudged up the hill. Both the growing number of rocks and the path's roughness suggested we were getting close to the outskirts of one of the old quarries.

If we were dealing with the same sorcerer and this was another of his kills, why here? The last time he'd terrorized Canberra, he'd shown a distinct preference for old warehouses. None of the kills had been out in the open.

Did that mean we *weren't* dealing with the same man? That it was all nothing more than a coincidence?

I honestly didn't believe that to be true, but we'd find out soon enough.

The scent of blood strengthened. The ghost lightly tugged at my left hand, guiding me off the track and into the trees. After a few more minutes, the light picked out a shoulder-height, curving stone wall.

"Whatever we've being sent here to find is behind that," I said.

"That's Mawu's hut, if I've got my geography correct," Belle said.

I glanced at her. "Mawu being a witch, I take it?"

She nodded. "She claimed she was a goddess of the sun and the moon and was basically as mad as a march hare. But harmless. She'd be pissed if evil has used this site."

"Could she be my ghost?"

Belle hesitated, scanning the area before shaking her head. "She's here—I can sense her presence off to the left—but she's definitely not the one who led us here." She cocked her head, expression slightly distracted. "She wishes us to know she is indeed unimpressed and asks if we can cleanse the site once we have finished."

"Suggesting that whatever we're about to find was indeed left here by dark magic." Ashworth stopped and undid his backpack. "I'm not feeling anything in the way of spells, old or new, but we'd better take some basic precautions."

He handed us each small bottles of holy water and a coin warding charm on a leather chain. Belle and I each wore a multi-layered charm around our necks that countered all sorts of spells and supernatural beasties, but this felt very different. The magic in it was an intricate mix of both Eli's and Ashworth's spells, but I didn't immediately recognize any of them.

"What does this do?"

"It'll counter any attempts to magically locate you," Eli said. "Be it via a summoning spell or a tracker."

My gaze jumped to his. "You think this could be a trap?"

"Well, I don't think it's a coincidence that whatever lies within the remains of the hut was placed here at the same time you're visiting the Sarr compound."

I remembered what Samuel had said about the magic circling the first murder being designed to collect and catalogue information and swore softly. I hadn't thought the implications of *that* through far enough.

I flipped the coin over in my hand. It was only small, but the weight of magic sitting on it made it far heavier. "There seems to be far more to the spells on this thing than just an anti-summoning spell."

"That *is* a rather meaty spell at the best of times," Ashworth said, "But we've also woven through a beacon spell so that if you are snatched, we can find you."

"How is a beacon different to a locator?"

"It's not as obvious and has more chance of escaping the notice of a wary witch or sorcerer."

The first thing any sorcerer worth his salt would probably do was smash the charm and thereby destroy any magic attached to it, but Ashworth was as aware of that as I was. And I guessed a small hope was better than no hope.

I slipped the coin over my neck, tucked it under my shirt, and then slowly cut through the trees, my eyes on the stone wall and the smell of blood thickening in my nostrils.

I followed the wall around to the left, found the entrance, and stepped inside. In the middle of the main circle was a second one, though it was only about a foot in height and probably would have contained the main cooking and heating fire for the old hut. In the middle of that ring lay the source of the blood—a rabbit.

Its throat had been cut and its blood had been trailed over the top of the stones and across the neat row of papers that lay within the circle.

I didn't have to get any closer to see what those papers were. In the bright beams of all four flashlights, it was pretty obvious.

They were photos of our sorcerer's targets.

Photos of my family.

CHAPTER FIVE

I forced my feet closer. The rabbit's blood gleamed in the multiple beams of light, an indication that it was definitely a recent kill. It also meant that Ashworth was right—the sorcerer had known where I was.

But had he known the ghost would lead me here? Was she somehow in servitude to the man? There was no sense of evil emanating from her, but maybe that was because she inherently wasn't. Maybe she was being forced to do his bidding, though surely if that *was* the case, I'd be getting some sense of distress or fear through our brief interactions. That I wasn't suggested she might be a "free" agent—but if she was, then how was she connected to these kills? Because I had a feeling she was, even if I didn't know how.

I stopped a few feet away from the old firepit and studied the photos within it. There were six in all—the same number of people he'd killed the first time. The decapitated woman I'd found this morning was the first in line and her image bore a bloody cross. The next in line was a woman I didn't recognize, though she did have the family features. The third was my brother, the fourth my mother, the fifth my father, and the final me. As Belle had suggested, I was his dessert—his final treat in his quest for revenge.

Under the photos, held in place by the dead rabbit's front paws, was a message that looked to be written in blood; *Revenge will taste as sweet as your bloodline.*

Belle stopped beside me. "Well, I guess this confirms our thoughts on who it is and why he's here."

"Yes." I flicked off my flashlight and shoved my hands in my pockets, more to conceal the sudden bout of trembling than because they were cold. "Why announce his plans like this, though? It gives us a chance to protect everyone."

"Could be he loves a challenge." Ashworth walked around the firepit, sweeping his light back and forth across the ground. "Remember we're talking about a dark sorcerer here—they're mad bastards at the best of times."

"And this one probably more so if he somehow survived what you and his demons did to him the first time," Eli said.

I glanced at him. "If he survived his injuries all those years ago, why would his demons have attacked him?"

"Because demons are generally only controlled by a sorcerer in peak health. They would have taken advantage of his weaker state."

"They obviously didn't kill him though," I said. "These notes weren't written by a ghost, nor was the first victim killed by one."

"True," Ashworth said. "But it's possible he's in an in-between state, especially given I'm finding no trace of prints on the ground and no indication that he's used a magical or practical means of getting rid of them."

"You're talking about a wraith," Belle said.

I glanced at her. "What's the difference between a wraith and a spirit or ghost? Aren't they basically variations of the same thing?"

She shook her head. "Superstition would have us believe that wraiths are nothing more than the tortured souls of dark witches or sorcerers, created when something goes wrong with their spelling—usually when they're trying to extend their life in some way. In reality, they're dark sorcerers or witches who have *actually* died, but who have 'unfinished' business that keeps them on this earth in an undead form."

"Meaning they're basically a zombie?" I said.

"No," Eli said. "They're far worse."

"Zombies are pretty damn bad." I knew this from having dealt with one.

"Zombies aren't magic capable and have no capacity for thought or reason. They are simply compliant flesh and bones. Wraiths, on the other hand, have all the skills and reason they had when alive."

"Well, fuck," I muttered, "we really get to play with all the good ghouls, don't we?"

Ashworth laughed. "It would seem so. On the bright side, wraiths are fairly easy to kill with either holy water or a blessed weapon."

"And using either means getting entirely too close to the bastards," Belle said. "You also forgot the side note on that— if you don't manage to kill them the first time, you just piss them off and make them more dangerous."

"Meaning if there's any killing to be done, it had better be done by me," I said. "He's already mad at me, so why extend it?"

"You can't and won't be going after him alone," Eli said, "so get it out of your head right now."

I didn't bother responding because there was little point. If push came to shove, we both knew well enough that I *would* confront this thing alone because the last thing I wanted was to endanger their lives as well.

Which *didn't* mean I wouldn't explore every other possible option first. I wasn't stupid and I certainly didn't want to die—especially when I almost *had* the last time I'd confronted this bastard.

And sure, I was a whole lot more knowledgeable and powerful now than then, but that upgrade might not make a jot of difference when confronting a man with decades of knowledge and who knew how many demons backing him.

I glanced back at the photographs. "I have no idea who that second woman is, but we need to find and protect her fast."

"Could it be Juli's wife?" Belle said.

Juli—Julius—was my brother and had taken the mantle as my father's heir after Cat's death. I wrinkled my nose. "That note says this is about bloodline, so being married into our family won't count."

"What about your dad's siblings?" Belle asked. "He has three of them, hasn't he?"

"Yes, but the last I heard they were all overseas. My father didn't appreciate the competition."

"That was ten years ago," Belle said. "A lot could have changed since then. Hell, we're evidence enough of that."

"True." I got out my phone. "I'll call Samuel."

"You might want to call your father, as well," Ashworth said, then held up a hand to counter my almost instantaneous retort. "I know, I know, but at the very least, you should ask him who that woman is."

"Samuel will be able to trace her."

"But they might not be fast enough. You're the one who said if he is following the same pattern, he'll kill again tomorrow night."

"Which gives the council and Samuel time to find her."

He gave me the sort of look a father would a recalcitrant child. I couldn't help grinning. "I'd reserve that expression for Eli's nieces and nephews—it's got far more chance of working on them."

He harrumphed. "I know you dislike the man—"

"Dislike is putting it mildly."

"But I'm thinking you also don't want him dead. At the very least, talk to your mother if you don't want to speak to your father. If there's one thing we've learned in the last few months, it's that death has its own timing and waits for no man or woman."

I sighed. He was right. And I didn't want my father dead, as much as I might have silently wished for it in the darker days when we'd first left Canberra. Which didn't mean I'd ring him—not unless there was no other option. "Let me ring Samuel, then I'll call Mom."

He nodded. "Eli and I will check the wider perimeter just to ensure he hasn't left any nasty little surprises behind."

As they left, I made the call to Samuel.

"Lizzie," he said, in a somber sort of tone, "don't take this the wrong way, but I was hoping I wouldn't hear from you again so soon."

"Oh, trust me, I was hoping for the same thing."

"I take it your ghost has made a return?"

"Yes, and this time, she's led us to a list of intended victims—all of them my family."

"Then I'll be there ASAP." He paused. "Send me a photo of the list. I'll get the team straight onto organizing protection for them all."

"Will do."

"Thanks. Are you able to stay there and protect the site

until I arrive?"

"Yes, I'm not here alone this time."

"Oh, good."

He hung up. I took the photo, sent it across to him along with my location details, then scrolled through my contacts list until I found my mother's number. But I didn't make the call. Not immediately. I *had* talked to her recently, and it was fine, considering, but there remained a deep reluctance within me to have too much to do with either of them.

"Which no doubt stems from a fear that doing so will eventually lead to you being sucked back into their toxic orbits," Belle said. "But you're stronger than that now."

"I'd like to think that, but there remains a part of me that's not so sure."

"No doubt that part is the inner unloved kid so hurt by the lack of parental care, and yet so desperate for any form of acknowledgment."

"No doubt." A somewhat bitter smile twisted my lips. "But that kid should have gotten well and truly over it by now."

"Why? Neglect is a serious trauma for any child, and you've spent most of your adult life running from it."

And was still running from it, in many respects. I sighed. "I just—"

"No matter what that inner child or the current adult thinks and fears, we both know you wouldn't be able to live with yourself if something happened to your parents and you made no attempt to stop it."

"God," I said, "when did you get so damn insightful?"

She laughed. "I've spent most of my life with you, my friend. I can guess how you're going to react better than I can guess how I might."

I drew in a deep breath, released it slowly, and then hit

the call button. It rang for what seemed forever, then a warm and yet somehow cool voice said, "Elizabeth, this is a surprise."

No doubt. "Has Samuel Kang or anyone from his team been in contact with you or Father?"

"Not that I'm aware of—why?"

If they hadn't been in contact, it meant they hadn't yet formally identified the headless woman. Which I guessed was not unexpected, given she'd been naked and didn't have any form of ID on her. They'd be relying on print and dental records to help with all that, and those things did take time, as frustrating as it often was.

"Have you heard anything about the murder in the park?"

"Your father mentioned it in passing, yes." She paused. "In case you are wondering, we remain on 'only when necessary' speaking terms."

Which I knew was Mom's way of saying they had a working relationship, not a physical one. It had happened on a regular basis in the past, when one of them got pissed off over something the other had done or decided. Not that anyone outside direct family would have known there was any sort of tension between the two—the family business and reputation were far more important than anything as inconsequential as emotion or sex or having to deal with a disappointing daughter...

I thrust *that* thought into the mental bin where it belonged and said, "Did he tell you we think he's on the hit list?"

"He did." It was said in a tone that very much suggested my father hadn't believed Belle. Whether Mom did I couldn't say. There was nothing in her voice that gave any indication as to her thoughts. "Is that what you're calling about?"

I hesitated and glanced at Belle. *Do I say anything? Or should I leave it to Samuel? I mean, it's not like they believed me the first time this bastard hit.*

Different time, different situation, she said.

But not different people. I sighed and said to Mom, "Sort of. If I send you a photo right now, will you be able to tell me who it is?"

"If I know them, yes. But why the urgency? Can't it wait until the morning? I'm about to go to bed."

"I wouldn't be ringing you if it wasn't important, trust me on that."

"Fine," she sighed, in a put-out sort of way. "Send it to me."

"Hang on." I switched over to the camera app and took a photo of the unknown second woman, being careful not to include either the dead woman's image or Juli's. "Okay, just sent you the pic."

A second later, a soft ding echoed down the line. "Received. Just a moment and I'll look at it." There was a long pause. "That's your cousin, Deni Marlowe."

I vaguely remembered Deni—or rather, remembered the fact that she'd had the misfortune of being born with green eyes and a splattering of freckles across her cheeks and nose, just like me. "I thought Aunt Frankie had moved to the UK for good?"

"She had, but she was offered a promotion back here and returned a few years ago."

My gaze went to the photo with the cross on it. Though my memories of her were rather vague, the headless woman could definitely have been my aunt—aside from the fact she had the family facial structure, her nose was just as proud and prominent as my father's.

"Has Aunt Frankie got white streaks in her hair?"

"A curious question, but I don't believe so."

Relief stirred, though in truth Mom's answer really didn't confirm the body I'd found wasn't my aunt. There were some demons who fed on their victim's life force, and the process of draining them unto death quite often rapidly aged them. That could have been what I'd seen, even if the victim wasn't a dried-out husk. "Have you got contact details for Deni? I need to speak to her urgently."

"What is this all about, Elizabeth? Surely if your father and any of our relations are in danger, the high council will handle it. They do have a special division for this sort of thing."

"That division fucked up so badly that Cat died before the sorcerer who kidnapped her was dealt with." *By me*, I wanted to add, *not the council and certainly not you or Dad.* "He's come back, Mom, and he's intending to take out the rest of us."

There was a long pause. I expected her to say something along the lines of *are you sure?* but she surprised me. "You've seen this?"

"I've seen his first kill."

She sucked in a breath. "Deni?"

"No. But Deni's next on his list."

"Then who..." She paused. "Frances? She didn't have white streaks in her hair, but still..."

"I honestly don't know, Mom."

"There would be a family resemblance."

"There was."

Another long pause. "I will contact Deni straight—"

"No," I cut in. "You need to contact Juli and warn him,

and you all need to go somewhere totally unknown to anyone in your contacts lists and start laying down multiple protections."

"There is no safer place than the home compound, Elizabeth."

"He drew Catherine from there," I reminded her. "He can draw you."

She didn't say anything to that. Perhaps she didn't believe she could fall prey to this monster as easily as Cat had, thanks to the fact that she was older and wiser. And that might well be true, but I'd still rather she not bet her life on it.

"I'll talk to your father," she said. "What of the court case? Will it still proceed? I haven't heard otherwise."

I hadn't even thought about the court case. I'd be seriously pissed if it was delayed and I had to come back at a later date.

"Neither have I," I said. "I'm presuming at this point that tomorrow's session will be on, but who knows what will happen after that."

"I'll send you Deni's details, but do please be careful, Elizabeth. No matter what you may think of me, I do not, under any circumstances, want to lose another daughter."

Tears stung my eyes, and I blinked them back furiously. Damn it, I was an adult, not that little kid desperate for a kind word from her parents.

"I have no intention of dying, Mom. I have a good life and a good man waiting for me to come home."

There was another of those long pauses. "That's good."

A smiled tugged my lips. I suspected the topic of my partner would be high on the list of items to be discussed at the dinner table tonight—though I doubted the news would squash my father's intentions, matchmaking wise.

"Keep in contact, please," she said. "I will see you in court tomorrow."

"You will," I said, and hung up.

A few seconds later, Deni's contact details arrived. I googled the address and saw she lived in Kingston.

"You going to ring her?" Belle asked. "Or go there?"

I hesitated. "Go. She's not going to take me at my word —not over the phone, anyway."

And especially not when it had been so long since we'd seen each other. She had no reason to trust me—no reason to believe me, especially after everything my father had said about my involvement in Cat's death.

Belle nodded. "We can borrow Mom's car. That way, I can be close enough to help if things go tits up without being close enough for my presence to offend Deni's sensibilities."

I raised an eyebrow. "Deni never had a problem with you."

"That was back when we were all kids. She's had plenty of time to develop all sorts of prejudices since then."

I'd like to think she wouldn't have but knew that was probably a faint hope up here. "Check with your mom that she's okay with us borrowing a car, and then we'll head over to Deni's."

Belle dug out her phone and made the call. I took several photos of the grim warning, then squatted near the rabbit's remains and tentatively touched its blood. It was as dead as the rabbit it had come from. I sighed. While I could use reasonably fresh blood as a means of tracking someone, I guessed I was being a little too hopeful that the skill might bleed over to animals.

I rose and brushed my fingers clean on a tissue. As Ashworth and Eli returned, I said, "Anything?"

Ashworth shook his head. "Not a footprint or anything else to suggest anyone has moved through this area. It all but confirms that we're dealing with a wraith or some other dark and deadly form of ghost."

I raised my eyebrows. "How many other kinds are there?"

"It's probably better not to know, lass."

It probably was.

"Right," Belle said, "Mom said we can use the Audi. No one needs it for the next few days."

"You're going somewhere?" Eli asked.

I nodded. "The woman in the second photo is my cousin, Deni. Mom sent me her address, so we're heading over to talk to her. You two will need to wait for Samuel."

"Be wary walking into her house," Ashworth said. "It's possible he's already laid a snare or two there."

"Not for me, he wouldn't have. I'm last on his list."

"Doesn't mean he won't grab you first and make you watch him murder everyone else," Eli said. "These bastards are nasty like that."

A reminder I didn't need.

"Don't forget to ask Samuel to cleanse the site once they're done," Belle said. "I suspect Mawu will make life a little more difficult for hikers if we don't."

Ashworth nodded and we left. Ava had the car out of the garage and warmed up by the time we got back—she would have been following our progress through the park telepathically—and repeated Ashworth's warning to be careful.

Belle jumped into the driver side while I set the GPS for the address. She lived in what Google told me was a boutique—read: expensive—residential development, and thanks to the fact that at this hour of the night, the streets were all but empty, it didn't take us all that long to get there.

Belle stopped just behind a fancy-looking SUV and glanced over at the building. "Art Deco style—nice."

"No doubt a nice price, too. Deni's top floor—can't see any lights on."

"Which might not mean anything, given we don't know how they divided the building when they converted it. Hopefully, she *is* home."

"Hopefully, the sorcerer hasn't gotten here before us."

Belle glanced at me. "If he's following the same pattern as before, he won't have."

"That's a big if, especially if the first victim *was* my aunt. The bruising suggests he snatched her days ago, which means the so-called pattern only exists in our minds."

Belle grunted. "Then be fucking careful. And yell if you sense anything untoward."

"I will." I touched her arm lightly—more to comfort myself than her—and climbed out. The icy wind stirred around me, and I shivered into my coat. The scent of rain hung in the air, strong enough to suggest that it was going to bucket down soon. Hopefully, we wouldn't be out in it when that happened.

Instinct whispered I should be so lucky.

I ran across the road and approached the building's double width wood and glass front door. There was an electronic keypad and a buzzer system to the right, the latter containing the surnames of all eleven residents. Deni's was ten, and one of two penthouses. I pressed the buzzer then waited for several minutes. No response. I pressed it again. Again, nothing.

I took a deep, frustrated breath and released it slowly. Why could nothing ever be easy? For all I knew, she had the bell turned down because she was asleep, but I couldn't risk leaving until I knew for sure. And that meant I'd have to do this the old-fashioned way—which, when it came to electronics, wasn't always easy. Or successful.

I wove the spell that would hopefully imitate an unlock command around my fingers, then pressed it into the mechanical lock. It was a spell we'd discovered in one of the books Belle had inherited from her gran, and it wasn't one I'd used all that often. I certainly hadn't updated its parameters to include the most up-to-date locks—mainly because to do that I had to have a working knowledge of said locks, and I didn't.

For several seconds, nothing happened, but just as I began to fear my spell was out of date, the door clicked open.

Lucky came Belle's comment. *I'd have thought apartments in this area would not only have the latest electronics, but also have taken precautions against unlock spells.*

For individual apartments, they might have.

It'd be easier to stop them from entering in the first place.

It probably would, but that would have cost extra money for building maintenance. And from the little I knew about them, most body corporates worked on extremely tight budgets. *I'm just hoping there aren't any overly alert witches in this place to sense my spell. I'll be in trouble if the police get here before I can speak to Deni.*

If the cops arrive, I'll send them elsewhere, Belle said.

I walked through the lobby, heading for the emergency stairs. There were two elevators, but they were also key coded, and I wasn't going to push my luck magically. Not until it was absolutely necessary, anyway.

The door into the emergency stairwell was one of those self-latching things, so it was just a matter of magically pushing down the inside lock to gain entry. Once I was through, I ran quickly—though not entirely silently—up to the fourth floor. I checked to make sure the door wasn't alarmed, then pushed it open and caught the edge of it, making sure it closed without force. Then I looked around.

The lobby was small but plushly decorated in dark wood and gold hues. The elevators lay in the center and there were only two other doors—one on the street side of the building, and one to my left. Deni's was left.

I spun on my heel and walked down. I couldn't sense any magical protection around the keycode lock, but there was definitely a weave of them around the door.

Trouble was, all of them had been shredded.

My pulse rate leapt. I swallowed to ease the sudden dryness in my throat and pressed the door buzzer. It rang inside, the sound soft and echoey.

As before, there was no response. Was she out, asleep, or dead?

Doubtful she'd be asleep, given the shredded protection spells, Belle said. *Maybe we'd better call Samuel and get some of his people here. Might be safer.*

I'm hesitant to do that until we know for sure what we're dealing with.

Who else could it be but our sorcerer?

Would our sorcerer have been so blatant and uncaring though? Nothing in his past suggests he's like that.

He wasn't a wraith in the past. Maybe he—or his demons —have grown impatient.

Maybe.

I shivered and pressed the buzzer again, even though I knew the result would be the same. Once its echoes had died down again, I tugged my sleeve over my fingers and lightly pressed them against the middle of the door.

It opened.

I didn't step inside.

Instead, I flared my nostrils and drew in the air that rolled out of the apartment even as I extended both my psychic and magical senses.

There was no blood, no smell of death, nothing to indicate anything *physically* untoward had happened.

My psi senses told a different story. As did my magical.

All hell had broken loose inside this apartment. Deni might not be here now, but a remnant of her magic was, and it had clashed against that of the man who'd broken into her apartment.

She'd been scared. Truly scared.

But anger lingered too, and its presence puzzled me more than anything else. That and the fact that the threads of magic still hanging in the air didn't *feel* the same as the magic that had surrounded the first murder. It was strong and filled with rage, but it *wasn't* dark.

We can't risk it not being our sorcerer, Belle said. *We need to find her.*

Yes, we did. And that meant going inside to find something that would allow us to do that.

I flexed my fingers, a repelling spell rolling around my right hand and the wild magic around the left. The latter was dangerous in a building filled with witches, but it was an automatic response to danger and not one I could entirely control. Hopefully, its pulse would be low enough that no one would feel it.

I carefully pushed the door all the way open and stepped into the hallway. To my right there were several doors, to my left a kitchen and dining area. While the vast amount of emotion and magic I sensed emanated from whatever rooms lay beyond the kitchen, I went right and checked all the closed doors. The last thing I needed was someone—or some*thing*—nasty jumping out at me. I discovered and checked a laundry cupboard, two linen closets, a bathroom, and a bedroom. All were empty. All were relatively free of the boiling riot of emotion and fear.

My stomach churned as I headed down the hall to the kitchen and dining area. I was well aware I wasn't about to find a body—the absence of blood and death scent told me that—but that didn't mean there couldn't be something else waiting. With all the broken magic still floating about the place, it was likely I wouldn't see a complete spell until I stumbled on it.

And then it might be too late.

I cautiously studied the kitchen and dining area before I entered, but the lack of anything untoward didn't ease my tension. I paused near the central island—which was as big as an eight-seater table—and studied the living area. It was generous in size and looked out over Lake Burley Griffin. There was a large, covered balcony to my left accessible through folding glass doors and another more regular doorway to my right—the main bedroom, perhaps?

I walked toward it, breathing through my mouth in an effort to avoid the increasing stink of fear and anger as I drew closer to the doorway. It told me one thing—Deni had known the person who'd broken in.

Shall I call the cops or Samuel? Belle said.

I hesitated briefly. *Samuel. We can't be sure that whoever snatched her hasn't been employed by our sorcerer. It would explain how he was in both places at basically the same time.*

Wraiths haven't got the same movement restrictions as we flesh beings have. He could have almost instantly gotten here from Mawu's hut.

This magic doesn't feel like his, though.

Belle grunted. *I'll make the call. Keep watching for traps, just in case.*

Tell him I'm going to try and trace her.

You know he'll just tell you to wait.

And given how often people tell me that, you know exactly what my response will be.

Yes, but I'll phrase it a little more politely.

Her voice was dry. I smiled and cautiously stepped into the bedroom. There were two more doors to my right, both open. One led into a large walk-in wardrobe, the other an ornate bathroom. The bed showed evidence of being slept in, suggesting Deni's intruder had indeed woken her.

I raised a hand and, using my psychometry skill, carefully checked the nearby makeup station for anything with a strong enough connection to use as a tracker. I didn't actually expect to find anything, and that's exactly what I found. I moved on to the chests of drawers on either side of the king-sized bed. A couple of gold rings registered a soft pulse, but it wasn't strong enough to use, especially given the head start her attacker had on us. I could form a deeper connection, of course, but I was loath to do that just in case something nasty happened when I was in Deni's mind. I'd heard too many tales of psychics losing their lives when in a deep connection and had certainly come close to it myself. Thank God Belle had been there to pull me out.

I moved on to the walk-in wardrobe. Like everything else in this bedroom, it was large, with not only multiple hanger spaces and drawers, but a shoe rack larger than my entire wardrobe and a jewelry station that would have had any thief drooling. I walked over and almost immediately found a strong pulse on a diamond-studded gold Piaget watch. If she used this as an everyday watch, she was obviously well off. There had to be at least twenty diamonds surrounding the asymmetrical dial.

I hesitated, then warily picked it up. Images and emotions assaulted my senses; fear, anger, and pain, all wrapped in flashes of darkness and light, the sensation of fast movement, and rope binding her hands and feet to each other in such a manner that her back was uncomfortably arched.

She was in the backseat of speeding car.

I let the watch go, tugged my sleeve over my hand to mute some of the sensations rolling off the watch, then picked it up and headed out.

Leaving the building was far easier than getting in, and I was back in the Audi within minutes. Thunder rumbled overhead, and in the distance, lightning flashed. The storm I'd sensed earlier was definitely on the way.

I buckled up as Belle started the car. "Where to?"

I gripped the watch's dial a little bit tighter, feeling a directional tug through the flow of sensory information. I didn't quite see the "guide rope"—a glittery silver thread that was a physical emanation of the connection between the watch and its owner—but I suspected I would once we were closer.

Of course, guide ropes were usually only visible when it came to *active* tracking spells, and even then, they weren't always in evidence. It definitely shouldn't be happening when it came to psi talents such as psychometry, but the wild magic had recently started blurring the line between the two.

"Head toward Capital Hill—I'll know more once we hit State Circle."

The latter being the name of the road that ringed the Hill and Parliament House.

She nodded, threw the car into gear, and sped off faster than was probably wise given that even when we'd lived here in Canberra, we very rarely came to this section of town.

"What did Samuel say?"

Her smile flashed. "Exactly what we expected."

"And his response to your response?"

"Impolite."

I laughed. "I take it he *is* heading over?"

"No, he said to update him once we find out where the idiot who's snatched Deni ends up, and under no circumstances are we to go in without him."

"Unless, of course, the situation disintegrates before he arrives."

"I did add that. He said it probably will."

I glanced at her. "That almost sounds like he knows what's going on."

"Deni apparently had a restraining order on her ex because he made several threats against her when she decided to break off their engagement."

"Sounds like she made the right choice." I directed her left. "Did he say anything about the ex?"

"Just that he has an explosive temper when things don't go his way."

"A typical Canberran royal witch then." And that meant *both* sexes.

I directed her to Adelaide Avenue. We sped past The Lodge and onto the arterial road. As we neared another big roundabout a few minutes later, I clenched the watch a little tighter and then said, "Left."

She obeyed and we sped on, through more roundabouts and a number of amber lights. Thankfully, there were no cops and not much other traffic about. Eventually, I directed her right, toward Tuggeranong.

Belle did so, then glanced at me. "Isn't the Tuggeranong district a bit too working class for a royal witch?"

"That makes it a perfect place to hide someone."

"Too many families, I'd have thought."

"Which Aiden would no doubt say is what makes it perfect, because families are often too busy with work and their kids to pay much attention to what else might be going on around them. Take the number of pot farms that are often found in residential homes, for instance."

"True, but a royal witch is going to stand out like a sore thumb in the midst of the everyday working class."

"The everyday working class is not going to sense a disguising spell."

She grunted in acknowledgement. We sped on down the empty road, the streetlights flashing by and the rumbling thunder getting closer. The storm would unleash when we finally found our target, I just knew it.

Once we neared the Tuggeranong area, the guide rope appeared, a gossamer thread that led us unerringly to Deni's location without me having to constantly deepen psi contact with the watch.

Belle stopped on the opposite side of a driveway that led into a long complex of two-story, red brick, red-roof-tiled homes. They were identical in every way except for the types of plants growing under the crab apples that dominated the small front lawn of every second unit, and the cars parked in their driveways. To the left of the complex lay empty land, while Google Maps said there were parklands behind it.

The connection ran down to the very end of the complex.

"Good location to hide someone—being the end house, there's less chance of neighbors hearing anything untoward." She glanced at the watch. "It might be worth trying to deepen the connection just enough to see and hear where she is without her emotions totally overwhelming you. It'll give us the lay of the land without getting close enough for him to sense us."

"Do you want to call Samuel first? It may take him or his crew time to get here."

She made the call. He didn't sound annoyed over the phone, but I couldn't see the man or his aura, so maybe he was just concealing it well. Working as he did for the high council, it was probably a skill he'd been forced to develop.

He again warned us not to go in unless absolutely necessary, said he was twenty-five minutes away, and hung up.

"He must be still at Mawu's hut. Wouldn't take him that long at this time of night otherwise." She motioned to the watch. "Remember, deep enough to connect, but not deep enough to feel everything she's going through."

Which was a fine line to walk even for the best trained psychics, and I certainly wasn't that.

"Yeah, but you have an advantage they don't—me."

I smiled, settled more comfortably in the seat, then tugged my sleeve away from the watch. Images immediately assaulted my senses. I drew in a deeper breath to fortify myself against what was about to happen, then opened the psychometry floodgates and dove right in.

The deeper connection was instant, and it happened so damn quick that I had to stop briefly and step back to control and reduce its depth. This was obviously yet another skill the wild magic was mutating and strengthening.

Once I was distant enough to see and hear without

Deni's emotions overloading me, I allowed her sensory inputs to flow over me again. Her hands and feet remained lashed together, and the cramps and pain that washed through her body were intense. It made me doubly glad I'd dropped the connection strength. Her neck burned, but I suspected it was some sort of magic counter rather than rope, because it pulsed in time with her attempts to spell. The room itself was dark and airless, and she was lying on her side across a bed. The man who'd kidnapped her wasn't in the room with her, but rather in the one beyond the door she was facing. He was pacing and speaking, his feet thumping heavily on the floorboards and his words tumbling together, full of rage and confusion.

I had no idea if he was talking to himself, someone else, or even to Deni, but one thing was certain—he was either drunk, on drugs, or mentally unwell.

If he decided to attack, we wouldn't get there in time to help her.

I pulled out of Deni's mind and glanced at Belle. "Is it at all possible for you to use my connection to slip into Deni's mind and telepathically control him?"

"Technically, given the strength of our connection, it should be, but it'd leave us both mighty vulnerable to an attack."

"Which might have been the point of the kidnapping in the first place. If this *is* connected to our wraith, the message he left at the hut could have been a distraction as much as a warning."

"It would hardly be a distraction—before we found the warning he left at the hut, we had no idea Deni was a target."

"True, but I suspect our undead sorcerer isn't above

fucking with our minds." That's what the message at the hut had been all about, after all.

"I still don't think this kidnapping is connected. I think it's more likely a coincidence and bad timing."

I hoped she was right. I glanced past her and studied the silent rows of houses again. The feeling that we were running out of time—that Deni was running out of time—stirred.

"I need to get closer. Something is off with this whole situation, and I'm not sure what." I handed her the watch. "Keep this safe, just in case things go wrong in there and we lose her."

Belle nodded. "I'll wait for Samuel. Shout if you need help... and be damn careful."

A smile twitched my lips. "Always."

She snorted. I grabbed the bottles of holy water Ashworth had given me, tucked them into my coat pocket, and climbed out. As I walked across the road, the first fat drops of rain began to fall. I hurriedly zipped up my coat, then padded quickly but warily past the long line of red brick houses. As I neared the end house, I paused, looking for magic or anything that suggested a trap had been laid or an alarm set. Thunder rumbled overhead, and the intensity of the rain increased. I shivered, gaze scanning the night, water dripping from the top of my hood and sluicing down to my shoes.

There was no sign of magic or anything else untoward. Then, beyond the house, close to the fence that divided this area from the field beyond, came a flicker of movement.

I had no sense of what it was, no sense of evil, and yet every psychic bit of me was telling me to run, to get the hell out of here and leave Deni to her fate.

I couldn't, of course, but damn, it was tempting.

I quickly stepped back, hit the trunk of the tree, then slid around it, using it a shield between me and whatever that thing was.

It must have caught the movement, because it stopped—something I felt rather than saw. I couldn't see it from behind my tree and had no desire to even attempt a peek out. But I had this weird feeling it was staring directly at me.

I licked dry lips, and, after a moment, the thing moved on. I cautiously peered out from behind the tree. It was heading for the house.

Not the nearby window or even the door, but rather the fully bricked corner of the building.

And then it went straight through it.

A heartbeat later, the screaming began.

CHAPTER SIX

B *elle,* I said immediately. *Ring Samuel and see where the fuck he is. And lock the car door just in case this is a distraction to grab you.*

I wasn't on the list—

And maybe that *was deliberate. Remember my premonition that it was a bad idea for you to come up here? This could be why.*

The screaming ramped up, becoming shrill and filled with horror and pain. I had to get in there. It was probably too late to help the man who was screaming, but Deni was in there and currently unharmed.

I had to keep it that way.

Around me, lights came on. Voices rose, filled with a mix of confusion and fear. I hoped everyone remained inside. Hoped they didn't get between me and this thing, whatever it was.

Car doors are locked, and the holy water is in my hand, Belle said. *Samuel is five to eight minutes away.*

Meaning he'd certainly put his foot down to get so close so fast but even so, it wouldn't be enough to help save the screamer. He might not even be close enough to help save Deni.

I grabbed a holy water out of my pocket but didn't uncork it. The bottles weren't particularly large, and I didn't want to risk spilling any as I ran.

The front door was locked, but a quick repelling spell soon fixed that, hitting the door with enough force to tear the thing off its hinges and send it tumbling into the room.

The screaming stopped, and the scent of death seeped into the wet night air.

Heart hammering somewhere in my throat, I slowed and approached the door more warily. The room beyond was bright, but I couldn't see anything—not the screamer, not the monster. But I could hear the latter—it was clomping up the stairs, heading for Deni.

I swore and stepped inside. Saw the blood and the body parts strewn all over the living room. It was a goddamn bloody mess.

Literally.

My stomach stirred but thankfully didn't rise—maybe because this wasn't the first time I'd witnessed the results of a body being all but shredded.

Is a wraith capable of doing this? I asked. *There's no magic here—this is the result of brute strength.*

Unless they had that sort of strength when—

Belle stopped abruptly. Fear surged through me. *What's wrong?*

Nothing. I saw some movement, but it was just a man heading into the subdivision next to yours.

Instinct wasn't entirely believing it was "just" a man, but then instinct was the suspicious type at the best of times.

Maybe you'd better leave, just to be—

Um, no.

You can park in the next street. Our connection isn't as distance restricted as it used to be.

That may be true, but if things go haywire in there and you need my physical help, me being in the next street will be a hindrance.

I sighed. She could be as stubborn as me sometimes. *Fine.*

The thing had reached the top of the stairs. I picked my way through the blood and body parts as quickly as possible, heading for the stairs in the far corner.

Above me, a door creaked open. I cursed again and bounded up the stairs. As I did, magic surged.

Not inside. Outside.

Belle.

She was being attacked.

When it came to a choice on who to save, there was none.

Sorry, Deni. I turned and all but flew down the stairs. Felt another surge of magic, heard the sharp clang of metal as something tumbled down the road. I bolted out the door. There were people everywhere—some heading toward this house, others staring toward the street.

"I'm with the High Witch Council," I yelled. "Get back inside and lock your doors."

Some obeyed. Many didn't. I didn't care. My eyes were on the road, on the car sitting opposite the driveway, and the seething mass of threads that now overran it. Some were Belle's; she was trying to counter what looked to be a retrieval spell of some sort.

It was testament to the increase in her magical strength that she'd muted the force of the spell enough to remain in the car.

Not sure how long that will remain the case, she said, her mental tones distracted and breathy. *This bastard is strong.*

Pull on my strength if you need to, I said. *I'll try to find him. He has to be nearby, given he's still feeding energy into the spell.*

And *that* meant he had to be close enough to see what was happening.

I swung left, leapt over the small brick wall that divided this subdivision from the next, and felt the stranger's magic surge again. Belle immediately deepened our connection and began drawing on both my physical and magical strength. It would drain me fast, but I didn't care. That last surge had given me his location.

The bastard was on the roof of the house directly ahead of me.

I raced through the trees, then across the long driveway that ran into the subdivision from the road, approaching from the rear of the house instead of the front in an effort to avoid detection until the very last moment. Thankfully, I couldn't see any sort of warning or protective spells from where I was, but I also wasn't about to take any chances.

I eyed the roof he was standing on, did a brief estimate of its height, then gathered all my speed and *leapt*.

As leaps went, it was pretty shit. But then, I was human rather than wolf, even if the inner wild magic was enhancing my senses, strength, and speed. My shins hit the guttering, and a yelp escaped as I sprawled forward, landing heavily on the slick wet roof tiles. Almost immediately, I began to slide back down. I twisted around and thrust my feet into the guttering. Felt the surge of magic, this time aimed toward me, and threw up one hand. A protection shield flared out from my fingertips, and the shimmering net fell around me. His spell hit a second later, flaring red against the silver and gold threads of my spell.

It was a leash spell, but a type I'd not seen before—no surprise really given my lack of "proper" training.

He didn't follow up with another attack, instead returning his attention to Belle. Which was odd in many respects—if this man was working for our wraith, why keep going after Belle when he now had me pinned?

Or was it simply a matter of him not seeing—or *knowing* —the bigger picture. Maybe the wraith had expected me to protect Deni, thereby giving this man enough time to snatch Belle.

If that was the case, then our former dark sorcerer really didn't understand the bond between a witch and her familiar.

As the stranger's assault on Belle ramped up, I called forth a simple repelling spell and cast it through the gaps in both my net and his. It sped across the rainswept night and was on him before he sensed it. He spun, raised one hand as if to ward off the spell, but it was already too late.

He was knocked off his feet and sent tumbling past the guttering to the ground.

His leash spell remained active, which at least meant the fall hadn't killed him. While the three-fold rule didn't usually apply in this sort of situation, it was always better not to risk it.

Belle? You okay?

Now that the bastard isn't trying to drag me out of the car, yes. I've got him telepathically pinned, though he's broken his leg and wouldn't be going anywhere anyway. What about you?

Still contained by his magic but otherwise, fine.

You able to unpick it?

I studied the glowing red threads for a second then said, *I think so. It's not that intricate.*

He probably didn't have the time or energy for anything more than simple.

I carefully plucked the spell's first line free from its brethren, checked there were no hidden nasties woven into its length, then deactivated and dismissed it. I repeated that process with the remaining five layers, until the whole thing was gone and I was able to release my protection net. As the last wisps of silver and gold floated away, Samuel arrived.

He stopped at the base of the building and stared up at me. "How the hell did you get up there?"

"I jumped."

"That's one hell of a leap."

"He was attacking Belle. It's amazing just how much fear and a little bit of magic can assist in these sorts of situations." I shrugged. "Is Deni okay?"

"My people are down there checking now, so I should have a report in a few minutes. Do you need help to get down? Shall I look for a ladder or something?"

"No, I'm good." I slid on my butt to the edge of the roof then jumped down, landing with surprising lightness next to him. "The idiot who attacked Belle is around the other side of the building."

"So she said."

There was a bite in his voice that had me looking at him. "What's wrong?"

"Nothing. Everything." He ran a hand through his wet hair, exasperation briefly evident in his expression. "This is on me. If I'd trusted your instincts and been here when all this went down—"

"It probably wouldn't have changed a thing." I lightly touched his arm. It was more muscular than I'd expected.

"The thing that attacked Deni and her kidnapper went through a goddamn brick wall and then proceeded to tear said kidnapper apart."

A smile twitched his lips. "My magic is a bit stronger than yours. It could have made a difference."

The former was definitely true if we weren't counting the wild magic.

"I've had more experience monster hunting." I paused. "Well, the supernatural kind, anyway. In many respects, the monsters you deal with are scarier."

He wrinkled his nose, amusement briefly evident. "Only sometimes."

We rounded the other end of the building and walked toward Belle's assailant. He was lying in the middle of a thorny-looking shrub and was obviously a royal witch of some kind, given the strength of his magic, though in the storm-swept night, his hair looked black. His silver eyes, however, were bright, and filled with equal amounts of fury and pain. It was just as well Belle was holding him immobile and silent, because I suspected if he'd been able to speak, we'd have gotten an education in swearing. He just had that look about him.

His clothes were torn, and there were scratches all over his face and hands. The lower part of his left leg was sitting at a weird angle, though there wasn't any obvious sign of blood or even bones sticking out from his jeans. Maybe he'd be lucky and the break simple.

Personally, I was hoping it wasn't.

I stopped a meter away. Samuel continued on and quickly patted the man down, pulled a wallet and iPhone from his pockets, then tugged a driver's license free. "Jacob Ashworth. Well, well, well."

I swiped a hand across my face to get rid of some of the

water, which, given the intensity of the storm, was pretty much useless. "I take it you know him?"

"Know *of* him. He's a freelancer who's come up on our radar a number of times."

"Meaning he's a witch for hire?"

Samuel nodded. "Jacob here has a reputation for not worrying about the legalities if the money is good enough."

"Huh." I told Belle to let the stranger speak, then said, "Who hired you?"

He swore at me. Colorfully.

Samuel kicked the boot on Jacob's unbroken leg. "Enough of that. Just answer the question."

"Aren't you supposed to read me my rights? And what about a fucking ambulance? I've got a broken leg here."

"Reading a suspect their rights is a gray area when it comes to magical crimes," Samuel said. "I would suggest you cooperate."

"And I would suggest you go fuck yourself."

"Belle," I said aloud, so that Samuel would know why Jacob suddenly became compliant. "Make him answer the questions."

Belle immediately put more telepathic pressure on him. Fear stepped into Jacob's eyes as realized that he had no choice but to obey.

"He didn't tell me his name," he growled. "He gave me the job, paid half upfront, and said I'd get the rest and a bonus if I could get it done tonight."

"'It' being kidnapping Belle Kent?"

"Kent?" Jacob frowned. "That's Belle Sarr in the car. I have her picture."

"Show me." Samuel handed Jacob the iPhone. The latter dutifully unlocked the phone, swiped through a few screens, and then handed it back. The fear in his eyes got stronger.

He should be fucking thanking me rather than fearing. I'm the only reason he's not a writhing mess of pain right now. She paused. *I've checked his recent memories— whoever called about my kidnapping didn't give a lot away. The voice sounded weird—Jacob suspects the caller was using either a modulating spell or the electronic equivalent.*

And that didn't raise any alarms?

From what I can see, freelancers basically expect it.

"Is this a recent photo?" Samuel asked and held the phone up so I could see it.

It was a picture of Belle leaving her mom's place. A fierce wave of anger rose, but I batted it away. It was harder to control the tiny hornets of magic that stirred around my fingers, however. "That was taken tonight, just before we found Mawu's hut."

"Meaning you're being followed."

I nodded. "It's becoming obvious our wraith has a living team working for him."

"Ashworth told me about your suspicions, but I have to ask... can wraiths do that sort of thing?"

"When it comes to the supernatural, anything is possible."

Which was a glib answer, but in truth, I didn't really know. There was no doubt information to be found in the books Belle had inherited from her grandmother—which we were in the process of transferring over to digital format— but accessing the files here, in Canberra, was dangerous. Legally, those books should have *all* gone to the National Library rather than only the half dozen or so that had. If the high council ever found out we had the bulk of them, they *would* confiscate them.

Footsteps approached, and we both glanced around. The two men walking toward us were big and solid, with a no-nonsense air about them.

"Ambulances are five minutes away," the taller of the two said. "You want us to look after this scum?"

Samuel nodded. "Restrain him first. He should be magically spent, but one never knows with these bastards."

"Do you want Belle to release him first?" I asked.

"Give my men a few minutes to cuff and put magical restraints on him, then yes, please." He touched my elbow, lightly but firmly guiding me away. "I need a statement from you, but let's get out of the rain first."

"I'd rather get down to the other house and see if Deni's okay."

"She's not. Or rather, she's missing."

My gaze snapped to his. "What? How do you know?"

He tapped his ear. It was only then I noticed the white earbud. "The team has been reporting to me."

"But she can't have disappeared. The thing that tore her kidnapper apart walked right through the wall—he wouldn't be able to do that with Deni in tow."

"He didn't have to. According to witnesses, he went out the front door. The one you tore off."

I swore softly. "Then we need to track her—"

"I already have men working on it."

"Yeah, but psychometry is far more reliable than feet and eyes."

He hesitated. "Are you sure you're up to it? It's been one hell of a night for you both already."

I couldn't help smiling. "Oh, trust me, this has been mild by reservation standards."

"Your reservation is definitely one out of the box."

In more ways than he knew.

"How do you want to proceed?" he continued.

"Deni's watch is in the car—it's what I used to trace her here."

"I take it you took said watch from her apartment?"

My lips twitched. "I'd normally say *that* would depend on whether anyone reports the break-in, but in this case, someone else *did* the breaking. I just entered and found what I needed."

"Considering who your boyfriend is, you have a very liberal take on the law."

A weird mix of doubt and hope slipped through me at the oh-so-brief mention of Aiden. I thrust it aside. I had too much to worry about here without piling on more.

Not that *that* had ever stopped it from happening.

"Don't forget he's a werewolf. They have very different rules and priorities than us so-called 'normal' folk."

Samuel snorted softly. "I have a suspicion no one would *ever* call you normal, Lizzie Grace."

I laughed. "I have a suspicion you might be right."

Belle was leaning against the side of the car but pushed away as we approached, and handed me the watch. "Do not think you're going anywhere without me. Not now, not tonight."

I didn't argue. I knew it would be pointless.

I wrapped my fingers tighter around the watch and reached again for my psychometry. Contact was fierce and fast, but Deni was unconscious, which meant I had no emotional or visual help. All I had was the fast-disappearing tether between the watch and her as a guide.

"This way," I said tightly, and ran into the subdivision, lightly dodging through the milling crowd.

Belle and Samuel were several steps behind me, the

latter informing his men what we were doing and telling them to stand down the search until we knew more.

Which was a good idea, given we had no idea what exactly we were dealing with.

The softly glowing leash continued to spool out through the night, but it had a decidedly stretched look about it now. The thing that had Deni was moving out of range. If I didn't speed up, I'd lose them.

I swore softly and reached for more speed. My feet all but flew over the ground, and the wire fence between here and the parklands loomed large. I drew in a deeper breath, increased my stride, and then leapt.

I cleared it by a good meter.

I hit the ground beyond a little too hard and fast, and stumbled forward several meters before I caught my balance and then ran on.

I'll keep within telepathic range, I said to Belle. *Guide Samuel.*

This time, *she* didn't argue.

She was in my head, so she was well aware the leash was on the verge of snapping.

I ran through the trees that divided the housing estates from the park and then straight across the field, each step on the soaked ground throwing up sprays of dirty water. The rain continued to pelt down, and if not for the leash, I would have lost them.

But I didn't.

In fact, I was gaining on them.

Maybe that was deliberate. Maybe all this was nothing more than part of an elaborate trap to lure me away from anyone capable of protecting me.

But something within doubted it.

The photos suggested our sorcerer intended to draw

this out and make me suffer. Capturing me *now* and forcing me to watch my family be butchered might allow him to bathe in my horror and grief, but would that make up for the thrill of watching me attempt to save them from being kidnapped and then murdered, only to fail at each and every hurdle?

As I'd failed to save Cat?

What this sorcerer wanted was a replay, except this time, it would end with my death rather than his.

The thread tugged me left onto a wide stone path. From up ahead came the scent of still water—a lake of some kind —though I couldn't see it through the rain. The path looped around to the left, and up ahead was an overpass. The path and the lake ran under it, and as underpasses went, it was reasonably well lit. No moths danced around the cheery yellow lights though—they obviously had more sense than to be out in weather this bad.

The thing carrying Deni tore through the underpass. In the brighter light he appeared misshapen, and there were two dark points rising from either side of his head—horns? Was he some sort of demon? One who could walk through walls?

Was he, perhaps, the *sorcerer's* demon?

Would such a demon do this sort of manual work? The little I knew of dark sorcerers and their ties to the under-world suggested not, but I guessed it depended on the strength of the sorcerer, the type of demon, and what sort of contract they'd entered into.

It had Deni around its shoulders in a fireman's carry, and though her hands and feet were now untied, something that felt dark and foul—even from this distance—ringed her neck.

As he swept back out into the storm, I entered the long

underpass, enjoying the brief respite from the shitty weather.

The lake and the path looped to the right and disappeared into the trees. I couldn't see the demon, and while the thread no longer had that stretched, about-to-snap look, it was also nowhere near as vibrant. Given how close I now was, the opposite should be happening.

Which could only mean one thing—she was dying.

And I rather suspected the black thing around her neck was the cause.

Which made no sense if he was replicating past kills, but maybe my earlier suspicion was only partially right. Maybe this wasn't so much about faithfully repeating history, but rather just the end result.

If that were true, then the first kill had been nothing more than a means of getting my attention.

God help us all....

I pushed aside the surge of fear and reached for more speed. There was nothing more left in the tank. I was running on sheer adrenaline now, and in all truth, might not have enough left to bring that thing down even if I did get closer.

If I was going to stop it, then I had better do it now, before exhaustion took full hold.

I rounded the corner and moved into the trees. The force of the storm was muted by their canopies, but fat droplets still fell, hitting the path ahead of me with enough force to eject tiny stones into the air.

Up ahead, the leash was pulsing, as if in distress, and the thing was again pulling away.

I swore. Vehemently. Then I quickly cast a repelling spell around my fingers, this time weaving a containment spell through it. I had no idea if it would actually work against the thing ahead or even if it would last for very long if it did, but that wasn't the point. I simply needed to get close enough to cast the holy water. If it was our wraith, then that should be the end of it. If it wasn't, well, holy water took a nasty toll on most other demons.

When the spell was done, I raised my hand and cast it, as hard as I could, toward the fast-disappearing figures.

At the last possible second, the thing seemed to sense it. He veered sharply to the left and headed for the water. My spell tumbled after it, but a heartbeat before it would have hit, the creature dived into the water and disappeared.

Leaving my spell to disappear into the night and Deni floating facedown in the lake.

CHAPTER SEVEN

I swerved through the trees, bolted into the water, and splashed like hell toward Deni.

Which was a stupid thing to do given the thing might still be there.

I grabbed her feet, tugged her toward me, then rolled her onto her back. She wasn't breathing, and I couldn't help her with that just yet. Not when I was in the water and the sense of danger was now so sharp it felt like my skin was being sliced open.

I tucked my hands under her armpits and dragged her back to the shore. As I was hauling her up the bank, a bony-looking hand and arm rose from the water and lunged for her feet. There was obviously a body attached to the arm, but between the night, the storm, and the water, it just wasn't visible.

It rather creepily reminded me of one of those cheap horror movies where the disembodied limbs of the dead crawled along the floor—or this case, though the water—trying to claim their prize.

I shifted my grip to free a hand, then grabbed the holy

water and uncorked it. As bony fingers curled around Deni's leg, I threw the contents of the little bottle.

The creature's sunken flesh instantly began to bubble and burn. As the stench of cooking skin stained the night air, a stream of bubbles rose from deeper in the lake, accompanied by the strangest sound I'd ever heard. It certainly *hadn't* come from a human throat.

The thing released Deni's leg and disappeared under the water. I dragged her the rest of the way up the bank and onto the path, well out of immediate danger if whatever the hell it was in the lake decided to come back.

I quickly felt for a pulse, then checked her breathing. Nothing. I ignored the stab of fear and started CPR, but as I bent to add two quick breaths, the thing around her neck reacted, unlashing at one end and lunging at my face.

I yelped and pushed back, landing hard on my butt several feet away. The magical leech or rope or whatever the hell it was around her neck snapped back and forth like an angry snake for several seconds, then swallowed its own tail and became inert again.

I warily edged forward. A ripple ran through the leech; it was ready and waiting to attack the minute I was close enough.

I hesitated, then crafted a retrieval spell and cast it toward the leech. Once the spell was attached to the creature's body, I gave a gentle tug. With an odd sort of sucking sound, part of the leech's body pulled away from Deni's neck. That's when I saw the bloody, hair-fine needles running underneath its body.

It really *was* some sort of leech, but I suspected it was feeding on her energy—her life force—rather than her blood. Her skin was gaunter now that it had been only moments ago, which meant that odd pulse of energy I could feel was the fading echo of Deni's life being drained away.

I tugged harder on my magical rope. An inch more of the leech came free, then Deni bucked, as if in pain, and sweat popped out across her pale forehead.

The creature was retaliating against my efforts to remove it by attacking its host. Doing anything else might just kill her.

But so would doing nothing.

I dismissed my spell, then uncorked a second bottle of holy water and poured it over the creature.

Nothing happened. It might look and feel evil, but it wasn't of demonic origin. Perhaps it had simply been enhanced—or more likely, twisted—by magic.

And not dark magic, either, because the holy water would have had some effect in that case.

Sharp footsteps had my gaze darting down the path, although I already knew it was Belle and Samuel.

"Call an ambulance," I said. "She's not breathing."

"Then why aren't you doing CPR?" Samuel asked as Belle got out her phone.

"Because there's a fucking leech around her neck."

"A leech? Flick it off with a—" He cut the rest of the sentence off with a sharp intake of air. "Fuck, it's a shushunjë."

"A *what*?"

He repeated the name. "They're magically altered leeches developed in the seventeenth century to drain bad energies from a body in much the same way that regular leeches supposedly drained 'bad' blood. Unfortunately, the spell worked too well, and the things drained *all* life energy."

Meaning they were a medical experiment gone wrong. "What the fuck is it doing here?"

"I don't know. They're not native to Australia, and they're illegal to import."

He knelt beside her and leaned closer to inspect the leech. Another ripple ran through its body, but it didn't react any further. Maybe it had been programmed to only retaliate against me.

"You'd better hope that ambulance gets here fast," he added, "because if she *does* survive the removal of this thing, she's going to be in a bad way."

"They're ten minutes away, according to the call center," Belle said.

Which would probably be eight minutes too late.

"How the hell do we get it off Deni's neck?" she added. Rain—or maybe even sweat—dripped off her nose, and she was puffing hard, which made me feel a little bit better given how much fitter she was than me.

"There's a removal spell, but it's complicated because these things have multiple sucker mouths and if you attempt to pull them out—"

"Which I did."

He puffed out a breath that was a mix of anger and frustration. "Then we have even less time. Stand back and keep watch. If this *is* the work of your wraith, then he's going to feel me disentangling this critter."

I stepped back and rubbed my arms, a mix of hopelessness and anger washing through me.

None of this is your fault, Belle said sharply. *You've done everything possible to save her.*

Maybe, but I should have known better than attempt to detach the shushunjë—

You weren't to know it had multiple suckers.

I knew it was dangerous. The damn thing attacked me.

I'm thinking it was more likely warning you off. After all, if this is part of our sorcerer's evil plot, he wouldn't want you dead just yet. Belle gave me the mental equivalent of a hug. *What he wants is your hopelessness and your rage, so don't you fucking dare give it to him.*

A smile tugged reluctantly at my lips, but I didn't reply as Samuel's magic surged. I crossed all things that his worked where mine had failed and watched him carefully weave a spell around the shushunjë that nullified its ability to move and feed. Then, with a second spell he applied with knife-sharp precision, he began removing the needle-fine suckers from Deni's neck.

It was a long and tediously slow processes.

By the time the leech was removed and had been sliced in half with what I presumed was a blessed silver knife, Deni had been without oxygen for nigh on six minutes. Brain damage usually began around four.

He started CPR, but it didn't help. The shushunjë had done its job too well, draining her life force to the point of no return.

Even now, her spirit was rising.

At least we gave her that, Belle said. *At least she can move on and live other lives.*

We don't know that wouldn't have happened anyway. I rubbed my arms against the increasing chill of weariness and fear. *From the sound of it, they leech energy, not souls.*

Except this one had been in the hands of a dark master— who knows what his magic might have done to it.

And might still do to us. Fear stomped through my soul, but I did my best to ignore it. Belle was right—that's what this bastard wanted, and even if I achieved nothing else, I would not give him that.

The ambulance crew arrived and took over from Samuel, but after another ten minutes, terminated treatment. While they couldn't officially pronounce her dead, they noted the time of death, then placed her covered body on a trolley and wheeled her away toward the ambulance.

I watched them go, tears trickling down my face.

"I'm sorry for your loss," Samuel said softly.

"Don't be," I said. "In truth, I really didn't know her."

"Estranged or not, family is family." He gently squeezed my shoulder. "We will get this bastard, you can be sure of that."

I glanced at him. "If you think I'll be sitting on the sidelines—"

He raised a hand to stop the rest of that sentence. "I think we all know the devil himself wouldn't stop you hunting this thing down now. I just want you to promise to keep me informed and to *not* go after it alone."

I hesitated and then nodded. "But if it grabs Belle, all bets are off."

"Then let's ensure it doesn't grab Belle."

"I can definitely get behind that," she said.

I glanced at her. "You do realize this means you—and probably Ashworth and Eli—will have to go into protective custody, be it at Hattie's place or somewhere else."

Belle snorted. "I think we both know what Ashworth's response to *that* will be."

Probably the same as what mine would have been. But they'd do it, simply to protect Belle. Besides, in this place there was no one else I'd trust to protect her. Not even Samuel and his people. To be honest, I would have preferred us all to pack up and leave this shithole, but that was impossible right now. I had both the magic reevaluation and the trial to attend tomorrow, and leaving would only delay, not end, both. Besides, it was better for everyone if I was out there, moving around. It would draw the wraith's attention, keeping him watching me rather than the people I cared about.

Which did not really include my blood family, but I guessed I couldn't let them die. My overactive sense of guilt would make me pay for years and years if I did.

I doubt you being out there will matter in the long run, Belle said. *This bastard has had years to plot his revenge, and I'm betting he's got every little detail planned out.*

Probably, but I've nothing to lose by trying.

Nothing except my life, of course, and if the images he'd left were indeed a hunting order, then I really didn't have to worry about him turning on me until my father was dead.

Your father is not going to react well to any attempt to protect him or curtail his movements.

No. Mainly because he was extremely confident in the superiority of his own magic—with good reason, of course, as he was one of the strongest witches in Canberra. I didn't know Julius all that well, but from our brief interaction at the café not so long ago, he was very much my father's son when it came to self-belief.

Even if he didn't quite have the same power levels and skill.

More people arrived. Samuel ordered the lake and the bank on the other side searched, then motioned a tall, thickset woman with dark skin and crimson red hair forward. After introducing us, he said, "Saska will escort you both home."

"There's no—"

"Oh, there's *every* need." His tone was dry. "The council would have my head if something happened to their star witness before the trial could reach its end."

I snorted. "Like anything I say will make a difference to their decision anyway."

"The mere fact your father has been hauled before the court at all has generated great consternation amongst the royal lines and great delight among the lesser lines," Saska said, her voice deep and almost masculine. "In many ways, the trial has already achieved its main aim."

"I still want the bastard to pay some sort of penance."

"The council might yet surprise you," Samuel said.

"That's extremely unlikely, and we all know it." I motioned toward the path. "Shall we go?"

Saska nodded and spun around, moving at a good clip down the path. By the time we came out from under the long row of trees, the rain had eased, though the night remained bitterly cold. Saska didn't say anything, but her gaze and her magic constantly scanned the night. Which was reassuring, even though I was pretty sure she wouldn't find anything. The threat had long since passed.

It took fifteen minutes of brisk walking to arrive back at the subdivision. The end house had been cordoned off, all the internal lights were ablaze, and multiple people walked in and out. Up ahead on the road, the yellow lights of a tow truck washed across the darkness as a man wearing a reflective vest loaded Belle's car onto the back of the vehicle's tray.

I glanced at Saska. "I take it you're driving us home?"

She nodded. "All part of the service. Besides, you can't drive a car that has a missing door. The cops would pull you over in an instant."

They could certainly try, Belle said. *But they'd suddenly find themselves turned in the opposite direction. I am not in the mood to deal with any more officialdom at the moment.*

A mood I could utterly understand. All I wanted to do

right now was get to Hattie's, drop into bed, and sleep so deeply not even dreams could find me. But that was unlikely to happen—Ashworth and Eli had to be updated, and I also desperately needed a hot chocolate with a good handful of marshmallows. My energy levels needed the sugar hit.

We were ushered into the back of Saska's SUV and quickly driven over to Hattie's place. Belle telepathically contacted Eli once we were close enough, so by the time we walked into the kitchen, our hot chocolates were ready and waiting.

It was after two by the time Ashworth and Eli were updated and plans made. I was so damn tired when I crawled into bed that sleep hit almost instantly.

But it didn't stop the dreams.

They were filled with images of bloody death that would not stop until the wraith was truly dead.

Or I was.

At breakfast the next morning, Eli slid a pair of gloves across to me and said, "Wear these in the testing room."

"Why?"

"Because they'll help contain the wild magic."

I raised my eyebrows. "Really? How?"

I mean, they looked like regular woolen gloves, even if they felt a little heavier than usual.

"They've got an internal lining that's been woven out of blessed silver thread. In theory, it should conceal the wild magic."

"In theory?" Belle said. "They haven't been tested?"

"Not against wild magic," Ashworth said. "I mean, how could they be?"

I warily slipped one on. The changes the wild magic had been making to my DNA had made me sensitive to silver when it sliced into me, but so far hadn't altered my ability to handle either my silver knife or even silver charms. The thread was scratchy against my skin, but there was no burning sensation or violent need to rip the thing off.

I tugged it off anyway. Better to be safe than sorry. "Concealing is only one part of the problem."

"They may well pick up its echo through your native magic," Eli said, "but it's doubtful they'll understand its cause."

"All witches know what wild magic is—"

"Only in theory, via what is taught at university," Ashworth said. "Most witches wouldn't come in contact with it during their lifetimes simply because they haven't the power or the training to deal with emerging wellsprings. The few who *do* certainly wouldn't be working in a testing station."

"Besides," Eli added, "the Fenna were all but erased from witch literature *and* consciousness eons ago. I'd hazard a bet there are none currently living here in Canberra who even would consider it feasible."

I hoped he was right, because if he wasn't, then we'd be making a midnight dash home and to hell with both court cases.

A car arrived to pick me up and I was quickly whisked across to the testing labs at the witch university. Ashworth and Eli had initially offered to take me, but after Deni's death and the attempt to snatch Belle, had agreed that it was probably safer if they all remained at Hattie's and watched each other's backs. They'd beefed up the magical security measures around the house, and Samuel provided additional security via magically null guards. Which meant, I discovered, that while they had no magic of their own, they were also immune to its use against them.

It was a weekday, so the uni was packed with people moving to and from classrooms. My driver escorted me across to the right building, then navigated our way through the various corridors until I reached the right set of rooms. Obviously, he was under orders to make sure I got there.

I'd never undergone the full testing process and accreditation, thanks to the fact we'd skipped town well before we turned eighteen, but the process was as tedious as I'd heard. Basically, you were seated in a chair in the middle of a dark room, where a crown-like inhibitor was placed on your head and various sensors attached to your body—thankfully, no one asked me to remove my gloves, but that was probably due to the room being damnably cold. According to one of the testers, the lower the temperature the better where the sensors were concerned.

Once the inhibitor was activated and curtailing all conscious magical response, spells were cast, their intensity initially low but increasing by gentle degrees. The sensors detected the instinctive response until the moment a witch's natural magic was overwhelmed.

Mine didn't fail as quickly as I'd hoped, but from the murmurs of surprise I could hear coming from behind the protection screen, I was also nowhere near the end of the test range. My testers had expected far more from a Marlowe, apparently.

I was mightily relieved they were disappointed.

One of the examiners came out and began retrieving the sensors.

"When will you know the results?" I asked.

"In about five minutes. We'll give you a copy, if you like."

Her breath was visible as she spoke. It really *was* cold in here. "Any initial impressions?"

She hesitated. "They were not what we expected."

I couldn't help smiling. "It's a well-known fact I am *not* my father's daughter."

"No." She hesitated again. "However, it would appear you are your mother's."

That had my eyebrows shooting upwards. "How?"

"While you do not have anywhere near the capacity for magic that she has, you do have the same anomalous strain running through it."

My heart began beating a whole lot faster. It was the wild magic. It had to be.

"Do you know what it is?"

The tester shook her head. "It could be a quirk in your mother's bloodline—your sister had it too."

"How do you know that?"

"We always check family records before a test subject comes in. It enables us to better understand and categorize the results."

If they'd detected the anomaly in both my mom and my sister, then perhaps we'd been right in guessing there were Fenna in Mom's background.

"Does that mean my brother hasn't got this aberration?"

She nodded. "It only appears in the females of the line."

Which suggested the Fenna had only ever been female.

She plucked the final sensor free, then motioned toward the small table tucked into the corner of the room, behind the locked door. "Feel free to grab a drink. You'll probably need the electrolyte boost after all that."

I hopped off the chair, retrieved my coat and shoved it

on, then poured a glass of the orange-colored liquid. It was as sweet as fuck, so I downed it quickly, then dropped the cup into the waste basket.

The other tester approached and handed me several sheets of paper. "We'll send the results electronically to your father, as he requested, but for your own information, you sit just above mid-range, at six point nine."

"Which is way higher than I'd expected." Even with the boost of wild magic, I'd thought that, at best, I'd register a high four or low five.

A six point nine put me on the low end of the scale when it came to my father's line, but for most "regular" royal witches, that was an acceptable level of competence.

Even if I remained an "underpowered disappointment" to my father, I had no actual reason to be disappointed in my native capacity for magic.

The tester's eyebrows rose. "I'm surprised you're pleased, given your family generally sits in the mid nines and your father is one of the few witches to reach a near perfect ten."

And was no doubt pissed off that he was *only* "near-perfect." "I left home when I was young and have never been trained—"

"Training has nothing to do with native strength, young lady. It only refines and sharpens your skill in using it."

I half shrugged. "That may be true, but when you've grown up being told you're useless, then these"—I shook the papers—"are an unexpected and quite brilliant result."

"I guess it would be." He stepped back and unlocked the door. "The results will be officially registered by tomorrow."

"Thanks."

I walked out to find Saska waiting for me in the hall. "Why are you here? Is there a problem?"

She pushed away from the wall and fell in step beside me. "The council have decided, in the light of recent events, to restrict the hours of trial to a couple of hours either side of midday and avoid the twilight hours."

Meaning it was going to be a short day today, given it was already close to eleven. "That won't stop this bastard's killing spree."

"To date, he hasn't been active during the day," Saska said. "Until that changes, the new timing will allow all witnesses time to return home safely and raise all necessary protections."

All witnesses primarily meaning my family rather than me, I was betting.

"That doesn't explain your presence. What's wrong with the driver who picked me up this morning?"

"Nothing at all. The boss just wanted a bit more beef on the detail, and I definitely fit that description." She glanced at me, amusement twitching her lips. "He likes you."

"Sadly for him, I'm taken."

"So he's said."

My eyebrows rose again. "He discusses his love life with you?"

"Only out of hours." My expression must have been somewhat horrified, because she laughed and added, "We've been besties since we were kids. Besides that, when you're dealing with the worst inclinations of royal witches on an almost daily basis, there *is* no one else you can really trust or confide in except your teammates."

I guess that made sense given the sensitive nature of the information—and the crimes—they were probably dealing with.

I rolled up the test results and tucked them safely into my purse. They might not be of any practical use to me in my everyday life, but I had a hankering to frame the damn things and put a big "he was wrong" over the top.

I looked up barely in time to quick-step around a student too busy looking at her screen to check where she was going.

Of course, she wasn't the only one so enamored with their phones—the corridor practically seethed with the distracted. I had no idea why there weren't a ton more crashes, but maybe they'd grown so used to being glued to their devices they'd developed some sort of radar.

I zipped up my coat as we neared the exit and said, "The council's still taking a big risk by not cancelling or delaying the trial."

"The chamber's defenses were strengthened overnight. It'll be fine." Saska glanced at me, amusement crinkling the corners of her black-ringed silver eyes. "Does this distrust of all things High Witch Council stem from your hatred of your father?"

"I don't hate him." I paused. "Well, I do, but I don't want him dead."

"Neither do we. That would mean Julius stepping into his shoes, and honestly? That would be a disaster for us all."

I laughed. "Is that coming from personal experience or observation?"

"Both. He's a very unpleasant man to deal with."

"Well, he'll be a very *dead* unpleasant man if he doesn't heed the warnings."

"Which he won't. We do have a detail on him though, just to be safe."

I hoped it would help. I feared it wouldn't.

As we came out of the testing building and walked

toward the parking area, the back of my neck prickled. I glanced around casually but couldn't see anything out of place.

No one appeared to be taking undue interest in us, and there weren't even any birds circling above us. But that didn't mean my watcher couldn't be a shifter of some kind. He could be some sort of rodent hiding in the nearby bushes or even one of the pigeons and starlings that currently lined the rooftops. While humanity seemed to have the impression that shifters were always majestic animals like wolves, lions, hawks or eagles, in truth most were simple, everyday animals that wouldn't raise suspicions—dogs or cats, parrots or crows, even roos, though I'd imagine the latter would come with some inherent restrictions. As much as many on the other side of the world seemed to think roos were an everyday occurrence in suburbia, they generally only came in during times of drought or when development pushed them off their normal feeding grounds.

"Something wrong?" Saska asked.

I started, causing wild magic to stir briefly around my fingertips, as warm as the day was cold. Thankfully, I still had the gloves on. "I think we're being watched."

She glanced around, her expression intent. "I'm not sensing anything magical."

"It's not magical."

She raised an eyebrow. "Then how are you... oh, psi."

I nodded. "Unfortunately, these sorts of warnings are generally undefined. In this case, it's not telling me who or where."

She grunted and pulled her phone out. "I'll call it in. They can send a flight up and see if there's any indication of a tail."

"Meaning you've shifters on the team?"

"Meaning a drone." She smiled. "They're far more efficient than a shifter, and you don't have to pay them."

I laughed. "You still have to pay the operators, so that cuts the benefits, doesn't it?"

"Well, yeah, but a drone doesn't get pissy if it's out in the weather."

Suggesting the shifters did. Belle came online, so I didn't question Saska any further.

How'd the test go? Belle asked.

You weren't following?

The room was psi shielded. I could have broken through with a little effort, of course, but Monty called.

Saska clicked her SUV open once we were near, and I climbed in while she made her call. I still wasn't seeing anything or anyone paying undue attention to what we were doing, but the sensation of being watched grew. *How's things in the reservation?*

It remains an unpleasant place for the O'Connor pack, apparently.

They're still being targeted?

Yep. Monty says the volume of the wild magic is definitely increasing, but at the moment, it's mostly restricting itself to the O'Connors' boundaries.

Which makes sense given the old wellspring is in their compound.

Saska climbed in and started the SUV. "They're sending up a drone, but Reggie will also head out."

"Reggie?" I asked, even as Belle said, *Drone? What's happened?*

Nothing. Just got a feeling we're being tracked.

With no further information, of course.

Of course.

"Reggie's one of our shifters on call," Saska was saying.

"He's a magpie and, much like the real deal, doesn't like to be messed with. If something *is* following us, he'll soon spot them."

I nodded, but didn't feel any safer. But that was more likely a result of my pessimistic nature than anything else right now.

How's Aiden doing? I asked.

Unhappy, apparently, and not just about what's happening in the reservation. His mom is delaying his confirmation as alpha.

No surprise there. She's probably figured out he's planning to bring me into the fold. At least, that's what I hoped he was planning. Katie certainly implied it, as did he.

Of course, implying and doing were two different things, and it annoyed the hell out of me that he still wasn't being open about his intentions.

Maybe he didn't want to get your hopes up.

I snorted. *I'm well aware just how far hoping will get me. Especially while his mother remains the other alpha.*

Maybe you should ring him. He probably needs to hear a friendly voice right now.

My eyebrows rose. *Meaning Monty isn't?*

Let's just say he's still not showing much in the way of sympathy to the pack's plight.

I couldn't help smiling. I'd really struck it lucky when the one cousin I could stand had been assigned to the reservation.

So did I, Belle agreed with a laugh.

Saska drove out of the parking area and joined the traffic headed back to the central business district. I looked out the side window and watched the CBD roll by. I might have been born and raised here, but this place no longer felt like home.

Because you've laid down roots elsewhere—quite liter-
ally, given your increasing connection with the old well-
spring and its deep roots into the earth. She paused. *I asked*
Hattie to pick up a pregnancy test. Ashworth and Eli are
beside themselves at the possibility.

Did you have to ask in their presence?

The minute I tried to have a private chat with Hattie,
they'd have suspected something was up. They're well aware
you've a puking tendency of late and had their suspicions
anyway.

Let's hope Aiden isn't as quick to pick up on it.

Doubtful. The only time you've lost it in his presence so
far has been at a horrific murder scene when your scent and
psi senses were overwhelmed.

True. And thankfully, even though a werewolf *could*
sense hormonal changes, they were unable to scent a pregnancy until near the end of the first trimester.

It gave us both breathing room—and him time to decide
whether he really did want the whole marriage and kids
thing with me.

Even if he didn't, and if I *was* pregnant, then I was
having our child. I'd dreamed of that blonde-haired, blue-
eyed little girl too often now not to bring her into this
world.

Of course, her birth would not be without risks, given
she'd be a hybrid. Most did not survive, and those who did
often weren't "right." Instinct might be saying that as the
first true Fenna born in centuries, she would be healthy and
hearty, but there were centuries of scientific evidence and
experiences to suggest otherwise.

Trepidation and perhaps a little fear washed through
me, but neither would change my decision if I did happen
to be pregnant.

I hope you haven't told Monty, I added, *because a blind person could see he was keeping a secret.*

Belle's laughter ran down the line between us. *I know, and it's endearing even if it is sometimes annoying. Besides, while I couldn't avoid Ashworth and Eli knowing, it's up to you who else you tell.*

Which will be no one. Not until it's absolutely necessary.

With Katie's connection to both the wild magic and you, I'm betting she'll figure it out pretty quickly.

She can't tell anyone so that doesn't matter. The last thing I need right now is Aiden's fucking mother accusing me of getting pregnant to entrap him.

And she would.

Because she really did hate witches—and me—that much, thanks to what had happened to her sister so many years ago. Nothing any of us said or did would change that. I doubted even Aiden taking over his father's mantle as pack alpha would alter her mindset.

Our one hope of a future together lay in the rest of the pack. While most believed otherwise, werewolf packs were a qualified democracy rather than an autocracy, so he could present the case of me becoming his mate to the pack and the wolf council, and their joint judgement would hold.

Of course, they could always say no. Karleen did still hold a lot of power and influence over the pack.

They won't say no, Belle said. *Not after that show we put on in front of the council and what's now happening in the compound. I'm betting they won't be able to move fast enough to install you as his mate.*

I smiled. It was a nice thought, however unlikely.

We arrived at the hearing room a few minutes before eleven and were quickly guided into the chamber. My father vehemently protested Saska's presence—not so much because he hated lower-class witches, though he did, but because he didn't want outsiders viewing and possibly reporting proceedings. Unfortunately for him, his objections had been anticipated. Saska produced a signed order giving her permission to remain "for the safety of all," and that was the end of the discussion.

My father's scowl of annoyance at being so easily thwarted cheered me up immensely.

The trial reconvened, and the first witness was called. The door opened, and Mom stepped in. It was the first time I'd actually seen her since arriving, and a strange series of emotions washed through me.

In many respects, the testers had been right in saying I was my mother's daughter, but not just because we shared the same anomalous thread of wild magic through our native magic. She could have been an older version of me—especially now that we both had silver eyes. There were more age lines around her eyes and mouth, of course, and her hair only had a smattering of gray rather than the two white streaks I now possessed thanks to the rusalka's attack, but otherwise she was the same height and build. Of course, she was far classier in dress and movement than I ever would be.

She strode past my father and his counselor with barely a glance and repeated the process with me. Once again, that weird mix of emotions tumbled through me. I wasn't entirely surprised by her actions, but I couldn't deny the disappointment. I'd spent a lifetime wanting recognition from my parents, but it seemed nothing would ever change.

Not even the latest test results were likely to make a difference, because they didn't show the power boost my father had no doubt been expecting. Even the anomalous strain wouldn't tell him anything regarding the wild magic, simply because Mom and Cat had the same result.

Of course, the question that did need to be asked was, why the fuck did I even care what he or Mom actually thought about me?

I had no answer to that. No answer I wanted to acknowledge, anyway.

Once Mom was sworn in, Anthony rose. "Mrs. Marlowe, you said in your witness statement that you were unaware of the arrangements made by your husband regarding your daughter's marriage to Mr. Clayton Marlowe, is that correct?"

"Yes." Her voice was calm and even, but her aura told a very different story. It was a seething mix of color—while guilt and regret were definitely present, the main glow came from annoyance. Whether it was aimed at me, at my father, or at being legally required to take the stand here today, I couldn't say.

If I had to guess, I'd say the latter.

"And is that usual? Did you, for instance, also leave the arrangements for your son's marriage to your husband?"

"No."

"Why is that?"

Her gaze flickered to me. Emotion glimmered briefly in her eyes, though I wasn't close enough to see what it was. "Because my daughter and I were estranged."

"And why was that?"

Mom took a deep breath and released it slowly. "We'd just lost Catherine, and I wasn't thinking clearly. I wrongly blamed Elizabeth for my oldest daughter's death when, in truth, she'd done far more than any of us to try and save her."

Her answer hit like a punch to the gut. Not because

she'd openly admitted they'd been wrong about me but, rather, what the answer implied as a whole.

Fuck, I said to Belle, *they're going to pull the "our grief made us do it" card.*

No great surprise, though in your father's case, it wasn't grief but a malicious need to both get rid of you and to make you pay for your perceived inadequacies.

Grief being the contributing factor to forcibly marrying me against my will would be hard to prove, though. Especially when the marriage deal included me inheriting a large chunk of Clayton's estate *and* a child bonus. Grief usually made bad bargains, not good.

Perhaps, but it'll be hard to disprove it, too.

"Were you at all aware the marriage was being proposed?" Anthony asked. "Did you venture any opinion as to the suitability of the connection?"

"It was mentioned in passing, but I said the decision had to be Elizabeth's."

"And when the marriage contracts were signed? What was your response? Did you question your daughter?"

"I didn't need to—Lawrence assured me she had agreed to the contract. I had no reason to question the statement."

Her gaze flicked across to my father. Theirs had never been a love match but rather a merger that had made them "the" power couple in Canberra. But that look suggested the alliance had fractured beyond repair. Of course, I had no idea if that was the truth or if it was simply an act for the benefit of the watching council.

I wanted to believe the former. I suspected the latter was closer to the truth.

"When did you discover otherwise?" Anthony was saying.

"This year, when I spoke to my daughter for the first time since she left Canberra."

"I didn't just leave, I fucking ran in terror," I said, unable to help myself.

The adjudicator banged the gavel loudly. "Ms. Grace, please refrain from comment unless requested to do so."

I nodded. Anthony gave me a somewhat sympathetic look, then continued to question Mom. Basically, her responses remained the same—she was grieving, she didn't see the marriage contract, didn't speak to me about it, she had no reason to think I was in any way being coerced.

Anthony handed over to Mr. Moderno, who fired off a range of questions that to me seemed only half-heartedly aimed at trying to trip her up. He didn't, of course, but that was no surprise. My parents had been dealing with legal aggravations like this for most of their lives.

The next witness called was the lawyer who'd drawn up the contract, and who basically confirmed that it was solely my father and Clayton he'd dealt with—my mother was not present at any of the meetings.

Which made me wonder if this was their way of clearing Mom's name so that she could continue the family business unbesmirched while Dad served whatever minor penance was handed out.

The final witness was the church chancellor, who wasn't present at the wedding and who couldn't do much more than confirm that the marriage had been recorded and was indeed legal.

The adjudicator declared the day's proceedings finished at one forty-five, and once again my father and his counsel left in a hurry.

As Anthony packed up his things, I rose and said, "Has

that witness you were waiting for arrived back in Australia yet?"

"No. Plane got delayed."

There was something in his tone that had my eyebrows rising. "Deliberately?"

"The conspiracy theorists in the team think so."

"And you?"

"While I'm aware of the existence of weather spells, it's a bit of a jump to think one could be arranged at such short notice."

I snorted. "If you have the power and the money, the impossible can very easily become probable—especially when said power and money are held by witches."

Amusement crinkled the corners of his eyes. "That's a very cynical attitude to have, young lady."

"I notice you didn't deny it."

"I really can't when I actually agree." He hefted his bag onto his shoulder. "Your father takes the stand tomorrow, so it should be an interesting day."

"Are we taking bets on the fact that, if he does make it onto the stand, he'll blame grief for the whole thing?"

Anthony laughed. "I've seen shorter odds on a Melbourne Cup favorite, but not by much. Oh, Clayton's brothers want another meeting at nine tomorrow."

I raised my eyebrows. "To make a counteroffer?"

He nodded. "They didn't say what. I suspect they're still hoping to browbeat you with the magnificence of their presence."

Behind us, Saska snorted.

"Yeah," Anthony said, "that was my initial response too."

"I am willing to discuss our options, but I refuse to take an insanely low offer, for Belle's sake rather than mine. She not only saved me from the bastard I married, but also spent years on the run with me. She deserves full compensation for what she went through."

He nodded. "I think you'll find their low offers have more to do with a lack of cash flow than unwillingness to do what it takes to make all this go away."

I frowned. "But Clayton had investments up the wazoo, and his family could never be considered poor."

"Investments aren't cash, and selling shares or indeed property in the wrong market can sometimes mean an unacceptable loss."

I raised an eyebrow, amusement twitching my lips. "This would be a bad thing in most situations, but in this one? I like the sound of it."

He laughed. "If you don't want mediation to drag on, then settle for a lower cash payment—maybe a mill each—and take some of his property instead. He has them all around the country, so there's no need for you to pick up anything in Canberra."

"Picking something in Canberra—a property my father wanted, for instance—does sound rather enticing though."

He laughed again. "Then definitely go for a mix."

"I will." I paused. "How do you want to play this? How many should I start with?"

He hesitated. "Start with eight or nine, then be whittled down to three or four. It'll seem like a win for them and still give you and Belle a good payout."

"I'll check the portfolio tonight and come up with a list."

He nodded and walked out.

I shoved my coat on, then collected my purse and followed Saska from the room. The halls were busy, but the sensation of being watched didn't start up again until we stepped outside. Whoever was doing the watching obviously didn't have the authority to enter the building.

As we followed the path around to the parking area, I said, "Our watcher is back."

She didn't glance up, which showed more control than I would have had in a similar situation. "Are you sure it's the same one?"

"Yes."

She grunted and got her phone out. "We'll change cars then. That should shake them for at least a little while."

I raised my eyebrows. "You have a spare car handy?"

"I'll just steal one. The boss can sort it all out later."

I laughed. "And is this something you do often?"

"Not these days." She raised a hand and wriggled her fingers. Tiny threads of magic stirred around them—the beginnings of some sort of break and enter spell, from the look of it. "Chances to hone my thieving skills sadly don't come by all that often nowadays."

"I take it they used to?"

She grinned. "Let's just say that Samuel and I walked a fine line when we were younger. It's actually what helps make him such a good investigator now."

We walked into the underground parking area, the breeze at our back pushing away any exhaust fumes that might have had my stomach protesting.

After a few minutes of looking around, she strode toward a Ford that looked decades old and more than a little worse for wear. She pressed her fingers against the lock, and her magic rose. Within seconds, the doors clicked open.

I walked around to the passenger side. "Did you choose this one because it's unlikely to belong to a councilor?"

"I'll have you know this car is a classic Ford Fairmont and would be worth a pretty penny if it was in decent condition." She leaned into the car and, a heartbeat later, the trunk popped open. "Best you get in the back until we're clear."

I eyed the rear dubiously. "Is that really necessary?"

"You're not claustrophobic, are you?"

"No, but—"

"Then in the back you get. Whoever is out there has had plenty of opportunity to arrange a little surprise for us, so let's try and spoil their fun."

"What's the point of me hiding when your unusual coloring will always make you stand out in a crowd?"

"I always travel with a fabulous hat to cover the glorious hair, and the jacket is reversible." Mischief twinkled in her eyes. "It only takes subtle changes to go from standing out to background material, especially when there's Sarr blood in your background."

"Experience speaking there?"

"Indeed. That line I mentioned was really only fine because we never actually got caught doing the dodgier stuff."

I laughed. "Which makes me even more curious as to what you and Samuel got up to when you were younger."

"Get me drunk enough one night, and I might just tell you." She motioned to the trunk again. "Now, in."

I sighed and obeyed. One good thing about these old cars was their sheer size, which not only gave you plenty of room in the cabin, but also in the trunk. It was almost big enough to party in.

Once I was as comfortable as I was ever likely to get, Saska slammed the lid down and, a few seconds later, started the car. I did expect her to stop and let me out at some point, but she didn't, and we arrived at Hattie's twenty long minutes later.

The minute Saska popped the trunk open, I scrambled out, then tugged my hood up. Melbourne's shitty and changeable spring weather appeared to have followed me up to Canberra, because it was damn well raining again.

Maybe the weather gods are simply trying to make us feel more at home, Belle said, amusement evident. *Eli said to ask Saska if she's coming in for something to eat.*

I repeated the question, and she nodded.

"I'll tuck this beast undercover first, though, then do a check of the grounds and buildings to ensure nothing is amiss."

I raised my eyebrows. "Isn't that the reason we have the null guards? To ensure nothing is amiss?"

"Yes, but I prefer to double check. Always better to be safe than sorry. Found that out the hard way."

She jumped back into the Ford and drove toward the large parking garage. I walked up the steps and made my way through the house to the kitchen. Belle was on the phone—to Monty, if her expression and happy thoughts were anything to go by—and Eli was pulling a quiche out of the oven.

I drew in a deep breath and sighed happily. "That smells divine."

"It's a potato crust bacon and onion quiche," he said. "One of Ashworth's favorites."

I looked around but couldn't see him. "Speaking of, where is he? I half expected him to start gushing all over me about the possibility of becoming a granddad the minute I walked in."

Eli laughed. "I think he's reserving that until we know for sure it's happening. He's in the study, doing some research on wraiths."

I walked over to the coffee machine. After quickly skimming the rather large selection of pods, I picked out a caramel cookie one. I had a bad feeling a pot of tea wasn't going to give me the energy boost I'd soon need.

"Any reason why? We already know how to kill it."

Eli shrugged. "He said he had a vague memory of someone once saying there was a way to track the bastards using the energy of their aura."

I shoved the pod into the machine and placed the cup in position. "Wraiths are technically dead, so they wouldn't have an aura. Zombies don't."

"That's because zombies are little more than flesh marionettes for whoever raised them. Wraiths are *returned* from the dead rather than simply raised, and they're fully capable mentally and physically. They should have some form of energy output, even if it is different to what they had in life."

"Huh." Once the coffee machine had finished doing its stuff, I did a quick clean, then picked up my cup and moved across to the counter.

As I did, a premonition hit.

Hard.

I stumbled and would have fallen had Eli not moved with lightning speed to catch me. The cup dropped from my fingers and smashed on the floor, the coffee spraying across the bright white tiles, glistening as brightly as the blood in the vision.

For several seconds, that was all I could see. Then, gradually, it dissolved into darkness, firelight, and magic so foul it made me gag.

I could hear Belle and Eli talking, knew I was being guided across to a chair, but the image was all consuming and I had no power to speak or move on my own. I could only watch as the image shifted abruptly, and my field of vision widened. I was in a wide green field. The fire I'd seen stood at one end of a stone oval. On a stone in front of it was a gutted rabbit, its carcass smoldering in the heat of the flames. Another gutted rabbit had been placed at the opposite end of the oval. The rocks connecting the two were covered in blood and entrails. As was the man who lay within the circle.

He was pale skinned, had crimson hair, and was well built despite the beginnings of a paunch.

The image swirled upward again and focused in on the stranger's face.

Only it wasn't a stranger.

It was my brother, Julius.

CHAPTER EIGHT

"It's Juli," I said, when I could. "He's the next target."

Eli squatted in front of me, his hands on my knees, as if to keep me from sliding off the chair. "We already knew—"

"No, I mean, yes, but he'll die *tonight* if we don't find a way to stop it." I drew in a sharp shuddering breath. "We need to find him. *Now*."

"Your mom will have his phone number," Belle said.

I was shaking my head before she'd finished. "Ringing won't do any good. He's not going to believe me face-to-face, let alone over the phone."

"I have his home address," Ashworth said as he strode into the room. "I got the address of their listed—and unlisted—residences the minute we knew what was happening."

"Such a clever man," Belle said.

"He does have his moments," Eli said, voice wry. "I'll go find Saska."

He pushed to his feet and hurried out. I drew in another

deep breath and then glanced at Belle. "You'll have to remain here."

She nodded. "Juli's mood was never improved by my fabulous presence."

"I think he always felt threatened by you."

She raised an eyebrow. "Why on earth would he fear me?"

"Did you not make him strip off and run naked around the street once?"

She laughed. "God, we weren't even teenagers then, and it happened well before he came into his full power."

"Yeah, but it left an indelible mark on his pride." I walked into the laundry to grab a mop. "His power has no counter for your telepathy, and he's never forgotten it."

"Leave that, lass," Ashworth said. "I'll deal with the mess later."

"The coffee will stain the white grout, so I'd rather get the bulk of it up now." Besides, it took my mind off the images that were still flickering through the darker recesses of my mind. If I didn't get to Juli *soon*, he'd die. I might hate my brother, but not to the point of death.

Ashworth took the mop from me and began to clean up the mess. "What did you see?"

"Juli naked in a stone circle." I hesitated. "He was lying in a forest clearing, but a different one to the two the wraith has already used."

"Was your brother's head still attached to his body?"

I nodded. "I didn't actually get a long enough look to see if he was breathing or not, though."

"What about his body? Were there any symbols drawn on it?"

"He was covered in blood, which made it hard to see, but I don't think so."

"Then he was likely alive. Dark magicians generally mark up their sacrifices before they kill. It ensures their demons only dine on the supplied soul."

"Would the same apply to a wraith, though?" Belle asked. "They've already lost their souls to their demons, so why would marking their victims be necessary?"

"He may have lost his soul, but he still has his flesh, even if it isn't anything we'd recognize as human."

Footsteps had me glancing around. Eli and Saska appeared, the latter just putting her phone away.

"According to the tail we have on Julius," she said. "He's in a meeting with three business partners at Cucurbita."

I wondered what sort of business he was involved in but curbed the instinct to ask. It wasn't important right now. "I'm guessing Cucurbita is a restaurant rather than an herbaceous fruit of some kind?"

Saska's smile didn't quite reach her eyes. "It's a very fancy and expensive one, and quite popular amongst the elite thanks to the fact that they have a number of function rooms and guarantee privacy."

Which probably meant they swept for bugs and audio acquisition spells regularly. "How long will it take us to get there?"

"You really should stay—"

I raised a hand to stop her and said, "If my brother gets snatched and your people lose him, my psychometry may be his last hope."

A statement that would no doubt cause Julius to snort derisively, Belle commented. *Is it wrong that part of me wants him to be snatched just so he has to face the humiliation of being saved by his "underpowered" sister?*

It won't change his opinion of me.

No, but it would nevertheless be delicious.

147

"Our people won't lose him," Saska was saying, "but the boss did say it'd be useless trying to stop you, because you'd just toss me aside and take off anyway."

I grinned and looked her up and down. "I'm fairly strong, but I'm thinking there'd be no tossing you if you decided to plant yourself."

"You have that right." She turned and motioned toward the hall that led down to the parking area. "Shall we go?"

I hesitated as instinct stirred, then held up one finger and said, "Give me a second," and then bolted for my room to grab my blessed silver knife. Holy water might well work against the wraith, but silver was a damned good backup when it came to most supernatural nasties.

I tossed it into my purse, grabbed a wooly hat from my suitcase, and tugged it on as I ran back out.

"Keep sharp, both of you," Ashworth said. "While I don't doubt the veracity of the vision, if they're watching Julius in order to snatch him, they might well take the opportunity to grab you instead."

"I'm more worried about them spotting me out and about and deciding it's the perfect time to grab Belle or you two," I said. "So kindly ensure you take your own advice."

"Oh, you can be sure of that, lassie. There's a prospective grandchild in the works, and not even a mad wraith intent on revenge will be robbing me of the opportunity to spoil her rotten."

I laughed, spun on my heel, and followed Saska out.

Cucurbita was located in an uninspiring but wide street lined with modern office buildings. Saska stopped in the parking area opposite but didn't immediately climb out.

Instead, she rolled down the window and lightly drummed her fingers against the roof of the car.

After a few seconds, a magpie swooped down, took a good look at us, then rose.

"Reggie, I take it?" I said.

Saska nodded. "He'll go speak to Julius's tag, then come back and report to us."

"That's all rather convoluted, isn't it? Why not just ring said watcher yourself? Or, better yet, just get out and talk to him or her?"

"Because we may still have a tail, despite all the precautions we've taken, and we can't risk outing the identities of Julius's protection detail."

It made sense but didn't help the growing frustration and need to be over there rather than here.

After a few more minutes, a thin man with bushy hair that was a mix of black and white approached. Saska wound down the window again and said, "Good afternoon, Reggie."

"Well, it's definitely afternoon, but I'm not sure what's good about it." He hunkered down in front of the window and glanced past Saska. "You'd be the woman causing all the problems then?"

I couldn't help smiling. "I am indeed, but hey, someone has to shake these bastards out of their staid existence."

He laughed and nodded. "I like you."

"Thanks," I said, not sure what else to say.

His gaze returned to Saska. "Your target is in the Cellar Room. No general means of access except through the main restaurant and down some stairs. No signs of anything untoward at this point, no one suspicious hanging around. Watcher one is in the restaurant, watcher two on the roof."

My gaze flicked upwards, even though it was unlikely

I'd see anything from this distance, especially if watcher two was some kind of bird shifter.

"When you say 'general means of entry' I take it you mean doors? What about windows?"

He looked at me again. His eyes were red-brown, the same color as his feathered counterpart. "Nothing a man his size is going to get through."

I nodded and studied the restaurant. The need to get over there was increasing in ferocity. No matter what Reggie said or how secure the premises seemed, something was about to happen.

"What about us?" Saska was asking. "Any sign of a tail?"

"No, but I'd be pulling up your coat hoods, both of you, just to be safe. It won't look out of place in this weather." He glanced up at the gray sky. "It's about to chuck it down again, so I'm off to find cover until you move this beast again."

"Thanks, Reggie."

He patted the edge of the window, then turned and walked toward the buildings behind us. I tugged my jacket's hood over my wooly hat. "We need to get over there ASAP."

"I'll just text the boss—"

"You can, but we're out of time, and I'm going in."

I opened the door and climbed out. Saska hastily got out and fell in step with me.

"Have you a plan?" she said, voice dry. "Or are we just doing the whole 'bull at the gate' thing?"

"Bull at the gate usually works perfectly fine if you're dealing with obnoxious people rather than obnoxious demons." I glanced at her. "You've ID, haven't you?"

"I do, but—"

"Then you can do the official thing while I go talk to my brother."

"The room will be magically locked to ensure privacy."

"Then I'll unlock it."

And hoped even as I said it that I could—though despite the restaurant's guarantee of security, I couldn't imagine their protection spells would be overly complicated. Bug scanners might not be all that expensive these days, but constantly renewing the various protection spells would be. So would keeping a witch on staff, though I couldn't imagine there'd be too many witches willing to work for the rates a restaurant—however fancy—could afford to pay. They were more likely to be using a simple charm system that could deter entry but be reused. What was the point of using anything more intricate when the royal witches using this place could—and probably would—raise their own spells if they were at all worried about security?

The restaurant's entrance was an understated affair built in the shadows of a large office building. There was stone-clad wall to one side of the path and a small garden area on the other. The door was warm wood and glass, with large windows either side.

The door opened as we approached, and an attendant asked if he could take our coats. Saska showed her badge, asked to speak to the manager, and was directed to wait near the podium while she was paged.

I touched her arm and said, "I'm going in."

"I'm not sure that's wise—"

"We don't have time to wait," I repeated, and walked away. Her frustration followed me, but she remained put. There were advantages to not having to follow protocol.

And it wasn't like I needed directions to find my brother. Even in a room filled with a riot of different and delicious aromas, I could smell both him *and* his aftershave. The latter was especially strong, and a strange and probably expensive aroma that was a mix of cigar smoke, old leather, and lavender. He'd had it when he'd made his grand appearance in the café, though at the time, my olfactory senses had taken a back seat to the sheer shock of finding him standing there.

I hurried through the various tables and strode toward the stairs at the rear of the building. Some sort of warding shield guarded the top step, but it wasn't a particularly intricate one, and it took me all of five seconds to disconnect it.

A waiter appeared from a side room and planted himself in front of me. I clenched my fists against the instinctive urge to push him aside and stopped several feet away.

He offered me a cool smile. "May I help you, miss?"

"We're with the high council." I motioned toward Saska, who was currently talking to a woman I presumed was the manager. "We need to speak to Julius Marlowe as a matter of urgency."

"I'm afraid that's imposs—"

The rest of his sentence was lost to a gigantic *whoomph*. He immediately spun and made a dismissive motion with his right hand—no doubt to deactivate the warding spell I'd already dismantled—then hurried down the stairs. As I ran after him, the shouting began, from both behind and below.

Thick dust billowed up the stairs, catching in my throat and making me cough even as visibility dropped to almost zero. The waiter stopped so abruptly that I cannoned into him, sending him tumbling down into the fog.

I swore and cast a light spell. It bobbed a few feet in front of me, highlighting the bits of plaster and wood fibers floating in the air. It suggested that a wall or a ceiling might have come down, but the fog itself was too thick to be natural. There was magic behind it, magic that didn't feel dark but wasn't entirely light, either.

I found the waiter sprawled at the bottom of the steps, his face etched with pain as he cradled his left wrist.

"You able to move?"

He grimaced and accepted the hand I offered him. Though he was bigger than me, I had no trouble hauling him upright. What I could see of his face in the dusty gloom said he was in a lot of pain, but he didn't swear, and that was more than I probably would have done in his shoes.

"Our guests—"

"I'll check on them. You need to get upstairs and get that wrist seen to. My colleague will have called in help."

He gripped the handrail with his good hand and began to climb. I ran on. While the lights were on, they weren't having much impact. People appeared out of doors to the left and the right, somewhat resembling bewildered brown ghosts. I ordered them to evacuate and pointed them in the right direction but didn't stop.

The bobbing light revealed a final door down the far end of the hall. Magic swirled around its frame, the color light, clean, and vaguely familiar. Juli's magic, I suspected. It had the same sort of energy pulse as my father's.

I was ten feet away from the door when a woman screamed, and the thick scent of fresh blood flooded the air.

I stopped abruptly, my gaze sweeping the door and the spell that blocked my entry. It was intricate and all-encompassing, and I simply didn't have the time to dismantle it.

The woman screamed again, the sound accompanied by an odd thumping, and a deep, deep rumble that had the hairs along the back of my neck rising.

It was a sound I knew. A sound I'd heard more than

once back in the reservation. A warning to back off or suffer the consequences.

I was running out of time.

Or rather, that woman inside was.

I gathered the inner wild magic around my right hand and flung it, as hard as I could, at the wall to the right of the door.

Unlike the door, it wasn't protected by magic.

The tumbling mass of threads and power punched straight through the wood paneling *and* the wall frame, spraying wood and dust back into the room while giving me direct access and a direct view.

The rumble I'd heard had indeed come from a were-wolf, and he was a *big* motherfucker.

Bigger than Aiden, even.

He was black coated and emaciated, though that didn't make him any less dangerous. He'd also been spelled. The threads of it shimmered closely around his body, its color a weird green that made my skin crawl even though I didn't recognize the spell or compulsion that had been cast on him.

He wasn't looking at me, though I had no doubt he would have been aware of my presence even before I'd broken into the room. He was too busy tearing into the flesh of the man who lay underneath him.

The screamer stood several feet away from the wolf, beating him across the back with a metal chair. That he wasn't responding to the attack hardened the suspicion he was under a compulsion.

I couldn't see Juli, but there was a big hole in the floor near the rear wall, and the air rising from it suggested it was either a sewer or stormwater drain.

I took a deep breath, then cast a net spell and flung it

toward the wolf. It wouldn't stop him consuming his victim, but it would at least stop him attacking the woman, me, or even running.

Though I doubted the compulsion would allow the latter.

My net hit the wolf and bounced away harmlessly.

I swore. The green glow of magic that had him enthralled was also protecting him. I'd have to do this the hard way.

"Lizzie?" Saska appeared, the light sphere bobbing above her head a pale yellow that not only pierced the gloom better than my light but appeared to push away the worst of the dust from her immediate vicinity. "What's happened?"

"They've blasted up from a stormwater drain to snatch Julius, and there's a fucking werewolf eating one of his guests," I said. "I'll deal with him but—"

"You can't deal with a werewolf alone—"

"Are you armed?"

"No, but I can spell—"

"He's warded against spells, and we haven't got the time to fuck around. Besides, you need to get your people checking the sewer exits ASAP."

"What about his guests? Any survived?"

"A woman."

"Can you get her out?"

My gaze flicked to the woman. She hadn't noticed me or the fact that she now had an escape route. Either she was too locked in horror, or too intent on trying to stop the wolf eating her companion. Either way, she was braver than many would have been.

"I'll try," I said. "Wait there."

I took another wary step forward. The wolf growled

without looking up, the sound a low rumble from somewhere deep in his chest. It was a warning to stop, and one I obeyed.

The woman lifted the chair, obviously intending to strike him again.

"Don't," I warned, softly but urgently. "Put the chair down and slowly but carefully back toward me."

Her gaze snapped to mine. Her eyes were wide, her pupils dilated, and her breathing rapid and shallow—she was definitely in shock, and that really wasn't surprising given what she was witnessing.

"I can't—Harry—"

"I'll look after Harry." I raised my free hand and made a come-here motion. "But you need to leave first."

She hesitated, then put down the chair and slowly backed away. The wolf's gaze remained on me, and the rumble was getting louder. I raised the knife and sent just enough wild magic into the blade to make it glow a fierce white blue. Normal werewolves didn't need a reminder of just how deadly silver could be, but this fellow wasn't normal.

When the woman was close enough, she grabbed my hand, her grip fierce and her fear so sharp it was all I could smell.

"You're okay. You're safe from him now." I guided her through the hole in the wall. "My colleague will take you upstairs."

Saska took her from me and directed her light ball back into the gloom. Then she glanced at me. "Don't go into the drain after your brother, and definitely don't get yourself killed."

"I won't."

"Famous last words," she muttered, and retreated.

I drew in a breath that didn't do a whole lot to calm the nerves, then warily stepped through the hole and into the room. The wolf glared at me, his muzzle bloody and his eyes unfocused.

He was definitely under a compulsion.

I took another step, the knife between us though I wasn't sure this wolf had enough awareness to recognize the danger it represented.

His lips curled, revealing bloody canines that glowed unnaturally in the remaining dusty light.

They were unsettlingly *large* canines.

I forced down the flare of fear, knowing well enough that the slightest show of weakness could result in an attack.

Not that I had any doubts that he would attack regardless.

"I don't know if you can understand me, but I need to remove the compulsion that controls you before the situation gets any worse. To do that, I need to get closer."

Another low rumble and a slight shift in movement.

I raised the knife. "I *will* kill you if I have to, have no doubt of that."

No response, but no attack either.

My gaze flicked to his victim. Harry's throat had been ripped out, his jugular and the thick muscles that usually protected it exposed and still pulsing blood onto the thick carpet.

Anger surged, and my gaze snapped back to the wolf. Beyond the dead madness and blood lust lay death. This wasn't his first human kill. He'd done it before, and he'd do it again.

I took another step.

He attacked.

I flung out a hand and wild magic spun from my fingers,

forming a shield between us. The wolf twisted away from it, landing heavily on the other side of his victim. In that moment, I realized the wraith's spell was not only controlling the wolf's actions but also enabling him to see through the wolf's eyes. There was no other explanation for the wolf's desperate avoidance of my shield. He shouldn't have been able to see it, let alone known what it was.

But the wraith did. And now he knew I was able to call it.

I swore, though in truth, it probably wouldn't alter his plans all that much. If anything, the wild magic in my blood would only sweeten the deal for him and his demons if they ever did taste my flesh.

The wolf leapt again, and this time he didn't divert. I braced my feet, raised my shield to protect my upper body, and gripped the knife hard. The wolf hit the shield so hard, it slid me back several feet. He was close enough that I could smell the foulness of his breath and see in his golden eyes the ungodly intelligence that controlled his thoughts and deeds.

Then, with a howl that was unearthly and unnatural, he twisted and dropped away. As he did, I drew back the knife and stabbed him as hard as I could in the flank. The blade sliced through his emaciated flesh so easily, the hilt hit his fur with bone-jarring force.

There was an odd flash, and the magic shimmering around him died, leaving a foul stench behind. The wolf dropped like a stone in an ungainly heap at my feet, the light and intelligence gone from his eyes.

He was dead.

But... how? I'd deliberately aimed for his flank to avoid damaging his heart and his lungs, and the silver in the knife should not have affected him so quickly.

Was it the spell? In destroying it, had I somehow destroyed him? Had the spell been tied to the wolf's life force rather than the wraith's, in order to... The thought died as horror stirred.

The wolf's already thin body was literally disintegrating before my eyes. It was as if someone had hit the fast forward switch on decomposition.

And that meant the magic that had surrounded him wasn't only about control. It was, quite literally, giving him life.

This wolf had been dead long before my knife had ever found his flesh.

I shivered, stepped over what was left of his body, and ran over to the hole. There wasn't much to see, and the only thing I could hear was the rush of water. I cast my light down. The drain was circular concrete, and there was probably just enough room to stand upright as long as you weren't too tall. The water running along the bottom looked to be a foot or so deep, and there was graffiti and tags all over the place. There was obviously an outlet fairly close by.

Juli's scent followed the flow of the water, but it was fading fast. I fought the urge to jump down and chase after him—aside from the fact I'd promised not to, I was just as likely to get lost as find him—and looked around the room. There were a couple of suit jackets hanging over the back of upturned chairs. The one farther away was Juli's—I could smell the strange scent that clung to it from here—and if luck was with me, there'd be something in one of his pockets holding enough of his resonance to track him.

I walked across and picked it up. It was silky soft to touch and, even covered in dust, looked expensive. I'd never heard of the brand—MJ Bale—but I suspected the jacket wasn't off-the-rack but rather tailor made.

Saska stepped through the hole I'd punched through the wall. "You're still here. I'm surprised."

"I did promise not to chase after him. Besides, me getting lost down there wouldn't help my brother any."

"No, but that's never stopped anyone doing dumb things before."

It certainly hadn't stopped me in the past, either, but I kept that to myself and went through the jacket's pockets.

She cast a quick gaze around the room. "What happened to the wolf?"

"He died. Again."

Her eyebrows rose. "Again?"

I nodded. "The wraith raised him from the dead. I merely put him back into that state."

"A zombie *werewolf*?"

"And not a freshly dead one, either. You can tell that by the extent of the decay."

Saska grunted and squatted beside Harry. "Poor bloke didn't stand a chance, did he?"

"No."

"Why do you think this bloke was targeted rather than your brother? Why kidnap rather than kill him?"

"Because for the wraith, it isn't just about the kill. It's about revenge, and about making me suffer as he did in the intervening years since his last appearance."

Saska's gaze narrowed. "Then it's not about finishing what he started, which is the council's—and your father's —theory."

"Oh, it definitely is, but you have to remember one thing—a seriously underpowered teenager defeated him. That would sting the pride of any witch, dead or alive."

Saska snorted. "Thankfully we don't have to deal with many dead ones up here."

"They're never fun, trust me on that."

She studied me for a second, obviously unsure whether I was kidding or not, but her phone rang before she could say anything.

While she talked, I continued to search the jacket's pockets. There was nothing in either of the external pockets, but the inside one held a plain gold wedding ring. Which was odd. I mean, why would he remove... the thought died as my psychometry sprang to life, hitting so hard that for a moment, all I could see were shadowy, man-like shapes, all I could hear was the rush of water, and all I could feel was the needlelike grip on my shoulder pushing me on and the warmth trickling down the back of my head.

I sucked in a breath and shut the connection. He was alive *and* conscious and right now, that was all that mattered.

Though I couldn't help but wonder why he wasn't using his magic to escape them. I hadn't felt any sort of restraint in that brief connection, but maybe the answer lay in the head injury. Maybe he was concussed and confused as hell. I might be able to spell under duress, but it was a skill I'd learned the hard way and not one Julius would ever likely have needed until now.

I grabbed several tissues from my purse and wrapped his ring in them. It wasn't as good as silk, but it did mute the force of the connection enough that I could keep control and not be dragged back down again. The softly glowing connection thread spun from the covered ring and dove into the hole. But like Juli's scent, it was fading fast.

The minute Saska finished her call, I said, "I've found a means to track my brother, but we need to go now."

"Not until the crew arrives with the proper equipment,"

she said, in a voice that suggested she'd brook no arguments on this.

"Going into that bloody hole is the last thing I want to do," I said. "Though a team down there would at least prevent his captors from doubling back."

Which I didn't think they'd do, but to date the wraith's actions hadn't followed any sort of logic, so who actually knew.

"You can still track someone even when they're underground and you're above?"

"Up to a point, yes. Consider it a radar that fades as the subject moves farther away."

It was far more than that, of course, but we didn't have time to discuss the intricacies of it now. The connection thread was now so faint it was barely visible, and while that didn't mean I couldn't continue to track him through the pulse in the ring, the thread avoided the use of a deeper connection and made things a whole lot easier both psychically and physically.

"How long will the team take to get here?" I added. "Because—"

I stopped as two men came through the door, both wearing those thigh-high wading pants with built in boots. They were also armed, even though the pulse of their magic was strong enough to fill the room with their power.

I suspected *that* was deliberate, because most witches were well able to contain any sort of magical leakage. Life would get uncomfortable in crowded rooms, otherwise.

"Keep up the magical amps when you're down there," Saska said. "We want the bastards to be aware of your presence, so they'll think twice about doubling back."

The taller of the two nodded. "Which direction did they head? Do we know?"

Saska glanced at me.

"Downstream," I said.

Saska returned her attention to the two men. "Be careful and keep in contact."

"Will do."

As they positioned the ladder and climbed down, I dismissed my light sphere and headed out of the room. The unnatural dust curtain no longer filled the corridor, though the walls and floors were covered in muck. I ran up the stairs and through the now empty restaurant, Saska three steps behind me.

It was raining outside, and though it wasn't particularly heavy, I was damnably glad it wasn't me heading into the storm drain.

"On foot or in the car?" Saska asked.

I briefly tightened my grip on the ring. "Car. They're too far away now to be chasing them on foot."

We dashed across the road. I jumped into the passenger seat, quickly did up my seat belt, and then deepened my connection to the ring so I could gather impressions of what he was feeling, seeing, and hearing without being totally swamped by his emotions.

The darkness remained, but the hand on his shoulder was gone, and the growl of an engine now filled my ears. His limbs were bound, the rope—real rope, not the magical kind—so tight it sawed into his skin every time he moved. His thoughts were chaotic, and his magic was present and yet not. I could feel it, but there was something between his mind and his power, a wall that prevented his ability to spell.

Everything he was feeling—all the impotent fury, fear, and confusion—were an echo of everything I'd felt the night my father had forced me to sign the agreement to marry Clayton.

Forced not by magic, but rather a drug that inhibited magic and ensured compliance.

I couldn't help but wish the wraith had visited this particular punishment on my father rather than my brother. Even if for only a few hours, I really wanted the bastard to feel exactly what he'd put me through.

"Which way?" Saska asked, as she started the big car up.

I jumped, pulled back from memory and sensation, and then said, "Right."

She nodded and swung out of the parking area. I drew in a somewhat quivering breath and then dove back into the connection.

It was then I noticed the burning around his neck. I frowned and deepened the connection a fraction.

And suddenly it felt like there were dozens of tiny needles burning into my neck.

It wasn't a spell. It was a fucking shushunjë.

Which made me wonder about the veracity of the vision I'd had. Why use a leech if the wraith intended to sacrifice him? Or was it simply an added precaution? After all, the wraith's first two victims were much lower on the magical scale than either my brother or father, even if they were relatives. Maybe he wanted to ensure my brother didn't have the *physical* strength to react even if he could somehow overcome the drug's effects.

I pulled back again, took a breath, and said, "Do you know how to separate a shushunjë from his victim?"

"Yes, but where the fuck are they getting those critters from?"

"I have no idea." And at this point, didn't care. "I think

they've only just placed the thing on Juli, because there was no indication of it before now. He's been shoved into the trunk of a car and they're heading out of town."

"And up into the hills?"

"Our wraith does seem to like his trees."

She cast me a quick glance. "Why is that, do you think?"

"It might have something to do with where he died the first time around. The warehouse where he killed Cat was located in the Eastern Industrial Estate near West Queanbeyan, and there's a river, large grasslands, and forests behind it."

"They searched that whole area and never found tracks or a body."

"Well, they wouldn't if his demons got to him first." I glanced down at the ring as it pulsed. "Left at the next street."

She blasted the horn and scattered the pedestrians just beginning to cross. A glance in the side mirror revealed several raised fists and rude gestures aimed our way. I wondered how many of them had noted our number plate and were currently reporting us to the police.

We were barely half a mile down the road when the psychic connection to my brother snapped.

I swore and tried to reconnect, but there was nothing. Not even the caress of death. He'd either moved beyond my range, or something had been placed on him to prevent psi tracking.

I swore again and scrubbed a hand across my eyes.

"What?" Saska immediately asked.

"I've either lost the connection or it's been blocked."

"How the fuck can you block a psychic connection?"

"You ask this while wearing a telepathy band?"

"You know what that is?"

I smiled. "Came across them once or twice. Powerful telepaths can still get past them."

"Meaning Belle."

"Indeed."

"I'll inform the team. We might have to upgrade." She slowed the vehicle down. "What do we do now?"

"I don't—" I stopped as an ethereal hand slid over mine and a feminine voice whispered, *I will guide. Keep going.*

I swallowed heavily and added, "Drive on. We have help."

She hit the accelerator again and then gave me a questioning glance. "Meaning what?"

"You afraid of ghosts?"

"She's in the car with us?"

"Her hand is on mine."

Saska's gaze jumped down but there was nothing to see. To be honest, it was surprising her touch was so real to me, given seeing the dead wasn't one of my talents and it usually only happened when Belle stepped into my thoughts. Of course, with the wild magic blurring and altering our talents, anything was possible.

As the ghost directed us around another corner, the sounds of sirens began to bite through the roar of the big engine.

I glanced around. "Cops are after us."

She grunted, dragged her phone out of her pocket, and made a call. All while driving one-handed at speed. It scared the hell out of me even though she didn't look for a second like she was in danger of losing control.

Maybe her "somewhat shady" adventures with Samuel involved cars, cops, and speed.

"Jackie," she said, wrenching the heavy car around a

vehicle that refused to get out of the way. The tail twitched back and forth, but she had it going straight in seconds. "I'm on Barry Drive speeding toward Belconnen Way in an old blue and white Ford Fairmont. Cops are on my tail—get them off."

"Number plate?" the woman said.

Saska gave it, then added, "Tell them Julius Marlowe's life is on the line and if we're stopped and he dies, they'll be held responsible."

"And that," I muttered, "is not an empty threat."

If my father lost his only son on top of losing the daughter who was his pride and joy... well, things would really get ugly for everyone.

I'd no doubt be included in that ugly, but at least I was better prepared for it this time.

Especially when it was no longer just me and Belle against the force of nature that was my father.

We sped on and, after a few minutes, the cops turned off their lights and dropped back.

The ghost's hand tightened briefly on mine and the ghost whispered, *Left now.*

Meaning the road we were just about to sweep past.

I yelled the instruction to Saska and gripped the "oh shit" handle tightly. Saska hauled the car onto the dirt road that led into the Black Mountain Nature Reserve, the rear end fishtailing violently for several seconds before she brought it under control.

"Tell your invisible friend," she said tightly, "that I'd appreciate a little more warning next time."

The ghost chuckled softly, her breath gently stirring my hair. I shivered lightly and wondered again who this woman was—and why she seemed intent on helping me. If it wasn't for the fact that the souls of all our dark sorcerer's victims had been consumed in the initial round of attacks, I might have thought it was Catherine. But that, sadly, was impossible.

Straight ahead, came the soft instruction. *They follow the dirt track.*

And had busted through a metal gate to do so. But at least it meant we didn't have to stop.

Saska didn't have to be told to keep going. Thanks to all the rain, the fresh tire tracks were very visible. She flattened the accelerator and drove on past the wreckage of metal. The dirt road was narrow, with scrubby trees either side that scraped the sides of the car. The trees a few meters further in were larger, their branches arching overhead, forming a tunnel filled with shadows in the gloom of the day.

You near them. The ghost's voice was breathy and distant, and yet there was something in its tone that tweaked at my instincts.

Of course, said instincts weren't playing the informational game right now.

"We're not that far behind them now," I said to Saska. "How do you want to play this?"

"Given we don't know who or what we're facing, I think we should use the element of surprise and ram the bastards."

I glanced at her, eyebrows raised. "You do remember my brother is in the trunk, right?"

Her grin suggested she did and that she didn't care. "I'm just talking a little love tap here. Nothing too serious."

"I'm thinking Julius would not appreciate such a tap."

"Maybe not, but I can't spell and drive, so unless you know a spell strong enough to halt a speeding car, we've little other choice."

I hesitated. "I do know one, but I haven't really used it much."

"Much" being defined as not at all. In truth, I'd only seen Ashworth use it, and while I was pretty sure I could repeat the spell verbatim, trying it out in a situation like this could be risky.

Although probably not as much as ramming them.

"Then we'll give that a go first, and if it fails, I'll hit them."

We roared toward a Y-intersection. The ghost sent us left with a whispered, *Be wary, they have stopped*, then her hand left mine and her presence faded.

We swept around the sharp corner, only to discover the other vehicle had stopped sideways across the track. Saska swore and punched down on the brakes, but the track was too muddy for the tires to get much grip. We slowed, but not enough, and ploughed into the other vehicle with metal-crunching force. The impact flung me forward hard before the seat belt snapped tight, preventing me from cracking my head on the dash but bruising my neck and chest in the process.

As white steam billowed from the Fairmont's nose, two men appeared from the trees to our right. But there was a third person to our left, and while he remained out of sight, he was raising a spell. One that didn't feel quite right.

I tried to warn Saska, but she was already out of the Fairmont and running toward the two men. I tried to do the same, but the damn seat belt was jammed. I swore, grabbed my knife from my purse, and cut the thing off. Then I thrust open the door and scrambled out.

The world spun briefly around me, and the scent of blood teased my nostrils. I touched the right side of my neck; my fingers came away bloody. The damn seat belt must have lacerated my skin. I guessed I was lucky it hadn't done anything worse.

The caress of magic sharpened in the air, snapping my attention back. I bolted for the trees, the knife gripped tightly in one hand and a repelling spell spinning around the other. I couldn't see the caster, but I could certainly smell him. The man obviously didn't believe in deodorant.

I crashed through the scrub, hoping like hell the howl of the Fairmont's still running engine overrode the noise I made. He continued to cast, but that might simply mean he wasn't all that worried about my approach. Maybe he had counters or trip traps set, though I couldn't feel anything else in the way of magic.

If he had physical traps set, I'd no doubt soon discover them.

I had no idea what spell he was crafting, but the closer I got, the more my skin crawled, and that very much suggested it was anything but benign. He needed to be stopped before he could unleash it.

I released my repel spell, skimming it across the ground so there was less chance of him feeling its approach. The one advantage this sort of spell had over more complicated ones like a cage spell was the fact it was low-end, power wise. If you weren't paying attention to your surroundings, they were easy to miss.

Which was exactly what happened.

As his spell reached its peak and he began to tie it off, mine hit. There was a yelp and then a thump, and the caress of his magic evaporated, though its fragments remained in the air, reminding me vaguely of an unclean version of a cage spell.

I leapt over a log, crashed through some scrub, and stumbled into a small clearing. The caster lay in an ungainly heap at the base of a gum tree. I slowed and cautiously approached. It was only when I was a few meters away that I realized "he" was actually a "she."

Magic swirled around my fingers in readiness, but she didn't move. Blood matted her hair and trickled from her hairline near her right temple. But she breathed, so I'd simply knocked her out rather than killed her.

I quickly crafted a binding spell and lashed her feet and hands together. It wouldn't stop her retaliating magically, of course, but given the inner wild magic's tendency to raise a shield at the slightest hint of either a magical or supernatural threat, a physical attack was the bigger problem right now.

I bent and felt for a pulse. It was thready and a little rapid, which wasn't surprising given I'd knocked her out.

I pushed back a little—more to drag in some cleaner air —and studied her. She was tall and skinny, with the dirty-blonde hair often seen in some Fitzgerald lines. While they tended to be more carnival tricksters than true witches, there were some bloodlines who could trace their lineage back to royal blood, and that power sometimes found its way through to the current generation.

This witch obviously belonged to one of them, because her magic was far stronger than most.

Her clothes—jeans, sweater, boots, and a coat—were all wet and grimy, as were her hands and her face. It was pretty evident neither she nor her clothes had seen any sort of soap and water in the last few days.

Was that a deliberate choice or a forced one? Was the wraith hiring these people through intermediaries, or was he somehow forcing them to do his bidding?

I couldn't imagine anyone willing to work with such a

man, but given demons could possess people, maybe he'd found a patsy to control and use.

And if that were true, we needed to find said patsy, and fast.

I quickly patted her down and found her wallet in the inside pocket of her coat. Her driver's license revealed she was Hazel Fitzgerald and lived in some place called Googong. I tucked the wallet back, then reached for Belle.

Her impatience rolled through me. *About bloody time.*

I grinned. *Sorry, but things didn't go as planned.*

What a surprise. Her mental tone was dry. *What happened?*

A zombie werewolf, a car chase, a shushunjë, and a witch.

She did the mental equivalent of a blink. *Wow.*

Yeah. I need you to jump in and telepathically read the witch's memories.

I take it she's unconscious rather than dead?

Yep. We need to know how the wraith is contacting these people, because it's not like he could advertise.

Is she a dark witch?

I hesitated. *I'd describe her as gray.*

Which means she's at least flirted with unnatural magic or minor demons.

"Unnatural" being a term used for anything ranging from performing spells that ignored the three-fold rule to using blood magic.

He'd still have to contact her through an intermediary, I said. *And given none of these people would be working for free, someone has to be financing the whole thing.*

Unless he—or whoever he's working through—offered them a power boost. Remember, in this neck of the woods, power is all that matters.

Maybe, but such a boost would come at a cost. Surely most would not be so eager if it meant losing their souls and any hope of rebirth.

I suspect gray witches might live by the old saying "a bird in hand is worth two in the bush." Or in this case, their future.

Then they're idiots.

Her laughter ran through me. *No, just products of a system that places power over all else. You ready?*

I shifted position and placed my fingers either side of the woman's temples. While telepathy didn't in itself require touch, Belle was doing this through me, and given it helped when I was reading the last memories of the dead, I figured it couldn't hurt here. *Right, go.*

Belle's mind slipped more fully into mine, then on into the other woman's memories, shuffling through them so fast it was little more than a blur to me.

After a moment, she said, *A broker she's dealt with a couple of times before contacted her several days ago to offer her a cash job.*

Did he tell her what it was?

Not over the phone. He said it was better if they met in person, as the job involved a royal blood and caution was required.

And that didn't send up any red flags for her?

No. As I said, she's worked for him before. There was a long pause as she sorted through more memories. *He arranged for her to meet him at the Mount Ainslie lookout at dusk. She's met him there once before, so didn't see a problem.*

I gather it wasn't the broker who actually met her?

It was, but she was hit from behind. When she came to, she was physically and magically bound in some sort of old sewer. Two men periodically checked on her, and she was left supplies she had to battle the rats for, but that was it until this today.

I'm betting the two who checked her are the same two in the car with my brother. I'd also place money on the fact her sewer was either the same or an offshoot of the sewer they'd used to get my brother out.

Possible, Belle was saying, *but they were using concealment spells, so she never actually saw them.*

They obviously spoke to her, though; otherwise how would she have known they were men?

If she was their captive, why did she agree to help them? There doesn't seem to be any sort of compulsion on her.

There's not. They threatened to take out her grandson if she didn't help them.

I glanced at her. She didn't look old enough to have a grandson, but maybe the grime was filling the cracks. *And if she did?*

She'd be released and compensated handsomely.

I snorted. *If she believed she could get away with helping to snatch Julius Marlowe, she really is a fool.*

She didn't know who the target was.

Has this broker got a name? Or a description?

She paused. *Those particular memories have been fudged.*

Suggesting our broker might also be a telepath?

Possible. The way he's gone about it is a little strange though. It's more a smear than an actual erasure and suggests he hasn't been trained.

You haven't been trained, and you don't smear.

Not officially trained, true, but my parents run the PAC and basically taught me control from the moment the skill developed.

"Lizzie? You out there?" came Saska's shout.

"Here!" I replied and then silently asked, *What was she supposed to do?*

Be on hand to stop you from rescuing your brother.

That suggests the wraith expected me to act as I did.

He would have gotten a good sense of your capabilities when you almost killed him, remember.

Yes, but to have a witch on hand, ready to retaliate, suggests he's foreseeing my movements and reactions before I make them.

All of which would explain why the psychometry line had all but died. He'd been ready for me to play that card. Maybe it was no accident that I'd found the ring—maybe he'd wanted me to make the attempt to find Juli and then fail.

His plan might have worked, too, if not for the interference of a ghost.

We don't know all that much about him, other than he's a psycho dark sorcerer, Belle said. *Maybe in life he was also clairvoyant. Magic and psi abilities are not mutually exclusive, as you rather aptly demonstrate.*

The crunching of twigs had me glancing around again. Though I couldn't see her, Saska was close. *Did she hear or see anything that could help us track the wraith?*

Belle dove deeper for several seconds and then said, *There's nothing to indicate she saw the wraith. It was one of the two men checking on her who strengthened the restraints.*

She couldn't tell which house he was from by the magic?

Not everyone has your ability to read the thread lines and pick up the house origins.

Not even me, I replied dryly.

You do it more than you think.

That was definitely debatable. A familiar scent began to

ride the breeze. *Saska's almost here. Can you ensure Hazel remains compliant if she wakes?*

Belle did so, and then added, *Yell if you need anything else.*

Always.

Belle snorted and left. I took a deep breath that didn't alleviate the sudden wash of weariness. Deep dive connections always took a toll on both of us, so I could only hope nothing else happened this afternoon.

Saska stepped into the clearing, quickly scanning me before glancing at my captive. "What were you just doing? Mind reading her?"

I nodded. "She arranged to meet a broker about a job, but it was a setup, and she was basically kidnapped. They told her if she didn't cooperate, they'd kill her grandson."

She grunted. "There's not that many gray-side brokers in Canberra, and even fewer who'd risk their reputations with a stunt like that. I'll order a search, but it's possible we're dealing with an out-of-towner."

"Hazel's worked with him before, if that's any help."

She grimaced. "Without a name, it probably won't be, but we can go through her financial records and see if there's anything. Nice bit of binding on your prisoner, by the way." She bent, grabbed the front of the woman's jacket, and hauled her upright. "Let's get back to the car."

I led the way. "How's my brother?"

"Loud and obnoxious."

Staying true to type then. "And the shushunjë?"

"I removed it. It's the reason it took me so long to get here."

"Will there be any lingering aftereffects?"

"He'll be as weak as shit for the next few days, but other than that, no."

176

"Shame," I couldn't help muttering.

"Normally a comment like that would shock me, because hey, loyalty is all when it comes to any royal line, even if they hate each other. Now that I know some of your history, I'm actually more shocked you're being so polite."

I grimaced. "As much as I'd love to unleash the inner fury, it won't do any good. In fact, it would probably only confirm their already low opinion of me."

"From what I've witnessed, it couldn't actually get much lower, so why bother with restraint?"

"Good point." And to be honest, I wasn't entirely sure the restraint would hold all that long if I had to interact with my family too much more.

Hell, even stepping out of the trees and catching my brother's gaze had my fists clenching. He leaned against the Fairmont's trunk, his expression as thunderous as his aura. The man was *not* happy, which not only eased a little of the fury but also had amusement running through me. You had to take your fun where you could, after all.

"I'm told," he said, his tone cool and distant, "that I owe you my life."

"And having saved said life, I'd appreciate it if you'd take my warnings a little more seriously in the future." I stopped myself several feet away and crossed my arms. He'd probably see it as a defensive gesture, but it was more a denial of the need to grab his shirt and violently shake some sense into his arrogant skull. "This isn't over yet, and he will come for you again."

"He wouldn't dare—"

"He's a dark sorcerer returned to this world in the form of a revenge-seeking wraith. I think it's pretty safe to say there's nothing he wouldn't do *or* dare to get what he wants."

Juli studied me for a second, silver eyes gleaming in the hazy light of the approaching dusk. "I will be more careful—"

"You'll stay home and do what you're fucking told until Saska's mob and I can stop this bastard."

A condescending smile crept across his face, but I held up a finger in warning.

"Before you say anything derogatory, may I remind you that it was me—not you, not Father, not even the high council's investigators—who found this bastard the first time. I was too late to save Cat, granted, but if you lot had listened to me, she might be alive today. Her death was *never* my fault. The blame lies with people like you—people who refused to believe that psi powers could do what magic could not."

He didn't reply but his face was a picture. My family's status in Canberra these days was such that they very rarely faced anything in way of criticism—not directly, anyway—so unlike my father, Juli hadn't cultivated restraint.

That said criticism was coming from the sister he despised made it all the more unpalatable.

"That is the most ridiculous statement I've ever heard."

"Only to someone with their head stuck so far up their own ass that they wouldn't see the truth even if it could slap them in the face." I took a deep breath and released it slowly. "Saska, how far away is transport?"

"Ten minutes." Though she was depositing the woman alongside the bound and gagged men, her voice ran with amusement.

"Good. I'll wait over near the trees. I need fresh air."

I strode to the trees and didn't turn around, even though Juli's gaze burned a figurative hole in my back and his silent demand that I turn and face him filled the air. I continued to ignore him, and instead dragged out my phone and used the time to cruise through social media and calm down.

Saska's people arrived, and Samuel wasn't with them, which surprised me given my brother's standing in Canberra. But maybe he was caught up dealing with my father. He would have been notified the minute the mess at the restaurant went down—news like that didn't take long to get around a place like Canberra—and my father would have demanded a direct update from the man in charge.

Once our prisoners were handed over and the team updated, Saska led me across to one of the cars while my brother was guided to another. It didn't take us all that long to get back to Hattie's, which was a relief because weariness was definitely sweeping in.

"I'll pick you up at eight fifteen." Saska halted next to the front steps then handed me a business card with her phone number on it. "Don't go anywhere without ringing me first."

I nodded. "Has extra security been placed on my brother?"

"Yes. And he's been ordered to cancel face-to-face meetings for the next few days." She studied me for a second. "For what it's worth, I think you're as powerful as any person in your family, just in a different way."

I half smiled. "There is only one power that matters to my family."

"Then they're fools. But you already know that."

I smiled, jumped out of the car, and dashed into the house. It had been a long day, and I needed to pee something fierce. Which reminded me... *Belle, has Hattie had a chance to get the pregnancy test yet?*

No. She got caught up at the court and the pharmacy was closed by the time she got there.

You can buy them in the supermarket these days.

I suspect Hattie is not the type to venture into a regular supermarket.

Given the amount of chocolate in her pantry, I suspect you're wrong.

Belle laughed. *Home delivery is a thing, you know, especially amongst the royal houses. Can't be seen mingling with the masses after all.*

Hattie didn't give me that impression at all.

No, but she mingles with the masses all day long, and tends to just want to come home and zone out at the end of it.

Meaning Belle had at some point read her mind. *Can you jog her memory? As much as I want to avoid knowing, I probably should.*

Will do.

Thanks.

After a long hot shower that washed away the grime, if not the weariness, we ate dinner, then spent the rest of the evening going through Clayton's property portfolio. We eventually came up with two lists—one with the properties we'd initially ask for, and the other with the ones we'd settle on. Which, if we included the cash, would leave us a couple of mil shy of the ten I'd demanded, but would nevertheless be a fucking amazing result.

By the time ten rolled around, I was all but dead on my feet. I bid everyone good night, then stumbled down the hall to my bedroom. I was barely in bed when the phone rang, the tone telling me in instant who it was.

My silly heart skipped several happy beats.

Aiden.

CHAPTER NINE

I shuffled up in the bed, tucked the pillow behind my back, and then hit the answer button.

"Aiden," I said, in a calm tone that totally belied the chaotic churn of thoughts and heart. "Everything all right?"

"No, but I'm guessing you already know that. Monty has never been one to hold his own counsel."

I couldn't help but smile. "That's for sure. Has anyone been hurt?"

"When it comes to the wild magic, there've been a few scrapes and bruises, but nothing serious so far. The lilin, on the other hand, are causing a great deal of consternation."

"What the hell are lilin?"

"Monty didn't tell you?"

"I haven't spoken to Monty. He might have told Belle, but she hasn't passed it on."

"Understandable, given you've more than enough to deal with, and it's not like you can do much from up there anyway."

"I know but—"

"It's fine, Liz. Monty is more than capable of handling

the situation. And the lilin are minor night spirits who attack but don't kill men. Monty's calling them a nice change of pace."

I snorted. He would. "Does he know how to get rid of them?"

"We've instigated a full night curfew. Apparently, they'll move on if there's no one out and about to harass." He paused. "Their influx has had one benefit though—it's made a mockery of my mother's attempts to blame you for the demon infestations."

"I daresay she'll find something else to blame me for." It was lightly said. I might hate the bitch, but she was his mom *and* the current alpha. If I wanted any hope of a long-term relationship, then I couldn't say too much about her when I was talking to him.

"Not if she wants to maintain her standing in the pack. But I didn't ring you to talk about her. How are things going up there?"

"It's been... interesting."

"Which is usually code for 'it's a shit fight, but you don't want to worry me.'"

I laughed. "Basically."

"Is it your family, or is something else going on? Because the vibes I'm getting from Monty suggest the latter, but he's refusing to say anything."

"Is that why you called?"

"I called because I miss you." His soft reply was filled with an ache that echoed deep inside of me. "I called because I needed to hear your voice. Because I miss your scent in my nostrils, talking to you in the mornings, and loving you at night. I just..."

He stopped. I waited, but he didn't go on.

"I miss you too, Aiden," I replied eventually. "But the reality is, nothing has changed."

Though he remained silent, a big "not yet" seemed to pulse down the line. Hope or imagination?

I wearily rubbed my forehead. "To answer your question, it's more than just my family. The past has come back to haunt the present."

"Meaning what?"

"The sorcerer who killed my sister is back in town, and he's gunning for my whole family."

"Fuck Liz, you can't handle this alone—"

"I'm *not* alone, and you can't be here. He's already made one attempt to grab Belle. I don't need to be presenting him with a second option."

"He couldn't possibly know that you and I are connected."

"He can, because I had to walk through a wall of his magic to find the body of his first victim, and it was basically a magical data scanner."

"Damn it, it's not in a werewolf's psyche to stay away and do nothing when their mate is under threat."

Mate. Goddammit, he'd called me his *mate.* And my stupid heart danced giddily even though I was well aware it was just a word. Maybe even a slip of the tongue.

"You can and you will," I said, somehow managing to keep my voice even. "There's too much at stake for us both. You running up here to me will not help the situation with your pack."

And it would definitely provide more ammo for his mother's attacks on me. She'd without a doubt use it as evidence that he cared more for me than he did his pack and his duties as alpha.

"I don't fucking care—"

"That's a lie, and we both know it," I said. "Your pack has been at the forefront of your thoughts from the very beginning of our relationship, and nothing will ever change that. I appreciate the sentiment behind the statement, but you can't jeopardize your future by acting rashly now. We both know you'll regret it when the inevitable consequences hit."

He sighed. "Honestly, there's a large part of me that just doesn't care right now. I'm over them all, Liz."

"And once again, we both know you'd never forgive yourself if you *did* walk away from it all."

I might have once hoped that if it came down to a choice, he'd choose me over his pack, but deep down I'd always known that such a choice would, eventually, also destroy us.

He couldn't change what he was. He'd said that time and again. It meant our only hope as a couple was his pack accepting me as his mate, and right now, with his mother in the opposition corner, that was very much a fifty-fifty proposition.

A bristly scraping sound echoed down the line, and the vision of him dragging a hand across his stubbly chin rose. Lord, how I ached to follow the motion with gentle kisses.

"When did you become the sensible one in this outfit?" he said eventually.

I laughed. "I can be sensible. On occasions. *Rare* occasions."

"Hmmm" was all he said to that.

I smiled, but it quickly faded. "The HCI are all over the situation, Aiden. They know what they're doing. They won't let this bastard escape them a second time."

"Are you saying that to convince me or yourself?"

"Both, I guess. But I do believe it."

"I take it you're helping out?"

"I have no real choice given I'm the one being hit by visions. Plus, I'm the only one who can communicate with or even see the ghost."

"Ghost? Whose ghost?"

"I don't know. She's yet to fully reveal herself."

"One of his past victims, perhaps?"

"Unlikely, given his past victims lost their souls to his demons."

"What about Catherine? Are you positive your sister's fate was the same as his other victims?"

"As positive as we can be. Her soul wasn't lingering, and it would have had she somehow survived being 'eaten' but not moved on."

And it wasn't like there was a third option in the mix, as much as I might wish it.

"Belle can't commune with her?"

"We haven't had the chance to try yet. But while she can feel the ghost's presence, she can't see her."

"Not even through you?"

"No."

"That's unusual, isn't it?"

"According to Belle, some do have the capacity to conceal their presence from spirit talkers."

"Have Belle's spirit guides had anything to say on the matter?"

"Probably not. They've a tendency to be unhelpful when it comes to these sorts of situations."

"What's the point of calling themselves guides if they don't actually guide?"

"This is a point I have made many times."

He laughed softly. "And the court cases? How are they going?"

"As well as can be expected." I gave him a full update and then added, "My father is on the stand tomorrow. I'm preparing myself for a shitfest of lies and a stream of 'the grief made me do it' excuses."

"Surely no one up there will buy that. They all know him too well."

"Yes, but I'm thinking they'll use it as an excuse to hand out a gentler sentence." A huge yawn escaped. "Sorry, you're not boring me or anything. It's just been a long day."

"And I shouldn't have rung so late. I just needed to know you were okay."

"I am," I said softly. "Hopefully I won't be away for too much longer."

"Good, because I need you in my life on a daily basis, Liz. It's just not the same here with you gone."

Tears touched my eyes, and I blinked rapidly. Damn them. Damn my heart. Damn him for saying everything but the one word I was desperate to hear.

But maybe he couldn't—or more likely wouldn't—say it until the mess with the pack was sorted and he had a clear way forward.

I couldn't help crossing all things while silently praying to any god that might be listening that it didn't take too much longer. I needed him in my life too.

I hesitated, then said, "If anything happens... If the worst comes to pass, then know—"

"Don't you dare finish that sentence," he growled. "Nothing will happen, and you *will* come home. I'll accept no other outcome. Hear?"

A smile tugged at my lips, even as my heart did those silly flip-flops again. "Hear."

"Good. Night, then."

"Night," I said. "I'll try and keep you updated, even if only by text."

"I prefer to hear your voice, but I'll accept a text if that's all you've time for," he said. "Please be careful, Liz."

"I will."

He hung up. I closed my eyes and hugged my phone to my chest, very much wishing it was him I was hugging. Then, with a sigh, I scooted down under the blankets and went to sleep.

And for the first time in ages, my dreams were filled with possibilities rather than bloodshed. It was a nice change.

The four men in near identical suits once again stared disdainfully at me across the table.

"You cannot be serious," Ryland said. He obviously still had the spokesman job. "The sum of these properties amounts to far more than the cash you have demanded."

I shrugged. "Yes, but given your obvious reluctance to pay said cash, I'm giving you a second option."

"It is too much."

"It isn't even a quarter of his assets." I met his gaze evenly. "And given you're so desperate to protect the reputation of your deceased sibling, I would suggest you step up and start taking me seriously. Because I will destroy your family's name if that's what it takes."

Anthony touched my hand in warning. I glanced at him briefly then returned my gaze to Ryland. I'm not sure what he saw in my expression, but the amusement running through his faded.

"We want this situation dealt with as quickly as you,

and we are certainly willing to make concessions on our demands." Anthony's voice was mild but nevertheless no nonsense. "But if you're not willing to take us or this situation seriously, then we shall see you in court."

No immediate response, though the four men shared a glance.

Anthony glanced at me and nodded. As one, we rose.

Ryland sighed. "Fine. But eight properties and that amount of cash is too much. We both know the court would not fall that far in your favor. Not when the marriage was never consummated."

Which was basically an admission that the court *would* fall in my favor.

Anthony placed his files back on the table but didn't sit. It was a not-so-subtle reminder we were willing to walk. "What do you suggest then?"

Ryland glanced briefly at his brothers. "One million each and two properties."

"One million each and six properties," Anthony countered.

"Three, and we have a deal."

Anthony glanced at me, his eyebrows raised in question. I nodded mutely, my pulse rate high and my heart thunderous. It was in truth more than I could really have hoped for despite all our planning last night, and it would set me and Belle up for the rest of our lives.

"We have a deal," Anthony said.

"Do you have a preference for which properties you'd prefer?"

I hesitated, pretending to scan the list when I already knew which three were our top picks. "The apartment in Melbourne, the residence in Apollo Bay, and the apartment in Coolangatta."

They weren't quite able to contain their joint relief. They'd expected us to go for the more expensive properties, like the one here in Canberra that my father was so desperate to get his hands on. And I admit, it had been tempting. *Very* tempting. But in the end, we'd fallen on the side of practicality rather than revenge. The three we'd chosen were all large properties that would easily house our two families—when we did eventually have families, that is —in locations that were practical and/or fabulous holiday locations. This also gave us the ability to rent them out to holiday makers during peak periods, which would help pay for their upkeep and rates.

"I want the Melbourne apartment solely in Belle's name, but the titles of the other two are to be placed in both my name and hers."

You can't do that, Belle said immediately.

I can and will. I know it will never make up for the time lost with your family and all the shit you've had to deal with—

I don't regret that shit, Lizzie. I'd do it all again if I had to.

I know, but I still need to do this for you, so shut up and just accept it.

She mentally harrumphed but otherwise obeyed. But love and appreciation washed through our link, and I found myself blinking back tears.

"It could take between four and six weeks for the title transfers to be finalized," Ryland was saying. "That's not something we can hasten, government departments being what they are."

"Send the paperwork across to my office as soon as it is completed," Anthony said.

Ryland nodded again, then switched his gaze to me. "It's been a pleasure doing business with you, Ms. Grace."

I bet it was, given they'd gotten the bulk of Clayton's assets without much of a fight from me. I gathered my coat and purse and somehow resisted dancing in utter joy as I left the room.

My father dominated the witness stand, both physically and magically. While the courtroom was guarded against all manner of spell craft, those spells didn't have the capacity to mute the glow of a witch in his prime, and my father was magically letting it all hang out.

A not-so-subtle reminder that *he* was the most powerful witch in the room.

He hadn't yet glanced at me, and I personally doubted he would. Not until he had a point to make and only then with a sickening amount of regret and sorrow. All false, of course. My father had mastered the art of playing to his audience long ago, and it was an ability that had kept him in power.

That, and his ability to manipulate, bribe, and otherwise force his opponents to do what he wanted.

Anthony walked across to the witness stand and stopped a meter away.

"Mr. Marlowe, we've heard testimony to the effect that, without the consent of either your wife or your daughter, you arranged a marriage between your daughter Elizabeth and Clayton Marlowe—is that testimony correct?"

"It is."

"Then you do not deny using both magic and medication to make Elizabeth compliant?"

"I do not."

My eyebrows shot upwards. I'd expected many things, but blunt agreement to the truth wasn't one of them.

"You are of course aware that underage marriages are against the law here in Australia."

"Of course."

"And yet you nevertheless proceeded with the arrangement. Care to explain why?"

"The merger was beneficial to all parties involved."

"I believe Elizabeth would disagree on that point," Anthony said, tone dry.

I waited for him to pull the "grief made me do it" card. Instead, he was silent for what seemed like ages, and then said, "I believed Clayton to be a good and caring man. I believed he would take care of her—provide her with the support and emotional strength I so obviously couldn't."

So, not the grief card, but rather the "I was only trying to do the right thing by her" one.

"How can you claim you had her best interest at heart when you drugged her, magically bound her to your will, and then forced her into the marriage? You seriously expect the court to believe any of that was in her best interests?"

My father sighed. It was a very put-upon sound.

Also, very fake. Not that it would be obvious to anyone who hadn't grown up with the bastard and seen him play this hand dozens of times.

"I am not the ogre many here would have you believe."

By "many," he meant me.

"Clayton and I had a gentlemen's agreement," he continued, all false sorrow and regret. "He was not to consummate the marriage until Elizabeth was both at a legal age *and* a willing participant."

I thrust to my feet so violently, my chair crashed backward onto the floor. "That's a fucking lie. You're a fucking liar!"

The speaker's gavel banged. "Ms. Grace, please sit down immediately. You are not to respond to the witness or the court unless invited to do so."

Anthony gave me a warning look. I sucked in my anger, righted my chair, and sat down. All the while glaring at my parent.

Said parent ignored me.

"Such an agreement does not alter the fact you forced an unwilling minor into a legally binding contract," Anthony said. "Tell me, was this agreement ever in writing?"

"As I said, it was a gentlemen's agreement. I did not consider it necessary."

"Rather conveniently, then, we only have your word that this agreement existed."

"My word," my father said, leaning forward to emphasize the point, "is not in question here. And I would tread very carefully, Counselor, if you intend to continue that line of questioning."

Anthony smiled pleasantly. "If you have spoken nothing but the truth, why then did you refuse to be truth read? It would have confirmed your version of events, just as it has your daughter's."

My father smiled, his expression cool, calm, and collected—everything the flash of red in his aura wasn't. It made me wish I wasn't the only one in the room who could see it, because it certainly painted a more accurate picture of the truth than anything coming out of his mouth.

"I allowed myself to be telepathically read once before on another matter before the court. The result was a leaking of personal information to the press and several bribery attempts—all of which are a matter of record."

"What the truth seekers and auditors do is not telepathy. They merely assess the legitimacy of your story through the telling of it. They cannot go beyond those restrictions and access other information."

"There is still a mental connection, and I will not risk it."

"Because you are afraid of what might be revealed?"

"Because my word is my bond, and everyone in this room is well aware of that."

"Everyone in this room no doubt believed the same of Clayton Marlowe, and yet he apparently broke your gentlemen's agreement the minute the contract was signed. I would suggest that there never was, in fact, a contract, and you are merely pushing the blame onto a man who is no longer capable of defending himself."

I pushed to my feet again. "Actually, that might not be true."

"Ms. Grace, you were warned," the speaker growled, her frustration evident. "Please sit down before I find you in contempt."

"Is this court about uncovering the truth? The *whole* truth?" I countered. "Or are we merely going through the motions so my father can receive his slap on the wrist and everyone else can move on?"

Anthony, I noticed, was making no move to silence me this time, though his raised eyebrows did suggest he was wondering where I was going with this.

"Ms. Grace, the court will weigh the evidence and apply the appropriate sentence—"

"Which cannot be done without knowing the *full* story. If he refuses to have his story checked via a seeker and auditor, then we have no choice but to call on Clayton and ask him directly."

"Via your familiar, no doubt," my father said in a dry tone. "How very convenient that would be for you both."

I flashed him a smile as cold as anything he'd ever given me. "I would not stain the integrity of the court in such a manner."

Red spun through his aura again. He really didn't like being spoken to in that tone—a tone that was simply an echo of his. "Then how do you propose—"

"The Psychic Advisory Commission," Anthony cut in. "They'd be able to provide a list of spirit talkers. The court could choose to prevent bias by either party."

He turned to face the bench. "While Mr. Lawrence Marlowe has not denied his part in contractually arranging the illegal marriage of his minor daughter, I think it behooves this court to understand the reasons why. If, as my client believes, it was used as a means of punishment and revenge, then surely that should be considered during any discussion on intent and sentencing."

"I have admitted wrongdoing," my father said, with just the slightest edge in his voice. The red flashes were now so strong they were nigh on blinding. Furious didn't even begin to describe his emotions right now, even if it was all being held well under the surface. "Intent should not matter."

"On the contrary," the speaker said coldly. "And I find it interesting that you fight this matter, Mr. Marlowe. It speaks to guilt more than anything else could."

"It is not guilt, but rather an unwillingness to waste the court's time with my daughter's foolish attempt to paint me in a bad light."

"Oh," I muttered, "I think you're doing a damned good job of that yourself."

Anthony cast me another one of those looks. I sat down and shut up.

The speaker glanced at the other councilors, then said, "We'll take an hour recess to discuss the matter." She glanced at her watch, then banged the gavel. "Court will resume at one."

The councilors rose and walked out. My father thrust to his feet and stepped toward me. Anthony quickly positioned himself between us.

"I suggest you rethink what you're about to do," he said quietly.

My father looked him up and down, then turned on his heel and stalked out of the room, his fury so fierce it left a heated trail of air behind him.

Moderno gathered his briefcase and said, "Well played, Anthony, but do not think for an instant you've won this game. We haven't yet played all of our cards."

My gut twisted. I had a bad feeling he was referring to my ability to use the wild magic, though to be truthful I couldn't see how it would get my father off the hook when he'd already admitted guilt.

Especially when the tests he'd insisted on had come back without the expected power boost.

Besides, the time to weaponize my ability to use the wild magic in order to get the charges dropped would have been before the court case had actually begun. Belle and I were the main witnesses, so the prosecution's case would have been far harder to make if we'd not shown up.

It could be a bluff, of course, though my father rarely bothered with such games.

"If you have a new witness, Jack, you're legally required to give us advance warning."

"I am well aware of that." With a nod that encompassed us both, he picked up his briefcase and left the room.

"Well," I said, "that doesn't sound ominous at all now, does it?"

"I would say that whatever they're intending is proving problematic. He has to get court approval to add another witness at this stage of proceedings, and we'd be automatically notified."

"Who do you think the witness might be?"

He shrugged. "Their only real hope now lies in proving you're an unreliable witness and that your memories can't be trusted. Did you ever see a psychologist when you were younger?"

"One, when the nightmares first hit me."

Anthony's eyebrows rose. "What nightmares?"

"Prophetic dreams—they set in with puberty. My parents initially thought I was either lying to gain attention or going crazy."

"Do you know the name of the psychologist?"

I shook my head. "It was a long time ago."

"Did you see him or her for long?"

"Her, and no, I think it was only three or four sessions. She was the one who recommended I be sent to the PAC to be tested."

Of course, Belle's parents had already arranged for me to be unofficially tested, more to reassure me that no matter what my parents said, I was neither insane nor a worthless attention-grabbing chit.

Anthony grunted. "Then they're likely to have some sort of record."

"Which Moderno would no doubt have already accessed."

"Probably, but he hasn't got the Lantern's access to trackers. If your psychologist is out there, we'll find her."

"I still don't see how it's going to help their situation. My father has already admitted his guilt."

"Only because your mother's testimony left him with no other choice. Claiming Clayton broke their agreement while proving your memories are unreliable is merely a means of lessening the sentence."

I snorted. "Do you still really believe that his penalty will be more than a slap on the wrist?"

"I certainly do, young lady."

"Why?"

"Because I have faith in the system." He collected his satchel and swung it over his shoulder. "Do you want to grab some lunch while we wait for court to resume?"

"Sure."

"This way then."

He turned and led the way out. I was three steps behind him when invisible fingers ran down my arm and clasped my fingers.

I stopped cold.

Move, the ghost whispered urgently. *He comes for Juli.*

Juli. Not Julius. *Juli.* The ghost had known my brother. Very few people outside the inner Marlowe circle called my brother that. So who, if not my sister?

"Anthony," I said. "We have a problem."

He swung around. "What?"

"My brother is in danger. We need to get to him—now."

"No, we need to remain here. Besides, he's very well guarded. No one will—"

"We're talking about a dark sorcerer returned to this

world in the form of a wraith. Trust me when I say that he *will*."

He hesitated and then dug out his phone. "I'll call Samuel. He can get extra people there."

It will not help, my ghost said. *He is already in the wraith's possession. He will die if you do not come now.*

I swore and scrubbed a hand through my hair. "Anthony, I'm going. Explain the situation to the bench and contact my father once you've made that call."

"Elizabeth, you cannot afford—"

I didn't hear the rest of it. I was already out the door.

As the ghost tugged me down the steps, I dug out my phone and called Saska.

"I take it there's a problem?" she said by way of hello.

"The wraith has my brother."

"Impossible. I would have been notified—"

"Impossible or not, it has happened."

"And you know this how? A vision?"

"No, my ghost."

"Are you sure this ghost isn't working for the opposition?"

"She hasn't led me astray so far."

"Doesn't mean she's not lulling you into a false sense of security."

"She's not. I'd bet my life on it."

"And you may well be. I'll be out the front in five minutes. Don't go anywhere without me."

The ghost's impatience washed over me, a wave so fierce it momentarily stole my breath. "Damn it, just stop. I'm not going to run into an unknown situation unarmed and alone."

You are not unarmed came the whispered response. *And you are certainly not without power. Not these days.*

Suggesting my ghost was aware of my ability to use the wild magic. Either she'd witnessed me using it or she wasn't a ghost but rather something else. But what?

"I can't use that magic against darkness," I replied. "I can't risk the possibility of staining the wellsprings."

You cannot stain what you are not in contact with came her reply. *What lies within you might have bloomed thanks to the presence of that unrestrained wellspring, but it nevertheless stands apart.*

"And you know this how?"

I'm not a ghost but a spirit guide. I'm able to access knowledge both past and present.

My head snapped toward her. "I don't have a spirit guide."

I didn't *want* a spirit guide.

Her laughter ran across my senses, warm and oddly familiar. It was a sound from my past, a sound I'd heard multiple times.

No, I thought. Impossible.

I am not your guide, she said. *In fact, I doubt there is a guide in existence who'd truly want the task. You have something of a reputation in the spirit world.*

Thanks no doubt to Belle's wretched guides.

Don't you be cussing them out when they have no chance of reply came Belle's amused comment.

It's nothing but the truth.

Perhaps, but why the sudden realization they chat about you behind your back?

My ghost claims to be a spirit guide.

Interesting. I'll see what I can uncover. Has she said her name?

No.

So ask her.

I hesitated, though I wasn't entirely sure why. I needed to know who this spirit was, if only to understand why she was helping us. And yet there was not only a deepening reluctance to take that step but also a growing suspicion that by doing so my world might be turned on its axis.

I stopped near the curb. Saska wasn't yet in sight, so I drew in a deep breath and said, "If you are not my spirit guide then why are you helping me and my family?"

Have you not guessed yet? came the amused reply.

"Obviously not."

Because I didn't want to give the fledgling wings of hope any weight, only to have them crushed.

Her laughter ran across my senses, warm and wicked. *Let me show you.*

The fingers clasping mine became visible even though they remained ethereal in appearance. The semi-solidity swept up her arm, down her body, and then finally reached her face.

It was a face I knew. I face I had once loved. A face I'd thought lost long ago, with no hope of any sort of afterlife or rebirth.

My sister, Cat.

CHAPTER TEN

J oy swept me. I took a step forward, wanting to sweep her into my arms and hug her fiercely, but she was already fading from sight.

Attaining any sort of physicality on this plane takes great strength came Belle's thought. *That she was able to do so after only a short time being a guide speaks to her strength.*

She always was the most powerful of the three of us. I gulped down air that did nothing to calm the excited racing of my thoughts and my heart, and somehow said, "I thought you gone, Cat. I thought the sorcerer's demons had consumed your soul."

They would have, if not for the wild light in our blood.

"The wild magic saved you?"

Yes, though at the time I did not understand what it was or where it had come from.

"But... how? It had taken an unrestrained wellspring to truly ignite the wild magic in my soul—"

Not so came Belle's reply. *Remember it was present when I was drawing on your strength to free you from Clayton. Fearing for your lives obviously allowed both of you to somehow shatter the barriers that divided you from the ancestral gift.*

My phone beeped. I glanced down to see a text from Saska. She was caught in traffic and remained three minutes away.

We cannot wait came Cat's response. *He'll die if you do.*

"I haven't the power to face him alone, Cat."

He doesn't want you dead yet. He wants you to suffer as he suffered.

"Doesn't mean he won't take the opportunity to grab me if I give it."

He won't. Trust me.

I hesitated. *Belle?*

Trust her, she echoed. *She is the real deal, according to my guides.*

You checked?

The minute you realized who she really was.

And is what she's saying true? About him not wanting me dead as yet?

Your own instincts have already told you that, but guides are able to see the paths of our future. If this path led to death, she would know.

But would she tell?

As a guide, she must advise the possibility.

She's not my guide though.

That doesn't matter. She hesitated. *My guides have said they will shadow her.*

Why? It's not like they can intervene if something goes wrong.

You forget how ancient my guides are.

Said ancient ones have repeatedly declared they are unable to do anything more than advise.

And for the most part, that is true.

Please came Cat's comment. *We must hurry. The wildness in his blood will not save him as it saved me.*

Because the Fenna were only ever females. Males might carry the gene or DNA adaption or whatever the hell it was, but they couldn't access it.

I sent a hurried text to Saska explaining the situation and telling her to track my phone, then took a deep breath and released it slowly. "Fine. Lead the way."

She immediately tugged me left, moving at such a pace that I had to run flat out to keep up. "Where are we going?"

Ferry terminal.

"He's on a boat?"

On an island. You need a boat to get to it. She paused, then added with just the slightest hint of amusement, *I'd suggest swimming but you were never very good at that.*

It was a comment that stung even though I knew she hadn't meant to hurt me. It was simply a reminder of just how many things I'd never been very good at as a kid. A reminder of just how many things I'd been forced to teach myself to do.

"Are we heading to Lake Burley Griffin or somewhere else? Because I had no idea it had islands."

We used to picnic there as children.

"Father? Picnic? Seriously?"

She snorted, the sound a bleak breeze past my ear. *Our father wouldn't do anything so common. Our governess took us.*

I couldn't remember having a governess, though it was likely she'd been hired for Cat and Juli, and I just tagged along.

"Did I detect a trace of bitterness in your tone just then, sister?"

Becoming a spirit guide has opened my eyes to many

truths about myself and our family. It has been an unpleasant reckoning.

You were young—

That is no excuse. I knew well enough that I was trained to replace our father, and I welcomed it. I wanted it. I was also aware that Juli was his backup plan. But I never saw anything wrong in how they treated you. It was simply the way things were, and I never questioned it.

"I never doubted you loved me, Cat."

But I was blind to the unfairness of his treatment. I could have—should have—spoken up, but I didn't. Sorry will never undo all the harm that blindness caused, but I nevertheless offer my apologies. She paused and laughed, the sound ironic. *Of course, the bitter sting in the tail for my father is the fact that he was training the wrong daughter. You have turned out stronger than Juli and I combined.*

"Which wouldn't have happened if I'd stayed in Canberra."

Your life would have indeed taken a very different path had you stayed, but you would always have landed right here, right now. There are immutable points in everyone's life. This moment is one of yours.

"If I was always destined to a second round with the wraith, does that mean I'm also destined to survive him?"

That, sadly, is not an immutable point.

Of course not. Fate had never been one to make things easy—why would she start now?

I spotted a black car speeding toward us, and a heartbeat later saw it was Saska. I stepped to the curb as she slid to a tire-smoking stop, then jumped in.

"We need to get to the ferry terminal." I buckled up as she took off. "He's on some island in Lake Burley Griffin."

He's on Springbank came Cat's immediate response.

I repeated this to Saska. She grunted and made a few calls; within minutes, she'd arranged for a boat to meet us at the Lawson Crescent Viewing Deck and take us across to the island.

I gripped the door as we turned sharply onto Edinburgh Avenue, then said, "How the fuck did someone snatch Julius from under the noses of your people?"

"I don't know. Samuel's on his way there now to find out what has happened."

"But wouldn't he have been notified the minute there was an attack or something?"

"Yes, so something must have gone seriously wrong."

Nothing has gone wrong, Cat cut in softly. *The man they had was a doppelganger, existing long enough to convince those escorting him that he was the real deal.*

Doppelgangers were a rare phenomenon and were basically spirit doubles said to be the harbingers of bad luck.

"It's not possible for a doppelganger to convincingly pass themselves off as the real person," I replied. "They're spirits, not flesh."

"I take it" came Saska's dry comment, "that you're talking to your ghost rather than me."

"Yes, sorry."

I quickly filled her in on what Cat had said, and she frowned. "Even if it were possible for a doppelganger to maintain legitimacy that long, when would the switch have happened? He was under full guard from the moment we rescued him from that car."

That wasn't Juli. That was the doppelganger, Cat said.

"Impossible." It was automatically said. "The contempt, the arrogance... it was all too perfect to have been an act."

Doppelgangers are the spirit double of a living person,

Cat said. *They do not often find flesh form but when they do, they are indistinguishable from their living counterpart.*

"But I used his wedding ring to track him—" I stopped, remembering my brief confusion over Juli removing his wedding ring. Obviously, the ring I'd found wasn't Juli's but rather the doppelganger's. We'd been following the fake rather than real man all along.

And I was blinded by my own fear and did not see through the veil until it was all too late, Cat said. *It will be my fault if he dies.*

"No," I said firmly, "The blame lays solely at the feet of our brother. He ignored my warnings and went to that meeting rather than stay home, as advised. His arrogance and refusal to listen is the reason he's now under threat."

But I saw the divergence of his path. I misread it. That is on my head. She paused. *Death sweeps closer. We must hurry.*

My heart rate leapt. I might not care for my brother, and I may have wished him dead dozens of times when we were kids, but he had his own children now. I couldn't let the wraith deprive them of a dad, even if I did think he was an overbearing piece of shit who deserved being taken down a peg or three.

"We're running out of time," I told Saska.

She grunted, and our speed increased fractionally as she skillfully wove the car in and out of the traffic. Within minutes, we were on Lawson Crescent, following the sweeping curve of the shoreline before speeding through a roundabout. A small hill with a strange, rusty red wave sculpture lay ahead, the road splitting around either side of it. Saska swung right, the tires squealing in protest. Directly ahead was a fenced-off boat ramp and several small buildings. A boat waited on the right side of the dock. Beyond it, not that far across the water, was the island. All I could see were trees, but with the weather once against descending and the treetops shrouded in fog, it looked wild and forbidding.

Saska stopped the car to the left of the metal gate. I opened the glove compartment and grabbed the knife and charms I'd left there earlier—everyone attending the court had to go through weapon and magical implement scanners, and I hadn't wanted to risk them being confiscated—then climbed out of the car. The wind was brisk and cold, though I didn't believe it was behind the goose bumps that danced lightly across the back of my neck. I hurriedly zipped up my coat, then hooked on my neck charm—to the unknowing, it looked to be nothing more than a bunch of leather and bronze threads through which had been strung a variety of pretty stones, but it was in fact the most powerful charm I'd ever created. Once I'd stuck the knife and my smaller charms into my purse, I followed Saska across to the gate. Cat remained near the car. Ghosts and flowing water were not often compatible.

Except she's not a ghost came Belle's comment. *She's a spirit. Those rules don't apply.*

Then why isn't she accompanying us?

Possibly because of that fog barrier. It's obviously not natural, and our sorcerer may well suspect we're getting spiritual help. Many witches do have spirit guides, after all.

Would a regular banish spirits spell work on spirit guides, though?

Saska unlocked the gate, then headed for the docked boat.

Yes, Belle said, *but only the strongest practitioner would dare perform them, as they can have serious repercussions.*

What sort of repercussions?

You'd basically be blacklisted by the spirit guide community.

I'm thinking that's a consequence our sorcerer wouldn't care about.

No. Mine are warning to tread carefully. There's magic afoot.

I'm not sensing it.

The fog is swallowing sound and sensation.

Which is just what we need in this sort of situation. Especially when the inner countdown was saying we were rapidly running out of time. That if we didn't find Juli soon, we wouldn't find him alive.

We're dealing with a wraith hell-bent on revenge. He was never going to make it easy for us.

None of them ever do.

The boat's captain looked up as we approached. He was a tall man with a thin face, a thick gray beard, and a cheery red-and-gold wooly hat. "You Saska Sarr?"

She nodded and flashed her ID. "Thanks for coming at such short notice, Mike."

"At the rates being offered, I'd be a fool if I didn't." He grinned, revealing neat rows of yellow-stained teeth. "Especially when it's only a hop, skip, and a jump to the island from here. The engines won't even get a decent workout."

He helped us both into the boat. I nodded my thanks, but the bulk of my attention was on the island. There was no indication of movement, no sense of anything untoward rising in the air, but my instincts twitched.

There might not be even the faintest whisper of magic riding the cold air, but the ceremony I'd envisioned had begun.

My brother had minutes, rather than hours, of life left.

I moved to the stern and wished I could ask Cat to scout

ahead. Traps awaited, I had no doubt of that, but it would have been handy to get some advance warning. I flexed my fingers as the boat reversed away from the dock, but it didn't do much to ease the growing tension.

After a moment, I asked, "How are we going to play this?"

"Cautiously."

I smiled and couldn't help but wonder if it looked as tense as it felt. "Beyond that."

"It'll depend on what awaits." She gave me a stern look. "You are not to go it alone, no matter what happens."

There was little point in arguing, given that until we were on the island, we had no idea what we were facing. Of course, if she actually knew me, she'd be well aware that she was pretty much wasting her time with an order like that. "What do you know about wraiths?"

"Not a fucking lot."

"I take it then you're not carrying any kind of blessed weapon on you?"

She raised an eyebrow. "Is that why you're carrying a knife? As a deterrent for supernatural nasties?"

"They do have a bad habit of treating the reservation as a drive-through restaurant."

It was wryly said, and she laughed.

"Then thank goodness I live here, where the only nasties I'm forced to deal with are the living kind." She paused. "Is there anything beyond a blessed silver blade that will work against this thing?"

"As far as we know, our only other option is holy water." I swung my purse around and plucked out one of the remaining bottles I had with me. "Use this if he attacks, and under no circumstances let him touch you."

She accepted the bottle somewhat dubiously. "It seems a very small amount to seriously threaten a demonic spirit."

"Evil cannot stand holy water. That's the one belief that generally holds true."

She glanced at me. "Generally? Meaning there are some beliefs that don't?"

I wrinkled my nose. "I'm not sure where the whole 'vampires hate churches' thing comes from, but I wouldn't bother running into one if you are ever attacked by a vamp. Stakes and silver do work on the bastards, though."

She studied me for a second, her dubious expression suggesting she wasn't certain if she should believe me or not. "I take it wraiths aren't immune to magic—we should be able to cage this thing, right?"

"Yes, but our wraith was once a dark sorcerer and powerful enough to evade some of the strongest witches in Canberra the first time round. Death would not have changed that."

In fact, I rather suspected it had enhanced rather than diminished his power.

"If all else fails, use a repelling spell against him. No matter the brand of practitioner or evil, they all underestimate the usefulness of a good repel spell."

Amusement crinkled the corners of her eyes. "Speaking from experience?"

"They've saved my life more than once."

"Then I'll keep them in mind."

My gaze drifted back to the island. We were approaching a small jetty that jutted out from near the end of the kidney-bean-shaped island. There were no boats tied onto the jetty or even moored nearby, and the island itself was strangely hushed. Though the breeze had picked up, it seemed to leave the island untouched. The fog that had hidden the treetops now shrouded their entire length.

There was nothing natural about that fog. I was certain of that even without entering it.

The boat slowed as we neared the dock. The captain expertly guided her in and then said, "You want me to remain here and wait?"

Saska hesitated. "We're not entirely sure what sort of mess we're walking into, so it might be better if you head back to the other dock and wait for our signal to return."

"And if things go sour and you need to get off fast?"

"If things go sour, then we more than likely won't be getting off."

"That bad, huh?"

"Yes indeed."

He helped us off, then backed out and motored away. I tried to ignore the premonition that we really should have left with him, and resolutely turned to study the wall of shrouded greenery that stood between us and whatever was happening to my brother.

Saska started forward. I followed her, scanning the trees warily, looking for the traps I suspected were close but couldn't see.

"I'm not liking the feel of that," she said as we neared the edge of the fog barrier.

"I believe it's designed to prevent sound and sensation from escaping while banishing spirits and maybe even certain people from entering."

"Meaning me?"

"Possibly." I shrugged. "He's not going to ban me, because this is just another means of twisting the emotional knife until he decides it's my turn to be tortured and consumed."

She warily pressed a hand forward. The fog briefly resisted her touch and then gave way. She shivered violently.

"Looks like I'm on the approved list, and I'm not entirely sure how I feel about that." Her expression was grim. "You're absolutely certain your brother lies beyond this wall?"

"No, but my sister is."

Her eyebrows shot upwards. "The ghost is your *sister?* The one who died at the wraith's hand the first time around?"

"Yep."

"And you're sure it's her and not some apparition he's conjured up to entrap you?"

"I'm sure." Or Belle's spirit guides were, and I trusted their judgement even if I'd never tell them that.

I retrieved my knife from my purse, unsheathed it, and then warily pushed its point into the fog. An odd blue-white light immediately flared down the length of the blade and the fog shivered away from it, creating a small pocket of "clean" air.

"Wow," Saska said. "I've heard tales of the 'godly glow' that happens with certain blessed silver items, but I've never actually seen it in action."

"It's a first for me, too."

But then, we'd only recently convinced the priest who kept us stocked in holy water to sanctify and bless our knives. He'd been more than a little reluctant to do so beforehand, despite the constant flow of demons entering the reservation. The brutal deaths of several of his parishioners at the hands of said demons had finally convinced him otherwise.

"Then you have no idea if it's capable of banishing evil

with the merest touch, or whether that's just another folktale?"

"None at all."

"Hell of a time to find out, then." She eyed the pocket free of the fog somewhat dubiously. "Though that tiny bit of clean air isn't going to do either of us much good."

"I suspect it might increase in size once we head in." I hoped like hell that *that* was the case. "Stay close, and keep your hand on my shoulder. I've a bad feeling you might not get back out if you lose contact."

She nodded. As I stepped toward the wall of fog, she gripped my shoulder and followed. The fog continued to peel away from the knife point and, as I'd hoped, created a pocket of fog-free air for us to move through. But we weren't alone in this place. Something kept pace with us in the gray beyond our bubble, though the only evidence I had of it were the tight swirls of fog eddying past the knife's point.

I shivered and pressed on, warily stepping around the ghostly trunks of trees that only became visible once we were in touching distance.

We were barely a few steps in when the howling began. It was a low, mournful sound that had goose bumps tripping lightly across my skin.

Saska's grip tightened on my shoulder. "What the fuck is that?"

"A werewolf."

"It doesn't sound right."

"Because it probably isn't." I flexed my free hand, briefly sending little sparks of energy dancing through our pocket. "I suspect it's probably another zombie wolf."

"Because why not," she muttered. "Do silver bullets work against them things?"

My eyebrows rose. "You have silver bullets?"

213

"Not on me, no, but I know Samuel has requested them from the Society."

"Officially, or via his sister?"

The smile that tugged at Saska's lips suggested there'd been more than a few occasions when the request had been unofficial. "Hanna hasn't been working with them long enough to risk inappropriate appropriation."

"But he nevertheless has a source within the organization, does he not?"

"One or three, perhaps." Her smile grew. "It's always wise to spread the love around."

A comment that no doubt referred to more than just shady silver bullet acquisitions. "To answer the question, yes, silver will work against the dead as easily as the living, but in this case, it'd be a waste. Just shoot their knees out to stop them moving, then aim for their brains to break the connection with the monster who raised them."

"I'm thinking those rather specific recommendations come from experience," she muttered. "It's an interesting life you lead, Lizzie Grace."

"As understatements go, that's right up there."

The movement eddying the fog sharpened abruptly, and my pulse rate jumped. My grip on the knife was now so fierce, my hand ached.

"What's wrong?" Sasha whispered.

"The wolf who howled before is looping around us again, and he's looking to attack. Get ready to defend yourself."

"Aren't werewolves afraid of silver?"

"Yes, but this wolf is already dead, and I don't know if the same rules apply."

We kept moving, despite the ever-tightening circuits by the unseen wolf. I had no idea how much distance we'd covered, because I'd lost all sensation of time and place from the moment we'd entered this fog. But the faintest caress of magic now whispered through the air, and it was coming from directly ahead.

"Oh, that doesn't feel very good," Saska commented.

"He's begun the sacrifice ceremony, which means we're officially out of time."

"That may well be, but we have to get out of this fog before we can be of any use to your brother, and this fucking tree line seems way deeper than it should be."

Which no doubt had something to do with the magic that pressed all around us.

We moved on. The swirls of movement increased, gaining an intensity that suggested growing frustration. Another howl ripped through the air, the sound hoarse and desperate.

Then, from the right, the wolf attacked.

I felt its approach a heartbeat before it hit, and swung around, sweeping the blade across the fog. The wolf must have realized at the last moment it was silver and twisted away violently, but the blade nevertheless scoured the mangy length of his pelt. He didn't bleed blood; he bled decay, and lord, it was foul. This wolf had been in the ground even longer than the one that had been sent in as a distraction during Juli's kidnapping.

More movement, then the muzzle of a wolf that was more skull than flesh appeared out of the gloom, lunging for my face. His teeth were as rotten as his scent, and his mouth impossibly wide. Once again, I retreated. His jaws snapped closed where my face had been moments before, and he shook his head in frustration, spraying drool and rotten bits of skin across my body.

Bile rose, but I gulped it back down and slashed the

knife across the wolf's decaying snout. He jerked away, but once again wasn't quite fast enough. The knife's sharp edge sliced through remnants of flesh, muscle, and bone, but it was the godly glow that caused the greater damage. It leapt from the metal to the creature's decaying flesh and spun down his length, quickly forming a glowing cage. The wolf howled and writhed, obviously desperate to escape, but the glowing net only got tighter. Then the stench of burning flesh stained the air. There was no smoke or fire, but that light nevertheless consumed him in his entirety. Within heartbeats, there was nothing left, not even tiny bits of ash or bone.

Another howl rent the air, quickly followed by several gunshots. It was only then I realized Saska's hand was no longer on my shoulder.

I spun and scanned the fog. The shots had come from my left, but the movement seemed to be coming from the right.

"Saska?" I shouted. "Where are you?"

"Here" came her reply.

"Here" came another, from behind me.

"Here" came the third to my right.

I had no idea which of them was real—and no time to find out.

The clock was counting down. I couldn't keep wading through this fog looking for Saska—not if I wanted to save my brother—and that was undoubtedly the wraith's intention. He was forcing me to make a choice, to choose one life over another. It was just another means of ramping up the anger and the guilt.

Maybe his demons were demanding a soul filled to the brim with all the dark, juicy emotions as their final feeding prize.

"Sorry, Saska," I said. "I have to keep moving."

Several more shots, then a quick "Go" echoed all around me.

The bastard had planned his trap very well indeed.

I spun and ran toward that gathering wall of magic, hoping all the while that it wasn't another trick. The fog eddied around me, suggesting I was still being tracked even if I wasn't yet being attacked.

I kept the knife in front of me, using its glow to spot and dodge the heavily shrouded trees and shrubs before I ran into them. Just as I began to think the fog was never going to end, the vague outline of what seemed to be picnic tables became visible in the near distance. There remained no sign of the sorcerer, but his magic now crawled across my skin, tiny gnats of power that made me want to stop and scratch. He was close, even if I couldn't see him.

Then, just as the fog started lifting and the hope that I was finally nearing its end surged, something moved to my left.

I swung round and raised the knife. Saw, in its godly glow, a decaying wolf launch at me.

That wolf had Aiden's face.

My eyes widened in horror, and for too many seconds I didn't move. *Couldn't* move, as the dead thing soared toward me, its mouth open and eyes hungry. Deep down, I knew it wasn't Aiden. Knew it was nothing more than an illusion, because it was impossible for *any* wolf to maintain any part of their human form once they'd shifted. And yet, I stood there, frozen, staring at the face of the man hurtling toward me with seemingly deadly intent.

Lizzie came Belle's internal scream. *Move! Now!*

It was enough to break the freeze. I threw myself sideways, but it was far too late to totally avoid damage. The wolf's teeth scoured my right arm, tearing clothes and skin instead of throat or face.

I swore, twisted around, and lunged at the wolf as he landed several feet away, thrusting the knife deep into his side. The godly light quickly did its work but the sight of Aiden's face melting away, his mouth open in a silent scream, had sobs rising.

It made me glad he wasn't anywhere near Canberra, because the sorcerer was showing me exactly what he planned to do if my wolf *did* appear.

I swiped at the tears staining my cheeks with my left hand, then thrust up and ran on. A dozen steps later, I was out of the fog and sucking in fresh air. Aside from a few picnic tables and rubbish bins, the grassland beyond was flat and empty. There were no trees, no shrubs, and definitely no sign of the sorcerer, his victim, or even a protection circle.

Had Cat been fooled? Or was she indeed nothing more than another lure by the bastard who now knew entirely too much about me, thanks to the goddamn barrier that had surrounded his first victim.

No, she was the real deal. Probably the only thing that *was* right now.

Besides, his magic *was* here. Not just in the fog behind me but also in the emptiness ahead. He was obviously using some sort of concealment shield, one that was designed to give no definitive hint of its location.

I ran past the picnic tables and bins so fast they were little more than a blur. But the knowledge it was all too late, that my brother was dying if not already dead, pulsed through me. Despair quickly followed.

No, I thought harshly. *No.*

That's exactly what the wraith wanted—my tears, my

desperation, and very definitely my despair. I couldn't afford to fall down that emotional rabbit hole, because it would only make him—and his demons—stronger.

I was maybe a dozen or so steps away from that middle point when a huge *whoomph* shook the ground and sent me stumbling. A heartbeat later, a blast of air hit hard, knocking me off my feet and tossing me back a good five meters or so. I hit the ground with a bone crunching "oomph," losing my knife somewhere in the wet grass as I slid backward a few more yards before coming to a halt.

Winded and bruised, I pushed into a sitting position and looked around frantically for my knife. It lay in the grass a few meters away. I scrambled toward it on hands and knees, then pushed upright.

A stone oval now lay ahead. The remains of a fire sat at one end, with the body of a butchered rabbit just in front of it. Entrails and blood lay across the other stones, though from where I stood, I could smell more than see them.

Within the oval lay the bloody, naked body of a man.

My brother.

As dead in this field as he had been in my vision.

CHAPTER ELEVEN

I pushed back the thick surge of anger and despair and quickly scanned the area. There was no sign of the sorcerer. No sign of whatever had caused that explosion. No sign even of the torn remnants of magic that should have accompanied it.

Just my brother, bloody and naked within that oval.

I sheathed my knife and then swung around, unable to face the brutal reality of his death just yet.

The fog that had shrouded the island had also disappeared. Saska marched through the last row of trees, her gun held at her side and blood smeared across her left cheek. I didn't think it was her blood, but I wasn't close enough to be sure.

She didn't say anything. She didn't need to. Not when her aura was a mess of conflicting emotions, and her face was set and hard.

I wasn't the only one who'd failed here today.

And yet, neither of us really ever had a chance of saving Julius. His fate had been set by his own actions, and nothing we did after his fateful decision to meet his friends in that restaurant could have changed anything.

I fell in step beside her, and we silently strode toward the stone circle, stopping a meter or so away from it.

My vision should have prepared me for what I was seeing.

It didn't, simply because that vision hadn't shown the half of it.

"Fucking hell," Saska said. "The bastard went all out this time, didn't he?"

He had indeed.

Because the blood and entrails that covered Juli's naked body didn't belong to the rabbits who'd been sacrificed here but were instead *his*. He'd been cut open from neck to navel, and all his innards pulled out. His rib cage had also been cracked open, and there was dark hole in his chest where his heart should have been.

It struck me then that there was a method—a deliberation—in the way the wraith was killing each of his victims.

If his first victim was indeed Aunt Frankie, the little I remembered of her said she'd valued her intellectual achievements over magical, and our wraith had taken her brain. Deni had prided herself on her fitness and her physical achievements, and her life force had been sucked away by a leech. Juli had always boasted that he would never let his heart, or his emotions, get in the way of a good deal, and now he had no heart to worry about.

The wraith's actions might well be based on revenge, but he was also very clearly killing them in a way that would have the most effect on them *and* on me.

"Why do this?" Saska waved a hand toward my brother. "Why use completely different methods to kill each person?"

"It's a message," I said bluntly. "He's telling me that he's done his homework and knows exactly what each member of my family prides themselves on."

And that homework had been completed well before I'd gone through that first barrier. He'd obviously been tracking my family for some time to know these sorts of details.

"Ah, now that does make sense," Saska said. "But it also makes me wonder what he has planned for your mother and your father."

Given both my father and mother valued themselves on their magical prowess, I had a fairly good idea.

"Let's hope we can stop this bastard before we find out," I muttered.

"At this point, you'd have to say the odds are with the wraith rather than us." Her expression was a mix of annoyance and frustration. "I take it you never saw how he got off the island?"

I shook my head. "It probably had something to do with the explosion that erased his magic; maybe he used it to conceal the fact he had a boat waiting on the opposite side of the island to the jetty."

"Do wraiths actually need boats? Ghosts can cross water, can't they?"

"Not in most cases. They're generally restricted by the location of their death and by moving water. But wraiths are very different to your average ghost, and it's pretty obvious he's not bound by the same rules."

Saska grimaced. "Well, if he *did* use a non-magical means of transport, Reggie will have spotted and followed him."

If he was, I hoped he was also maintaining his distance. The wraith was probably aware that the HCI had shifters working for them.

Saska got her phone out. "I need to call this in and then take some photos. You got anything in that purse of yours to treat that wound on your arm? You're dripping blood all over the place."

I glanced down. The wound was ragged and deep enough to see muscle and even a hint of bone. He'd obviously missed anything major, given I could still move all my fingers, but I suspected it hadn't been luck but rather deliberation. The wraith didn't want me dead yet. He wanted me frustrated and angry and maybe even sick—a thought backed by the fact that the wound was already festering around the edges. I had no idea what diseases or foulness a wolf raised from the dead might carry, but those yellowish globs forming deeper within the wound did not bode well for my health. Thank God I still had some holy water with me.

"I do have a small first aid kit in my purse."

She half smiled. "Most people wouldn't."

"I'm not most people."

"I'm definitely seeing that."

I smiled and pulled my sleeve over my hand to catch the worst of the bleeding, then returned my gaze to my brother. In all truth, the rising anger and despair came more from the fact that I'd failed to save another sibling than anything deeper emotionally. I had no desire to cry for him as I had Cat, but maybe the emotional impact would hit me later. I *did* feel sorry that his kids would now grow up without their father, but other than that? Nada. I was numb. Worse than numb, perhaps, because there was a large part of me that just *didn't* care.

I tore my gaze away again. "After I've treated the wound, I'll do a ground search of the wider area and see if there's any other evidence to find."

"Don't touch it if you do find something."

I half smiled. "I know the drill, trust me on that."

She nodded and made her call. I moved well away from the stone circle then dug out a bottle of holy water and poured it carefully into the wound in an effort not to waste a drop. The water bubbled and steamed almost instantly, and pain erupted. This was the first time using blessed water as a sterilizer actually *hurt*, but I guessed it *was* also the first time I'd used it against a wound caused by a zombie.

I kept dribbling the water on until the pain eased and the wound stopped bubbling, then carefully recorked the bottle. There wasn't that much left, but I wasn't about to waste it.

Once it was tucked safely back into my purse, I bandaged the wound, put the first aid kit away, and then began a studious sweep of the area. A few minutes later, I spotted something glittering in a small, blackened circle.

I walked over and squatted on my heels. It was several small shards of glass, though the rainbow reflections that ran across their surfaces told me they were most likely the remnants of a diamond spell stone. While Belle and I used quartz because it was far cheaper, most witches went for diamonds simply because they held any spell placed on them in a more precise and powerful way. They weren't indestructible, though, despite what most thought. Put enough force through them or *on* them, and they could be shattered or destroyed. That's obviously what had happened here.

I held a hand just above the remnants, but the pulse of whatever spell had been cast upon them had fled. Nor was there any indication that our wraith *had* even held the spell stone long enough to leave a spark I could trace.

I rose and kept walking, finding four more burned out

circles. I suspected they were the source points for the fog we'd encountered, but the destruction was so complete that we'd never actually be certain of that.

I was about to give up when another faint twinkling caught my eye, though it was well out of line with the other stones. I walked across and squatted down beside it. This time, it was a whole stone rather than a shard. Maybe, just maybe, luck had finally fallen on our side.

I held a hand above the raw diamond, fully expecting it to be as dead as the earlier shards.

It wasn't.

The spell still pulsed though the bright heart of the stone, but for whatever reason, had failed to execute. Maybe the caster hadn't set it properly. Or maybe it had been set too close to whatever magic had shielded the sacrifice oval and *that* had caused a malfunction. Either way, it said a lot about the strength of the spell that the remaining stones had still activated when one section had been somehow kicked out of alignment.

But its failure meant I could now use it to trace whoever had set it, though that person wasn't our wraith. The spell was gray rather than black.

"Saska," I said. "Found something you might want to look at."

She immediately walked across and squatted opposite me. "A spell stone, complete with a spell attached."

I nodded. "It was part of a ring of six, and the only complete stone that's left. Do you recognize the spell on it?"

"It's a weather-based curtain spell—no doubt the source of the fog that shielded the island. Our wraith didn't cast this though."

"No, but we can trace whoever did through this stone."

She raised an eyebrow. "I'm thinking you don't mean

via any of our usual methods for tracking the creators of inert or misfunctioning spells."

I had no idea what their usual methods were, so simply said, "I can use my psychometry to trace the creator, but it'll have to be done now rather than later, as the more time that passes, the weaker the connection will become."

She nodded, took a couple of photos, then handed me a pair of gloves. "Do your thing. I'll go meet and update the troops, then we can go."

"They're here?" I glanced around in surprise but couldn't see anyone else.

"They just pulled in. I also called in the paramedics, so make sure you get that arm checked out."

She rose and headed toward the trees. I pulled on a silicon glove, then carefully picked up the stone. Though it wasn't touching my skin, images nevertheless stirred. They were fleeting and distant, running across my senses like a broken picture reel. There was one snapshot of a shadow-haunted shop that was dominated by old wooden shelving. Another of faded charms and glassed potions, all of them thickly coated with dust. A man in a chair, his hair gray and wild-looking, his clothes threadbare and old, wearing purple glasses so thick his closed eyelids looked huge. He didn't look dead, but he didn't exactly look alive, either.

I gripped the stone a little tighter and tried to pull a location. After a few seconds, the picture reel jumped, giving me the image of a run-down, two-story shop. A second jump revealed a street name but not a location. Which was annoying but better than nothing.

As the images faded, I dug out my phone and quickly googled the street name. Thankfully, there was only one Gartside Street, and it was located in Erindale, a good twenty minutes away.

I pulled the glove off around the stone to keep it secure, tucked it into my pocket, then rose and walked through the trees. Our boat was once again sitting at the dock. Saska was talking to Samuel and a couple of other people, and two paramedics were also dockside.

Saska must had said something to them about me, because they immediately headed my way. There were no seats, so I made do with one of the old concrete bollards and let the medics do their thing. They tsked over the state of my arm, insisted it needed stitches, and looked less than pleased when I told them using Steri-Strips would do exactly the same thing. But then, they had no idea one of my DNA adaptions was the fast healing of a werewolf.

With a few more grumbles, they patched me up, gave me some painkillers, and told me to go see my doctor the minute there was any sign of infection. I thanked them, took the painkillers, and headed down to the boat.

"Seems like you did hit a wee bit of trouble," the captain said, offering me a hand in.

I nodded. "I don't suppose you saw anyone else leaving the island, did you?"

He wrinkled his nose. "A boat appeared from around the far side and headed over to the other shore, but I couldn't say whether it originated from that side of island or was merely passing through."

"Any idea how many people were in that boat?"

He hesitated. "Two for sure, but there was this weird shadow near the stern that might have been a third person. Hard to be certain from such a distance."

I was betting the weird shadow was our wraith, and the fact he was partially visible suggested that there were at least some limitations to his powers and his strength. Why else wouldn't he have created a spell to fully hide his form?

"Are there any docks over there?"

"Several, but a boat that size could basically stop anywhere along the shoreline."

And probably had, given the wraith and whoever was helping him wouldn't want to be seen.

Samuel finished talking to Saska, then jumped into the boat and gave the captain a nod.

I gripped the overhead bar as we backed away from the dock. "I'm surprised you're not staying to lead the investigation into my brother's death."

"Saska's more than capable of doing that. I'm under strict orders to bring you in."

I raised my eyebrows. "Bring me in where?"

"To the council's secure bunkers."

I snorted. "We're dealing with a dark sorcerer who deals with demons. Do you really think there's any such thing as a secure bunker? Because I'm here to tell you there's not."

Which was something of a lie, because there were plenty of spells that could prevent demons entering places unasked, but I was betting on the fact that Samuel wouldn't really be certain of that. While minor demonic banishment spells were taught in high school, most of the more dangerous ones were taught in a specialty course in university. Belle did know many of them, but only because she was a spirit talker and had to deal with the demonic presences that sometimes took the place of a called spirit.

"Maybe," Samuel was saying, "but it'll be a better option than the house you're currently in."

"That house is being guarded by two men very experienced in hunting supernatural and demonic nasties. I'd trust their magic and experience over anything or anyone from the high council. And let's be honest here, they don't have a stellar reputation for protecting the likes of me."

"They're protecting your father—"

"Well then, you can definitely count me out. There's no way known I'm about to share air space with that bastard for any longer than necessary."

"But—"

"The sorcerer isn't going to come after me until he's dealt with my mother and my father. Protect them by all means but let me get on with the business of finding and stopping the wraith."

He studied me for a second, his expression worried. "If you're wrong, you could pay a very high price."

"I'm well aware of that. But I'm not wrong." And crossed all fingers, real and figurative, that I hadn't just tempted fate.

He grunted. It was not a happy sound. "They've also relocated the trial."

"Not to the same bunkers, I hope, because I don't trust the council one iota, and if I get locked underground with my father, I hold no responsibility for the outcome."

His lips twitched. "Were you always this difficult?"

"My father would say yes."

"I didn't ask your father."

Amusement ran through me. "It's a trait that's developed from having to deal with bloodthirsty entities and insane exes."

He shook his head, though his expression gave me little idea whether it was in frustration or amusement. "Did you manage to get anything from that spell stone you found?"

I nodded. "The caster has a shop in Erindale."

He glanced at his watch. "We'll have to deal with it after the court hearing. We're due back there in twenty minutes."

"If we don't go to Erindale now, we might as well not go at all. Besides, aren't we already late for the hearing?

"They rescheduled."

"Then they can do so again. This is more important."

Amusement crinkled the corners of his lovely green eyes. "I'm thinking they'd disagree."

"And I'm thinking I don't really care."

He laughed. "Yeah, I get that impression. But pissing off the council is not something sane people generally aspire to."

"It's more about pissing off my father than the council, but if he dies, then the court case dies with him."

"No, it doesn't."

He climbed out of the boat, then offered me a hand. I accepted the offer and let him pull me up. He might not have the strength of a werewolf, but the man obviously worked out. His arms were damn fine.

"What makes you so certain of that?"

"The Society has warned the high council that they require a judgment on this case, even if it is given posthumously. If that judgment is guilty and nothing comes of it, they have warned that they will make every scrap of evidence they have on underage contracts available to the HCI and ensure *all* those involved are investigated if not charged." His lips twisted. "It's a fair bet that all the major families would be caught up in the ensuing mess."

"The Society can't actually pervert justice to ensure a guilty verdict though... can they?"

The ghost of a smile touched his lips, though the amusement didn't reach his green eyes. "That depends on who you ask. And it helps to remember their motto—by fair means or foul, justice will be served. They want this practice stopped, and stopped it will be."

Samuel pulled a business card from his wallet and handed it to the captain. "The team will be in contact to confirm payment details, but if there's any problems, give me a call."

"I will. Thanks," the captain said, a happy smile creasing his weatherworn features. Obviously, today's business had filled up the kitty nicely.

As the captain made his way back to the island, Samuel made a couple of phone calls, informing both the court and the high council of our situation. From their responses—which I wasn't hearing as clearly as I would have liked, thanks to the fact that I was following Samuel up the ramp and the wind was at my back—they weren't best pleased.

I can't say *that* displeased me. Quite the opposite in fact.

Samuel unlocked his car and then said, "The next court session will be postponed until tomorrow morning."

I frowned as I climbed into the passenger seat. "Wouldn't calling the whole thing off until the danger has passed be better? The Society may want a result, but even they can't want my father and mother dead."

"It's not them pushing for this continuation, it's your father. He wants the whole thing over with so he can get on with his life and, I presume, mourn the loss of his only son."

"He has grandsons. He'll be fine."

Which was a harsh thing to say, but it was also the truth. Juli's death wouldn't affect him in the same way Cat's had, because Juli had never held all his hopes and dreams in the same way. I had no doubt he *would* grieve to some extent, but Juli had done his duty to the family and ensured the Marlowe line would continue, and that was all that mattered.

Cat... I suddenly realized she was no longer with me. It

was unlikely she'd be over on the island, as she was already holding too much guilt over her failure to see the doppel-ganger early enough to save our brother's life. Maybe she'd decided to supervise my father and mother's move to more secure quarters. If she *was*, that would at least give us insider knowledge on the location and the methods being used to protect them.

"You want to punch the address into the GPS?" Samuel said as he started the car and drove out of the parking area.

It took us nearly thirty minutes to reach Erindale and Gartside Street. It was basically a shopping and restaurant strip with a drive-in parking area one side of the street that made it look larger than it actually was. There wasn't much in the way of foot traffic, but most of the parking spaces on the right were full, suggesting the area was well attended.

The old man's place was at the end of a long row of two-story brick and glass buildings, with a lane separating it from the row of single-story buildings.

Samuel pulled into the parking strip, then stopped and ran a search on the address. "Owned by one Martin Fitzger-ald. No priors, though he's a known dealer of gray spells."

"How can he have no priors if he's selling illegal spells?"

"He might enjoy the protection of a royal line. It's not unusual for some of the lower caste families to have someone like him on the payroll. On a cash basis, of course."

I'd never heard the term "lower caste royal families" before, but he obviously meant those who held the name but were only indirectly linked to the three main houses. There were enough of them.

"If that's *not* the case," he continued, "then he'll no doubt run the minute we approach. It'll be better to take a two-prong approach. I'll head around to see if there's a back entrance, while you take the front."

I nodded. "If the front door is locked, do I have permission to break and enter?"

He raised an eyebrow. "Yes, but I'm thinking you don't ask your wolf for permission prior to an act of criminality."

"My wolf has given up on keeping me to the letter of the law."

My comment was wry, and he smiled. "I'll meet you inside. But please, be careful."

"It's my middle name."

"From what I saw in the brief time I was in the reservation, I very much doubt that."

I laughed and climbed out of the car. As Samuel disappeared down the small lane between the buildings, I walked over to the front entrance. The door was locked, so I cupped a hand against the glass and peered inside. While shadows crowded the room, enough light filtered in through the tinted windows to see. An old wooden counter lay to the left, while the free-standing shelving units I'd seen in the vision dominated the remaining space. Toward the back of the room lay stairs up to the next floor, and to the right of these was a door. Given this room was only a fraction of the building's overall size, it was a fair bet his practice and storage areas lay beyond it.

I couldn't see any evidence of protection spells, but that didn't mean they didn't exist or that there weren't physical alarms installed. Especially when the lock on the door looked as old as the building itself. Even the dodgiest human thief could probably have had it open in seconds.

I looked around to ensure no one was paying me any undue attention, then quickly cast an unlock spell and pressed it against the handle. The door clicked open, but I didn't step inside, checking again for security measures. Most casters who kept charms and potions so openly on display usually had some means of not only preventing theft but also accidental activation.

I didn't spot anything obvious, so I warily stepped inside. No alarms went off, magical or mechanical. I closed and locked the door, then moved across to the counter. The air smelled musty, no doubt due to the fact there didn't appear to be much in the way of ventilation, and tiny dust devils stirred around my boots. This shop obviously hadn't seen much traffic in recent weeks. Either that, or the old man really hated dusting.

I moved behind the counter and did a quick search through the various shelves and drawers that lined the wall, finding the usual variety of charms, potions, and other minor magic memorabilia these sorts of shops usually sold. Hell, we stocked many of the same ones in our café, even though it wasn't a main part of our business.

What I didn't find was anything in the way of gray magic, but that was hardly surprising. He wouldn't risk keeping such items openly on display or even close to hand. Not when he was dealing with the public and had no idea who might walk through his door next.

I turned to check under the counter and discovered, tucked in the back corner of the top shelf, a black metal box. I glanced up sharply and finally saw the camera. It was attached to the ceiling just above the end of the shelving unit and was pointed directly at the old till. Obviously, the old man had been more worried about losing cash than losing stock.

The door at the back of the room opened and Samuel stepped though. "Found several spell rooms and a storeroom with an interesting—and illegal—array of items. No sign of our caster yet though. You had any luck?"

"I haven't checked upstairs, but I did find a DVR security system."

"Ah good. We'll requisition the drive and see what we can find."

"If it hasn't already been erased."

Our wraith—or whoever he had doing his leg work for him—constantly seemed to be two steps ahead of us, so it was more than possible that might be the case.

"Yes, but depending on the drive being used, we still should be able to recover the files and information. But just to be safe, we'll make sure there's no interference from this point on."

He pulled the plug out of the power point, then cast a quick spell to protect the unit from external interference. With that done, we walked across the room and headed up the stairs. As the scent of age and dust faded, the smell of "old man" increased.

But again, I had no sense of any kind of protection spell, which was decidedly odd for someone who walked the grayer side of magic.

Samuel reached the landing then paused. "We've a bathroom directly ahead and two doors, left and right. You got a preference?"

"You're the official in this investigation. You choose."

"Why is it you only acknowledge my authority when it suits you?"

I grinned. "My werewolf has asked the very same question."

He snorted and went left. I went right, walking down the short corridor to the closed door. After checking for any sort of spell work, I carefully opened it.

And found the old man still and silent in his chair.

My heart rate leapt even though this was exactly what

I'd seen. But despite initial appearances, he wasn't dead, because his chest moved fractionally even as I watched. One breath didn't mean anything, of course. One breath, or two, or more, didn't mean his mind or memories were whole.

I visually checked the room again to reassure it was safe to enter, then walked across. The old man breathed through his nose, the sound wispy and quiet. I gently touched his arm, but there was no response. Either he slept *really* soundly, or he'd taken something to help him sleep, either by choice or not.

I stepped back and reached for Belle. *You there?*

Well, of course I am. What a stupid question.

I smiled. *Sorry, but with the frequency Monty has been calling these last few days, anything was possible.*

There must be more problems in the reservation, because he's only made one call so far today. Besides, keeping connected to you and updating Ashworth was the only way to ensure he stayed put.

I frowned. *Ashworth knows better than to rush into a situation like this.*

Except he hasn't been in a situation like this before, she replied. *This is the first time he's been forced to sit on the sidelines when someone he cares about has faced any sort of danger, and he hates it, even if he understands the reasons.*

Eli worked for the Regional Witch Association and must have been in more than a few dangerous situations.

Difference is, Ashworth only knew about them after the fact. He didn't have to face real-time fretting and worry.

I smiled and once again thanked the day he came into our lives. As found family went, you couldn't get any better. Hell, I doubted my goddamn biological father was losing any sleep over my safety.

I take it you want me to read this Martin fellow? she continued.

Yes, but be wary. I have no idea whether he's been spelled, is under the influence of drugs, or has been telepathically tampered with.

I'm not the one needing to be cautious, because I'm not physically there. Besides, if he was spelled, you'd feel the energy of it.

It's more the prospect that he's been given telepathic orders that worries me, especially given someone had already messed with Hazel's mind.

Whoever did that isn't capable of setting a trap strong enough to grab me. I'll be perfectly fine.

That's like me saying I'll be careful.

Her laughter reverberated lightly through our connection. *If it's safe to touch him, do so. It definitely makes remotely reading him easier.*

I stepped to the front of the chair and, after a brief hesitation, touched my fingers to either side of his temples.

It was at that precise moment he came to life.

With an almost inhuman roar, he thrust me away from him with enough force to steal my breath and knock me off my feet. I hit the floor hard, looked up, and saw him launch at me. I didn't have time to get up, so I twisted and swept one leg around, hitting him just below the knee and knocking him sideways.

He didn't fall.

He might look frail, but the bastard had the balance of a cat.

He lunged again. With little other option, I grabbed his hands, then rolled back and lifted my knees, using his momentum to fling him over my head and across the room. He crashed into a table and fell onto a chair with enough force to break one of the legs. As he hit the floor, I scrambled upright and unleashed a containment spell. Heard footsteps and spun, a second spell already swirling around my fingertips. Samuel slid to a halt and threw up a hand. "Don't unleash."

I took a deep breath and relaxed. "Sorry."

"Understandable. You okay?"

"Yeah." I let the second containment spell drift away and walked across to the old man. He was fighting my net physically rather than magically, but maybe he wasn't awake enough yet to form any sort of counter spell.

Of course, the threads of wild magic woven through the spell might also have something to do with his reluctance to counter the spell. Any sane witch—gray or not—tended to be very cautious around wild magic.

Samuel stopped beside me, studying my captive and, no doubt, the magic that contained him. "Don't suppose you'd care to explain why threads that look an awful lot like wild magic are running through your spell?"

I wrinkled my nose. "I could, but it'd take too much time right now."

"Have they anything to do with the reevaluation tests your father ordered for you?"

"Yes, but the only thing he'll discover is the fact that both my mother and my sister carry the same anomalous gene responsible for those threads."

He glanced at me sharply. "I've never seen anything like this in your mother's spell craft."

"And you won't. We believe it takes trauma to activate it."

His expression said he suspected there was more to the story than that, as his next comment proved. "One day, when this mess is over and you're back home safe and sound, I'll visit, and you can tell me a story."

"Unofficially and over cake?"

"Definitely."

"Agreed then."

"Good." He returned his gaze to my captive. "What happened?"

"He attacked. I responded."

"Obviously." Samuel's voice was dry. "But why did he attack?"

I shrugged. "I'm presuming he was primed to do so, though I'm not sensing any sort of spell on him."

"No." Samuel studied the still struggling older man for a second. "His pupils look normal, but that doesn't rule out drugs."

"Or some other means of control. He only attacked when we were going to read him."

"Telepathically via your connection with Belle, I'm gathering?"

I nodded. "I can still do that, unless you want to question him the old-fashioned way."

"Your way will be faster. Besides, witches who walk the gray line are rarely bosom buddies with the truth. Just let me secure him properly."

I thought he meant physically but instead he overlaid my cage spell with a more intricate one of his own, wrapping it around the old man's body so tightly he resembled an Egyptian mummy. What was more interesting though was the fact that it not only restricted movement, but also prevented the formation of magic. A very handy spell indeed, I thought, taking mental notes for future use.

He then produced his ID, read Martin his rights, and told him what was about to happen. The old man's only response was furious blinking and a rumbly growl that found no real release. Samuel's spell had apparently locked his ability to speak as well, and that was probably a good thing, given we'd probably be getting nothing more than obscenities from him right now.

I released my containment spell, then stepped forward and pressed my fingers either side of the old man's temples. Samuel's containment magic buzzed around my fingertips but otherwise didn't restrict my touch.

Go, Belle, I said.

She immediately deepened our connection, the force of her thoughts seeming to flow from my mind to my fingers and then into his mind. It was a weird sensation.

His surface memories are as messy as Hazel's, but the deeper ones remain intact. She paused. *And it's the same telepath responsible.*

Out of habit more than necessity, I repeated everything she was saying to keep Samuel in the loop. *How can you tell?*

Every telepath leaves some trace of themselves behind—a tell, if you like—especially if they haven't been trained.

You don't... do you?

I daresay I do, but it'd take a stronger telepath than me to detect them.

And there weren't all that many around. Or at least there hadn't been when we'd left Canberra all those years ago now. *Does that mean you'll be able to recognize this telepath from the feel of his thoughts?*

Yes, because his tell has a rather weird vibe.

Weird in what way?

Hard to explain, but it's making my skin crawl. It's almost otherworldly.

Could that be a result of him dealing with the wraith?

Maybe.

Maybe not, her reply seemed to imply. *Was the old man primed to attack me?*

She hesitated. *Nope. That was all him. We're not exactly dealing with a stable mind here, and you frightened the hell out of him.*

An experience that was mutual. *Why is he still raging, then?*

He knows he's in deep trouble. He just doesn't understand why, because his memories are a stew.

Meaning there's no hope of pulling anything useful?

Not from the last forty-eight hours. Whoever did this used the mental equivalent of a jackhammer and broke every memory up.

That suggests the spell stones were purchased sometime within that time period.

And might well mean that the DVR I'd found would have been erased. The other telepath would have skimmed the old man's mind for any pertinent security information before mushing his memories.

Yes. Belle paused. *But luck is with us, because the old man keeps a private record of all high-end spell stone sales in a safe in the other room.*

As Samuel immediately left to investigate, I said, *The other telepath would have picked that up in his sweep before erasure though, wouldn't he?*

Not if he was looking for standard security measures and records. It's rare these days for someone to keep a hand-written personal account of sales. The old man did it for his larger cash sales. She paused again. *Here's an interesting tidbit—he's done work for a Marlowe line.*

Not mine, surely? My father was many things, but he wasn't stupid enough to get involved in any way with gray magic. He was well aware that even a whiff of gray magic would forever tarnish his reputation.

She did the telepathic equivalent of a shrug. *The information is sitting right on the edge of the destruction zone, so I'd have to do a deep dive into his memories to pull out a name and description.*

I hesitated then shook my head. *Samuel knows the old man is working with royal lines, so if it's relevant to the case, he can dig for it. Is that it?*

'Fraid so. As I said, it's one big mess in there. It's going to make pinning any charges on him rather hard, I would think.

Given the gray paraphernalia Samuel has already found, he's going to face jail time regardless.

Which, given his age, will probably see out whatever time he has left.

I glanced around as Samuel reentered the room carrying one of those old-fashioned ledger books.

"It looks like luck is finally with us." He placed the book on the table, then opened it at a tabbed page and ran his finger down to near the end. "These are all the entries for the last week. He sold two sets of primed diamond spell stones—well above market price, I might add—to one Russel Martingale."

"I take it you know him?"

"You could say that." Samuel's voice was wry. "We've charged him multiple times over multiple offences but have never made anything major stick. The bastard is too cunning."

"Is Russel a witch? Or a telepath?"

"Most brokers aren't witches—in fact, many of them are magic immune to some degree. He is, however, telepathic, though not a particularly strong one."

"He doesn't have to be to make memories unreadable."

"I take it that's what he's done to Martin here?"

I nodded. "Does the ledger say what spells were attached to the stone?"

He ran his finger across the line. "A fog barrier and, ah fuck, an incendiary explosive spell."

I frowned. "Most government buildings are protected from such spells, aren't they?"

"Yes, as are most high-profile residences. That doesn't make them any less dangerous, particularly if they're used as a diversionary tactic."

"Then I guess we need to find this Russel Martingale before he has the chance to unleash that second spell."

"I'm personally hoping that's the spell they used to break through the basement and grab Julius. But I'll put an APB on him and have his residences searched, although there's a good chance he's gone to ground."

More than a good chance, I'd say, given he was working with our wraith. "There is another way."

He raised an eyebrow. "Involving you, I take it?"

"Unless you've someone on your books gifted with psychometry—or can ask the PAC to provide you with someone ASAP—then yes."

"We don't, but I will contact PAC and see what they say." He grimaced. "I'd rather keep you away from the front line as much as possible."

"A goal I can totally get behind."

Any sensible woman would.

Of course, I had never been sensible.

And I'd certainly learned in recent times that offense is sometimes the best defense—not that *any* of us had been doing much of that so far.

"I'm hearing a 'but' in your tone," Samuel said.

I smiled. "But I don't believe I'll be allowed to. The

wraith seems intent on having me witness every bloody victory."

"You could ignore his lures."

"Would you, if your family was being picked off one by one?"

He didn't answer that, but then, it was a rhetorical question. "I'll let you know tomorrow how we go. If we have no luck finding Russel, we'll try it your way."

"Fine." I paused. "Will Saska be picking me up in the morning?"

"No, I will."

My eyebrows rose. "Really? Haven't you got better things to do?"

"Indeed yes, but the high council have ordered it, so I have little choice."

"Seems a waste to put their best investigator on babysitting duty."

Amusement glimmered in his bright eyes. "I believe I said something along those lines. Don't take it personally though."

I grinned. "So why did they order it?"

"Because they appear to think that you'll take more notice of orders coming from me than from Saska."

"I'm not listed to take the stand tomorrow, so it really doesn't matter if I'm there or not."

In fact, I would have thought it'd be better if I wasn't, because there was no way known I'd hold my tongue if my father unleashed another litany of lies and half-truths.

"From the little I overheard, I believe they're actually intending to hear all final arguments and make their judgement tomorrow."

That raised my eyebrows. "But my father hasn't finished testifying, and I haven't even been called."

"I know, but your father did change his plea. Maybe that has made your testimony unnecessary."

I snorted. "My father's lawyer implied that would not be the case."

"Maybe your brother's death has changed things. Maybe he's agreed to expedite the trial rather than draw it out any longer. It would be viewed favorably and, more importantly, enable the council to hand out a more lenient sentence."

"So we're back to the proverbial slap on the wrist."

"Given the Society's threat, that's unlikely."

"Well, they're not likely to dump him from the council, are they?"

A smile ghosted his lips. "Dump him? No. Suspend him? That's more than possible and would send the necessary message."

It was also an outcome that would hit my father's pride more than his standing, but I'd take that over a slap on the wrist.

"Boss?" came a call from the floor below.

"Upstairs, Landry," Samuel replied, then returned his attention to me. "Once I update the team, I'll take you home."

I nodded and, as his people appeared, casually strolled around the room, looking for anything that tweaked my instincts. Unsurprisingly, nothing did. Russel might have mushed the old man's mind, but he'd left very little evidence of his presence behind.

Ten minutes later we were in the car heading back to Hattie's place. Thankfully, the traffic was fairly mild considering the hour, and it didn't take all that long. Belle had a pot of tea and a stack of thick beef sandwiches waiting for me when I walked into the kitchen.

"You read my mind. Strange that." I perched on a stool and reached for a sandwich. "Where're Eli and Ashworth?"

"Researching."

"Is that what they call it these days?"

She laughed and tossed a spoon at me. I ducked but caught it before it could hit the floor.

"The arm obviously isn't causing you much pain," she noted.

"No doubt because of the painkillers. Hopefully the fast healing will have kicked in by the time they wear off."

"Which is definitely one of the better results of your wild magic's immersion with the old wellspring."

It certainly was. Before the whole DNA adaption thing had started, this sort of wound would have landed me in hospital for days, and the arm likely unusable for weeks.

I bit into the sandwich then said, "What are they researching?"

"Demonic possession."

"Why?"

"Remember I said the telepath had a very odd vibe?"

I nodded and kept munching. I might have eaten earlier, but my stomach was acting like this was the first food it had seen in days.

"Well, I mentioned it to Ashworth when I was updating them on events, and he and Eli immediately said 'possessed.'"

"Again, why?"

"Because the easiest way for a dark sorcerer to control someone's actions is to have one of his demons possess them."

I finished my sandwich and reached for another. "Demonic possession basically erases the soul and mind of the host, though, and in this particular case, that would make Russel unusable."

It wasn't as if a demon would be familiar with the ins and outs of a human world, and that would result in odd behavior noticeable to anyone close to Russel.

"That's true of a full possession, but it's possible we're dealing with only a partial one."

Even a partial did horrible things to body and spirit, and despite the success rate of exorcism, the possessed were never the same. "Aren't they quite rare?"

"Yes, but it does depend on whether the demon or dark spirit is free or entailed. It happens more often with the latter."

"Meaning they leave him with enough mental capacity to ensure there's no unusual actions, but he's given no real control over what he does or says?"

"That's what we're thinking."

I licked the mustard from my fingers and then picked up the teapot and poured a cup. My nostrils twitched as the sweet scent of pear and jasmine teased the air. My favorite tea. "So how is this going to help us find the bastard?"

"I'm a spirit talker, remember? We create a protective circle and force the spirit inhabiting his body to come to us."

"Forcing the spirit from Russel's body will kill him, and that'll inform the wraith what we're doing."

"Death would be a kindness given the state Russel's mind and body will be left in after the demon leaves," she replied, "but if the summoning is both fast and very tightly woven, the wraith will have no idea what has happened."

Instinct hated the very idea of it. "It's still a damn dangerous move no matter how many protections you raise."

"Yes, but the risk will ultimately be worth it. Besides, it's no more dangerous than gadding about willy-nilly to ensure the wraith's attention is on you rather than us."

"That's not what I'm doing—"

"Yeah, it is, and we both know it."

I wrinkled my nose but couldn't entirely deny the accusation. I *did* want his attention on me rather than the three of them, but I wasn't going out of my way to present myself as a target. That was just a consequence of events.

Events *he* was orchestrating.

"Even if you do successfully summon his demon, it's unlikely it can be compelled to reveal any information about its master. The contract between them would surely be watertight."

"Maybe, but it's possible we can compel it to reveal the names of any other demons working with our dark sorcerer. If we can also banish *them*, it'll leave him with the choice of either summoning new demons to deal with or continuing his bloody revenge on his own. Either way, it gives us additional time to find him."

I grunted. Belle knew what she was doing when it came to the spirit world, and anything she didn't know her guides could undoubtedly help her with.

That didn't make it any less dangerous. Didn't make me any less scared for her safety.

I reached for a third half-sandwich. "There's one thing that's making me uneasy about this whole scenario—"

"The fact that he's been one or two steps ahead of us all the way?"

I nodded. "I know it's unlikely he'd guess you could sense his demon remotely, but I don't think we dare discount the possibility either."

"Which is why Ashworth and Monty are researching broad-based summoning and banishment spells."

"If we banish this demon, won't it just mean it'll be free to answer the wraith's call again?"

"Not if we find the right banishment spell. And if we can get the names of his other demons, we can repeat the process with them."

"The wraith isn't likely to sit around twiddling his fingers while you deprive him of his demons."

"No, but if we've prepared the summoning circle properly, he won't be able to track our location."

"That suggests you not going to perform it here."

"We're not. This place is too big, has too many distractions, and would be too hard to protect. Besides, the moon's full tonight, and her power would help the strength of our spells."

Which meant we'd be heading outside at around eleven to take advantage of the witching hour, which was between midnight to one.

"It's not so much the summoning that's worrying me but rather the fact you'll be doing it alone. Wouldn't it be better to disperse the load and any possible counter the wraith or his demon might have set?"

She hesitated. "We haven't time to—"

"Your dad is a strong spirit talker and could undoubtedly get hold of another at short notice. Not only will three of you disperse the overall load of the summoning, but if the demon does come at you, you've two other summoners present to stop him."

She hesitated and then nodded. "That's sensible. Besides, my dad would have my hide if I tried this alone and things went wrong."

I smiled. "It seems the years he spent drilling in the need for caution has not been totally undone by time spent

249

with me and my somewhat cavalier attitude to self-protection."

She laughed and pushed up from the stool. "I'll go contact Mom and get things started. You might want to grab a shower and rest up after you finish that last sandwich. It could be a long night."

I nodded and, as she headed into her bedroom to start making calls, poured myself another cup of tea. Then I pulled out my phone and called Aiden.

I just needed to hear his voice.

"Hey," he said softly. "How's it going?"

I closed my eyes and did my best to ignore the ache in my heart. "As well as can be expected, I guess."

"Meaning it's still all going to hell and you're hanging on by your fingernails."

I laughed. "Could be. But the council has apparently decided to hear final arguments tomorrow instead of calling my father and me to the stand, so I might be home sooner rather than later."

"Good" was all he said to that.

But everything he *didn't* say seemed to echo down the line between us. I bit my lip against the words that pressed against them. Words like *I miss you, I love you, I need you.*

Words that would only make the situation worse than it already was.

Words that couldn't be spoken out loud again until he had been ratified as the alpha for his pack. Only then did our relationship stand a chance of gaining the approval of his pack and the greater council.

Because without any of that, there was no "us."

After a long pause, he added, "That'd suggest your father has changed his plea, and from the little I saw of the man, I wouldn't have thought that likely."

"Except that we lost Juli today, so maybe he's had a rethink."

"Ah, Liz, I'm sorry to hear that."

I hesitated. "I'm not sure how I should feel, Aiden. I didn't love him, but he was my brother and... well, you know."

He'd lost his father *and* his uncle recently, so he, more than anyone, would understand, even if he was far closer to his family than I'd ever been to mine.

"Have you spoken to your mother? It might help."

"I haven't had a chance."

And in truth, really didn't want to. The depth of her grief would contrast starkly against my own and make me feel lacking yet again.

I scrubbed a hand across my face. I didn't want to think about my family or grief or even the wraith right now. I just wanted to talk to the man I loved and forget all about the danger that loomed.

"How's things going there? Belle said Monty has only made one call so far today, which sounds rather ominous to me."

"The situation hasn't really changed. The wellspring continues its rumblings, and Monty has declared there's nothing he can do to prevent it and that we'll all just have to live with it until you come back to see if it settles."

I hadn't even thought of *that* possibility. What if the wellspring's conniptions had nothing to do with my absence but a deeper problem involving my connection to it or even Katie's immersion with the other wellspring?

"As for him not calling," Aiden continued, "I dare say it has something to do with the welcome home surprise he's planning for Belle."

My eyebrows rose. "What sort of surprise?"

"I've been sworn to secrecy and cannot possibly say."

"Well, that's just annoying."

He laughed. "You can't warn her. Tuck the information deep in your memory banks and don't let her see it."

"I will. But do warn him that she hates surprises."

"Which will make it all the more interesting."

I grinned, and we talked some more, keeping it light while a hundred different emotions swam under the surface, unspoken but nevertheless weighty.

I had no idea what would happen when we returned home or even if the situation with his pack would be settled by then, but that spark of hope I'd felt at the airport was brighter by the time I said goodbye and hung up.

I drained the last of my tea, then rose and walked down to my bedroom.

And there, sitting on my pillow, was a goddamn pregnancy test.

CHAPTER TWELVE

I walked across the room but didn't pick the kit up. I just shoved my hands into my pockets and stared at it while large parts of me wished it would disappear.

I needed to know. I was well aware of that.

But I also had no desire to uncover the truth right now. Knowing for certain I had another life to care about when the specter of death dogged my heels might just make me second-guess my actions at the wrong damn time.

Was that selfish? Irresponsible?

Maybe. But in this particular case, when there was so much already at stake, I just didn't want or need something else—someone else—to worry about.

I tucked the box into the top drawer of the bedside table, then grabbed fresh clothes and headed into the shower.

My phone rang just as I'd finished getting dressed, and a quick glance at the screen had my stomach flip-flopping.

Mom.

I took a deep breath that didn't do a whole lot to fortify my nerves, then hit the answer button. "I tried, Mom—"

"I'm well aware of that." Her voice was cool and very, *very* composed. It was the exact same tone she'd used the day I'd tried to save Cat and had failed, and meant she was holding on to her emotions very tightly.

I just had to hope that *this* time, they didn't slip. And if they *did*, that I was nowhere in the vicinity.

"I'm not ringing to accuse or place unwarranted blame, Elizabeth. Julius's refusal to believe the danger he was in combined with a certainty that his magic could protect him from *any* assault is the true reason for his death. His overconfidence is not your fault but rather ours."

I swallowed heavily. I hadn't expected her to see that, let alone admit it, especially when she'd always had a soft spot for my brother.

"But I will not allow this dark bastard to further decimate my family," she continued. "I want to help you track him down and kill him."

I sucked in a breath, caught utterly by surprise. "I understand the need, Mom, but you're next on his list, and I really don't think it's a wise course of action."

"I've lost two children already, Elizabeth, and I will *not* lose a third. I don't care if you hate me. I don't care if we're estranged and we remain that way. You are my *child*, and I will not stand idly by any longer and let this monster take you as he has taken Catherine and Julius."

Tears stung my eyes. I blinked rapidly and tried to get a grip on my tumultuous emotions. "I understand, Mom, but—"

"No, I don't think you do. Not until you have children of your own."

Which might be closer than either of us knew. "Have you talked to Dad?"

"Indeed, I have. He believes my decision is both foolish

and unwise, and I believe I have no choice in this matter. Not if I want to live with my conscience and make amends for past decisions."

The tears threatened again. I said, in a voice that was slightly constricted, "Mom, Juli's family is going to need the support of you *both* to get through this. His kids—"

"Could well be next in the firing line," she cut in. "Who is to say this bastard will stop at me or your father or even you? Who is to say that Catherine's death didn't give him a taste for our family? Especially now it is evident the females of our line carry an unusual gene."

Meaning they'd not only received the test report but suspected my ability with the wild magic had to come from that anomalous gene. There was a part of me—a vicious, still hurting part that just couldn't let the past go—that believed her determination stemmed more from a need to understand my "special nature" than to keep me alive.

But *that* was unwarranted and unfair.

If it had been my father, however...

"Mom, this is what I do. I stop bastards like this from destroying lives and families. You have to step back and let me, Belle, and the HCI—"

"I will *not*," she cut in again. "You are many things, Elizabeth—possibly far more than any of us might have imagined—but you are not fully trained, and you do not have the family's power at your call even if you do have your own. I am one of the strongest witches in Canberra, and this bastard will feel my fury, even if I have to hunt him down alone. I would rather not, however."

In that moment, I totally understood where I'd got my stubborn determination from.

"We will be there in in ten minutes," she added.

"We?" I said, with a whole lot of dread. God, the last

thing any of us needed was my father's negativistic and superior presence looming over everything that we did.

"I'm talking about Henry, of course."

I relaxed a little. Henry had been her chauffeur and bodyguard for as long as I could remember. He also happened to be a shifter and magic immune—very handy when both my parents had run up a good number of enemies over the years. "Isn't he getting a bit too old for protection duty?"

"He's only sixty. In shifter terms, that's middle age more than over the hill."

True enough. While witches did tend to have a longer lifespan than humans, shifters and werewolves outstripped us all.

"I take it Samuel and the HCI are aware of this development?"

"Indeed, they are. I believe Samuel is arranging for additional guards and defenses to be deployed around Henrietta's premises as we speak."

I could just imagine what he'd said about the whole situation, too. Something about "like mother, like daughter," no doubt.

In less polite terms, of course.

"We'll see you soon," she continued. "We can discuss our plan of attack over coffee."

"We already have a plan of attack, Mom."

"Good. We'll discuss it when I get there."

She hung up. I shook my head, shoved my phone into my pocket, and headed for the kitchen. Belle remained in her bedroom organizing things, but Ashworth and Eli were there, the latter in the middle of making hot drinks.

"Coffee?" he asked, when I appeared.

"No, thanks." I walked across to the kettle and flicked it

on. "But you'd better add a fourth cup. Mom's about to turn up on our doorstep."

"To remonstrate or commiserate?" Ashworth growled. "Because if it's the former, her ass will be back out the door so damn fast her head will spin."

"Neither. She wants the wraith dead and has offered to help us achieve this any way she can."

"And the HCI has approved this course of action?"

I smiled at the incredulousness in his voice. "No, and my father thinks it's foolish."

"I take it he's not accompanying her, then?"

"No. He's listening to advice and keeping safe."

"No doubt to keep the family business viable if something does happen to your mom," Belle said, as she came into the kitchen. "Don't for an instant believe that he wouldn't be leading the charge to find our wraith if he thought there'd be some personal benefit to the action."

"I don't like the man, but that's a little harsh," Eli said.

Belle shrugged. "True though. Did you find any new information regarding summoning our demon?"

"A couple of additional spells we can try." Ashworth glanced at me. "And actually, your mother's decision to help out is fortunate—we had discounted using the strongest spell we'd found because it was an interwoven one."

I frowned. "We've used interwoven spells to tackle demons before—what's so different about this one?"

"It requires the blood of a powerful royal witch in her prime."

"*Blood* magic?" Trepidation curled through me. "I'm not sure that's a good idea."

Especially when I'd already dabbled in it to protect Belle from Clayton. These things tended to add up and have consequences further down the line.

"To counter darkness, you sometimes have to step into the shadows," Eli said. "This isn't a dark spell, per se. It just uses the power of blood to lure and entrap the demon."

"Meaning Mom is bait because the demon—or the wraith who commands him—has a taste for the family blood."

Ashworth nodded. "While our wraith undoubtedly wants revenge for whatever hell he spent time in until he could regain power and some form of flesh, there's also no doubt he and his demons would have gotten stronger with each kill."

"There's no evidence they were feeding on the blood of their victims."

"We haven't seen the coroner's reports, remember, but your aunt's brain was missing, as was your brother's heart. Neither was found, but there are demons who consider such things delicacies."

I shuddered. That was information I really didn't need to know.

I made a fresh pot of tea, then carried it over to the counter, claiming a stool before grabbing one of the Tim Tams that had been plated up for afternoon tea.

"Why not use my blood, then? I'm the one he's ultimately after."

"But your mom is next on the list, and the demon will be aware of that."

"Yes, but this demon is in Russel's body and therefore not likely to be our wraith's strongest."

"A fact we hope will actually make him an easier target."

Presuming the wraith hadn't already figured that out and countered that possibility. "So how do we summon it without a name? Belle got a feel for its energy, but that usually isn't enough to summon a spirit, much less a far stronger demon."

"That," Eli said, "is where you come into the equation."

I raised my eyebrows. "I take it you mean for me to use my psychometry skills, but unless you can get hold of something personal from Russel's belongings, I'll be little more than a power source for Belle."

"Hopefully this summoning won't drag so much strength from me that I need to lean on yours," she said. "Not now that we have Dad and at least one other spirit talker coming to our aid. And Mom, of course, though she'll be using her telepathy to keep an ear out for movement and problems."

With all the people already protecting us, Ava's presence probably wasn't necessary, but I nevertheless felt easier knowing she'd be here. She was one of the few people from the "lower class" lines who had no fear of Mom and who Mom actually respected.

"It's going to get quite crowded in this house," Eli said, amusement evident. "Because Samuel is also turning up to help out."

"The man obviously doesn't believe in time off or sleep," I said. "He and Aiden are two peas in a pod."

Who both had the good sense to be attracted to you, Belle commented.

I smiled. *Samuel came onto the scene way too late. Besides, from the little I've gleaned from Saska, he's a bit of a player.*

Because he's been hurt.

That raised my eyebrows. *You've rummaged through his thoughts?*

When he first appeared and showed interest. Had to protect my witch, after all.

I snorted and returned my attention to the conversation.

"Samuel has collected a number of personal items from Russel's apartment," Ashworth was saying. "Hopefully there'll be something amongst them holding enough of an echo for you to trace."

I wrinkled my nose. "My psychometry generally requires me to physically look for the owner's location. I can't just point to a map and declare X marks the spot."

"You've never actually tried to do that though, have you?" Ashworth said. "Given the upscaling that's been happening, it's more than possible you could at least give an estimate of location even if not his exact position, and that might be enough."

"Is it worth the risk, though? Our wraith is aware of my psi skills—it's how I found him the first time, remember. He might well have primed his demon to watch out for such things."

"Demons generally aren't sensitive to the use of psychic skills," Eli commented. "And there's no spell that I'm aware of that can protect against them."

"And if there is?" I asked. "Have we got a plan B?"

"We always have a plan B, even if there's a less than optimal chance of it working."

Meaning we all had to hope we didn't need to use plan B.

I poured my tea then glanced around as the doorbell rang. Eli went to answer it and I heard polite conversation. Mom, not Samuel.

She appeared a few seconds later, greeting everyone in a measured tone before moving across to the counter and perching between Belle and me.

"I wish to thank you all for your effort to protect my family," she said. "I know the situation with the court case has complicated things, but let me assure you all that we will do all that we can to expedite that situation and let you get back to your lives."

I took a sip of tea. "Does that mean Dad will no longer fight the court case? That he has no intention of introducing additional witnesses to challenge the state of my sanity?"

She glanced at me, her features controlled and eyes giving nothing away. The same couldn't be said of her aura, and it certainly gave evidence to the conflicting nature of the emotions swirling beneath the calm exterior.

"Indeed, he has. We both agree, given the testimonies that have already been given and the weight of the evidence so far, it would be for the best. Prolonging the court case benefits no one."

"Wouldn't have anything to do with our side's request to hold a spirit talking with Clayton, now would it?" Belle said, voice dry.

A small smile touched one side of Mom's mouth but just as quickly faded. "That did come into consideration, yes."

"In other words, he's well aware that contesting things further will only harm his reputation," I said.

"Well, a man is only respected as far as his word can be trusted."

"I would think," Belle said dryly, "that after all this time being top of the tree here in Canberra, most blue bloods would be well aware just how far Lawrence Marlowe's word can be trusted."

Mom gave Belle a sharp glance but didn't reply. Ashworth slid a cup of coffee across the counter, then offered her the milk and sugar.

She shook her head and took a sip. "Lovely, thank you.

Elizabeth tells me you have a plan for capturing this wraith."

"We do," Eli said, and proceeded to explain.

Mom pursed her lips when he finished. "Blood magic is a dangerous path to take, especially when dealing with darkness."

"Yes, but it's also the best way to guarantee the demon will answer. We haven't got his name, and while we do have the name of the person he's infiltrated, there is no certainty the demon can be lured from the shelter of its host's body."

"Not even when you have a sense of the demon's energy?"

"Not even," Belle said.

Mom nodded. "Okay then, we'll do it. When, is my next question."

I blinked, not expecting her to agree so quickly. "Midnight. We can incorporate the strength of the moon in our protection spells."

She nodded. "Sensible. Will you be performing the ceremony alone, Isabelle?"

"No. Dad and another spirit talker will be assisting with the summoning. Liz will be connected to me but not part of the circle. You and Mom can be our last line of defense if the demon breaks out of our protections or the wraith attacks." She glanced at her watch. "We'll meet them at the location at eleven."

Mom's eyebrows rose. "We're not performing it here? Is Samuel aware of this?"

"He will be once he arrives," Belle said.

"And the circus that protects the place?"

"Will continue to protect it," Eli said. "In fact, they won't even be aware that we've left."

Meaning there had to be some sort of escape tunnel

built into the house. My parents certainly had one, but I hadn't been aware it was something other blue bloods did. I know my aunt didn't—I'd asked Deni about it as a teenager.

We made small talk for half an hour or so, and it was remarkably easy. Which really *shouldn't* have surprised me, because Mom was basically the "people" person of the Marlowe "firm."

The doorbell rang again and this time it was Samuel. He accepted Ashworth's offer of a coffee, then stopped at the counter and slid a large evidence bag across to me. Inside were a variety of separately bagged personal items, from jewelry and watches to a few smaller bits of clothing, and even a toothbrush.

"I wasn't sure what would work best, so I gathered everything I could." He reached for a Tim Tam. "I was gloved while collecting them, so my imprint shouldn't be on anything."

"Excellent. Thank you."

As I opened the larger bag and tipped them all out to examine, Samuel said, "Mrs. Marlowe, the high council wish me to pass on their disapproval of your current course of action."

"The high council," she replied evenly, "can disapprove all they want, because there is little else they can do. All must be present to ratify a course of action against a sitting member, and they are currently one down."

Meaning Dad. Juli might have been Dad's successor for the high council role, but he hadn't yet stepped into his shoes. And it made me wonder what they would do now— name a cousin, or wait and see what sort of power Juli's children developed as they grew up.

"Which is no doubt why your husband so unexpectedly agreed to full and complete isolation," Samuel commented.

Mom's smile was cool. "As has been recently noted, we've been playing in the power pool for a very long time now and are very aware of the currents and its dangers."

"Hmm" was all Samuel said to that.

There was nothing useful amongst the contents of the larger bag, so I spread the rest out, then opened the psychometry gates and carefully ran my left hand over the top of them. It wasn't until I neared the last few that I got a response.

I picked up one containing an expensive-looking gold watch. "This holds enough of his essence to track him."

"Is it strong enough to give me an approximate location?" Samuel asked. "It might be beneficial for us all to have a team ready to hit the place the minute you've summoned the demon."

"No guarantees, but I can try."

It really depended on two things—the first being whether my psychometry *had* mutated to the point where a map was a viable option. The second, of course, was whether Belle needed to pull on my strength at any stage during the summoning. What we were about to attempt was very dangerous, and I didn't need to be distracted, however briefly. It could mean the difference between Belle and her parents being safe or in deadly danger.

Ashworth glanced at the clock and then said, "We had best get moving. It's going to take a good twenty minutes to reach our location."

"And bring your raincoats," Eli said. "Fifteen of those minutes will be spent in a less than pristine abandoned tunnel. It might not be raining tonight but there's no guarantee the tunnel won't be leaking like a sieve."

"What's our destination?" Samuel said, "I'll need to notify our protection detail—"

"No, you won't," Ashworth said. "If the wraith is going to hit us, he'll hit this place, not the summoning circle."

"You can't be sure—"

"Oh," Ashworth said softly, "I certainly can."

Meaning some sort of spell had been set to ensure the wraith's attention would be drawn here rather than our summoning location.

Samuel studied the two older men for several seconds, then nodded. "I do hope you know what you're doing."

"This is our field of expertise, remember," Eli said. "And I would add that in the past year, both Lizzie and Belle have gained more familiarity with demons and their foibles than you or most others here in Canberra would ever get in a lifetime."

A smile tugged at Samuel's lips, but he didn't dispute the claim. "I'll tell the team we're headed down to the basement and under no circumstances are they to come inside."

Eli nodded. "No demon will easily get past the protection barriers this place is laden with, so it is more likely a physical attack they'll be faced with."

"Do warn them our wraith has shown a liking for using undead werewolves," I added.

Samuel made the call to his people while the four of us gathered everything we needed. When that was done, I slung one of the backpacks over my shoulders and then glanced at Mom.

"I don't suppose you brought your spell stones along?"

"While I was not aware that a demon summoning was in the offering, I thought they might come in handy while you were attempting to track him psychically." She paused. "My knowledge of you and your skills is shockingly light."

"Perhaps one day we could remedy the former."

It wasn't forgiveness, but it was a step forward, and the

brief flicker of surprise through her expression said that Mom was well aware of that.

"I would appreciate it."

I turned away before the damn tears stinging my eyes could fall. Maybe I didn't need that pregnancy test after all. Maybe the roller coaster my emotions were on was evidence enough.

Not necessarily came Belle's comment. *Historically, your emotions have always been all over the place when thinking about your parents and your relationship with them. At least since Cat's death, anyway.*

And it was a situation that probably wouldn't improve anytime soon, if truth be told.

I followed Ashworth and Eli out of the kitchen and down into the basement. They walked past several doors, then stopped at what appeared to be a tall fire hose cabinet. Eli opened it, revealing that it did, in fact, hold a fire hose, but reached past and pressed his hand against something I couldn't quite see. A heartbeat later, a solid-looking section of concrete wall slid open just enough for a person to step through.

Eli switched on the flashlight he was carrying, then said, "Ira, hit the release as you enter."

We followed him in. Initially the going fairly straightforward—the tunnel was concrete-lined, and while it sloped steadily downward, it was clean and dry.

That changed the minute we stepped through a second door into the old stormwater tunnel. Water dripped from the ceiling and dribbled down the walls, the air smelled foul, and the base of the tunnel—through which a trickle of water currently ran—was full of refuse. I swept my light across the graffiti-tagged walls as we waited for Ashworth to appear. A couple of them were relatively new, which suggested that while this tunnel might officially be abandoned, it wasn't unused or unknown.

We continued on. I tugged up my hood to avoid the constant drips soaking my hair and kept a close eye on where I was stepping. The rubbish and the slippery nature of the mossy tunnel floor meant our pace was far slower than it had been.

Thankfully, it wasn't all that long before fresh air started sweeping the foulness away and, a few minutes later, we reached a junction. The main drain went left, but we followed the smaller branch, which inclined steeply before reaching a metal grate. Eli magicked it open, pushed the covering to one side, then helped us all out.

Not only were we greeted by a steep, well-treed slope but also, rather oddly, what looked to be a Tardis.

"If you tell me that's bigger on the inside than the outside, I will order the drug squad out," Samuel said, his tone amused.

Eli laughed softly. "Wish it was, because it'd provide the perfect cover."

We followed a series of rough dirt steps that wound down the hill and eventually reached a plateaued area. The vegetation here was much thicker, and from deeper within the trees to our right came soft conversation. Belle's parents and an older man, from the sound of it.

We followed the sound and a few seconds later entered a small but perfectly formed circular clearing. One that, given the scent of lemongrass and sage that teased my nostrils, had already been cleansed of any negative energy in preparation for the summoning.

Edward greeted us softly and then introduced Brian, a gnarled, no-nonsense-looking fellow.

"You'll have to take the lead on this one, Belle, as you've

got the feel of his energy," he added. "Just give us the incantation to memorize and tell us what we need to do."

Belle nodded and preparations began. We created a pentagram, placed candles on each of the cardinal points, and then circled the entire thing with salt. Belle and I circled the salt ring with our spell stones, then Ashworth, Eli, and Edward interwove theirs around this. Then, just for good measure, we did another salt ring around the edges of the clearing to ensure that if the demon did do the impossible and break through every other barrier, we had one final level of protection. It might be overkill, but as Ashworth noted, it was always better to be safe than sorry when dealing with these dark bastards.

He handed our summoners two sheets of paper—one containing the summoning, the other the banishment spell —and handed me a map of Canberra. He then pulled what looked to be two metal eggcups secured in a plastic bag and a pocketknife from his backpack, handing the former to Mom.

"Righto, I need you to prick your finger and put half a dozen drops of blood into each cup so Belle can use them for the summoning."

"Why two cups?" she asked as Ashworth sterilized the blade.

"Because it's possible the wraith has more than one demon working with him," he replied. "The stronger dark witches often make multiple bargains to improve their power base."

"I would have thought that impossible, given even a dark sorcerer only has one soul to give," Mom said.

"Which would be the prize for the strongest of his demons. But he could have multiple lower caste demons that exchange power for the souls or life force of his victims."

"But this Russel surely could not be possessed by more than one demon," she said.

"No, but this wraith is doing many things he shouldn't, so we dare not take the chance."

She nodded, calmly accepted the knife, then cut the tip of her finger, letting the blood drip into each cup. Once there was enough, Ashworth took them from her and carefully placed the offering in the center of the circle, being careful not to disturb any of our protection lines.

I dug out the nearly empty bottle of holy water from my pack and washed the small wound. The knife had been sterilized but it never hurt to be cautious.

"Is that one of your potions or something else?" Mom asked, with just a touch of curiosity.

"It's holy water and treats all manner of demon and supernatural wounds."

"I thought it was only useful as a demon repellant?"

"Oh, it does that too, but it can't be beaten as a disinfectant. I recommend you get some for the first aid kit, especially when you're on babysitting duties."

She raised an eyebrow but didn't say anything. It struck me that I had no idea how close she and Dad were to Juli's kids, let alone if they actually babysat them.

To be honest, I couldn't actually imagine my dad having the time or the patience.

I slipped the near-empty bottle back into my pack, then walked across to where Belle stood at the spirit point of the pentagram and took off my boots and socks. Being grounded wasn't necessary for this sort of ceremony, but there was something within that just said "Do it." I wasn't about to gainsay it. Not when the last time we'd summoned a demon had almost ended in disaster.

The warm pulse of the earth's heat pressed against my feet, the sensation oddly welcoming. I dug my toes into the soft but gritty soil and somehow felt connected to the deeper, wilder power of the earth.

Illusion, of course, but it was nevertheless a comforting one. Especially given what we were about to attempt.

The four men took the other points while Mom, Ava, and Samuel positioned themselves close to the outer salt ring.

We lit the candles, then activated our protection spells. The air filled with so much power the hairs on the back of my neck stood on end. Ava had placed a containment dome over the clearing to mute the force of the magic we were raising, but I had to wonder if she'd known just *how* much power this many protection circles would emit.

If it wasn't successfully contained, it *would* be a beacon to the wraith if he became aware of what we were attempting, and it would definitely override any draws or subterfuges Ashworth and Eli might have placed at Hattie's place.

Belle placed the two sheets of paper at her feet, lightly stood on them to prevent them blowing away, then linked to me.

"Right," she said, more for the benefit of everyone else than me, "make the connection, Liz."

I drew the watch from the plastic bag, wrapped my fingers around it, and then unleashed my psychometry. This was the tricky bit—the bit we were uncertain would actually work. As my "other" sight leapt across the psychic lines, chasing the faintly pulsing thread that connected the watch to its owner, I raised the map and stared at it, trying to force a location reveal via the map rather than my usual method of physically chasing the link in a car or on foot.

For several extremely long seconds, nothing happened.

Then, without warning, something within me shifted, and a line on the map began to glow, moving across its surface, following the network of roads in the same manner I might have had I been in a car, working its way from our location to an area on the other side of Canberra.

Then it stopped and spun, as if trying to recatch the trail. The sharp movement had my stomach churning, but I gripped the watch tighter and, after a second, the spinning stopped and pointed at a street, then a house. Against all the odds, it had worked.

"I have his location." I quickly gave Samuel the address and then added, "Now, Belle; start now."

She deepened the connection between us, telepathically following the faintly pulsing psychic line to our target as she began the summoning.

As the four men echoed her words, the connection sharpened, and just for an instant, I felt the caress of evil.

The demon now knew it was being summoned, but the spell was far enough along that it could not warn its master.

Despite my connection with Belle, I had no insight into the mind of the man the demon inhabited. No idea if Russel still existed, or whether, despite all our conjecture, his soul had been consumed the minute the demon had taken him over.

In all honesty, I didn't care either way. The man brokered dangerous spells, and if he was stupid enough to make a bargain with a dark sorcerer, then he deserved his fate.

Light speared up from the pentagram's five points and met above the metal eggcups to form a cage-like structure.

As the summoning spell deepened and the force of its demand grew stronger, the center of the pentagram began to shimmer and boil.

The penultimate line of the summoning began. As the weight of the spell grew heavier and the thick scent of evil now stained the air, a figure began to form in the center of the pentagram, just above the metal cups. It was small and scaly, with taloned fingers and toes and a body that was twisted and odd-looking. It was still fighting the summoning, the air around it a churning mass as it twisted and turned, pulling at Belle's strength but not her determination. As she spoke the final line of the summoning, the demon screamed and took the offering. He was ours.

"Three answers you have," he said, his voice a harsh scratch of sound that hurt my ears. "What you wish?"

"I need the name of the other demon or demons your master has with him."

It hissed but nevertheless gave us a name. Relief stirred through me. One was better than the two or three we had feared.

"And where is your master now?" Belle asked.

"Know not. Release restriction."

The restriction being the summoning's leash on his ability to communicate with our wraith.

Belle smiled coldly. "That's not going to happen. Tell me where he was the last time you connected."

He gave us an address. I had no doubt Samuel was now ordering another team to that location and hoped like hell they had someone from the Heretic Investigation Center with them. While the HIC didn't deal with wraiths, per se, they did hunt and kill dark witches. If anyone had the experience to deal with our wraith, it would be them.

"That three," the demon scratched. "Release now."

"Sorry, that's not how this game ends," Belle replied, and began the banishment spell.

As the words of power rose in the air, the demon once again screamed, twisting and fighting the spell that curled around him. His sharp movements pulled at the glowing cage and the protections that kept us safe, but he wasn't strong enough to either slip past them or destroy them.

With a final high-pitched scream of fury, he was cast back into the hell he'd come from. The wraith couldn't recall him. Not without making a new bargain, and that would severely weaken him. Plus, the cost of a new agreement would likely be far higher now, given demons apparently lost face and power every time they were banished. Or so I'd read in one of the books Belle's gran had written about the critters.

Belle took a deep breath, pulled lightly on my strength to replenish her own, then began the second banishment spell, this time using the name the demon had given us.

This spell was trickier, as we had no idea where the demon was located and no idea whether distance would lessen the potency of the spell. There'd been no mention of it in the incantation book Ashworth had drawn it from, and it was normal procedure to list all necessary warnings. It would, of course, have been easier to just summon it as we had the first demon, but not only would it have pulled too much strength from everyone, it also gave the wraith a chance to protect his demon.

As the banishment spell reached toward its peak, the air stirred oddly beyond our protective barrier. I frowned and glanced around, my nostrils flaring to find some hint of what might be happening

No unusual scent or sound touched the air, and yet... And yet, the psychic part of me said that was all a lie.

We were about to be hit.

I opened my mouth to scream a warning to Mom, Ava, and Samuel, but I was too late and too slow.

With a roar that sounded like an avalanche, the three of them disappeared under a cloud of dust, magic, and death.

CHAPTER THIRTEEN

T he wind was so strong it pushed Belle several feet sideways. I grabbed her just before her foot slid through our protection circle, and screamed—both physically and telepathically—for her to keep spelling.

She nodded. I kept my grip on her and scanned the clearing. The four men remained at the cardinal points, their bodies braced against the force of the wind. The dust beyond the outer protection circle was so thick that I had no hope of seeing Mom, Ava, or Samuel.

The little I *could* see chilled me to the bone.

Shapes.

Skeletal shapes. Unnatural shapes. The supernatural and the dead. Summoning this many en masse would normally have required a huge sacrifice, but perhaps the wraith's desperation had broken the "unnatural" order of things.

Either way, it looked as if the wraith had broken open the doors of hell itself, and then raided its cemetery for good measure.

They battered the protection circle's wall with fists and

claws, each blow not only weakening the barrier but also the men who'd raised it.

The wraith obviously did *not* want his remaining demon banished, and that meant that was exactly what we had to do, no matter what.

But there were too many of them and too few of us. They would break through the outer protection circle, if not the inner, by the time the banishment spell was completed. We had to do something. *I* had to do something.

And for me, there was only one viable option.

I dug my toes deeper into the soil and called.

The wild magic answered.

It burned up from the deep recesses of the earth's inner core and ripped through every part of me, burning through flesh and muscle and bone, sweeping away all that made me human while making me so much more.

This power was life itself. And she was mine to control.

Lizzie came a distant shout. *Don't take that path. Come back.*

That voice didn't belong to Belle. It belonged to Katie.

She was hearing me, reaching me, through the energy we were both forever bound to.

I blinked and became aware of the dust, the wind, and the scent of blood once again. Aware of the trembling in Belle's limbs, the leaching tiredness in her mind, and the dire pulsing of the outer barrier protecting the four men.

I sucked in a breath, then gathered all the earthly fire boiling through me and cast it over the pentagram. As tempting as it was to protect the entire clearing, doing so would not only entrap whatever hell the wraith's spells had unleashed but also the creatures he had called.

I could kill them all, of course, but as much as I wanted to do so, I couldn't use the wild magic to do it. I might never fully understand this connection or what it meant for me long term, but I was certain of one thing—killing, for whatever reason, when I was so intimately connected would forever stain her with darkness.

And *that* could change the earth itself.

The glowing curtain of wild magic fell between the protection circle Belle and I had woven and the one the four men had done. A heartbeat later, the outer circle went down, and the ungodly and the dead surged forward with a scream. I could barely see them through the dust that continued to batter the clearing, but every one of them hit my wall and was flung away.

They scrambled up and threw themselves back at the barrier again and again, but it was powered by the earth itself rather than my own inner wild magic, and there was no end to its strength as there was to mine. I would undoubtedly feel the effects of calling it to me later but, right now, I had bigger things to worry about.

Like forcing more strength into Belle so that she could remain upright and finish the banishment.

As the last words of the last line of the spell echoed across the night, a distant scream filled the air, the voice harsh and male.

Our wraith? Or his demon being dragged back to the hell from which it had come?

I had no idea, but we'd undoubtedly find out soon enough. Even without his demonic friends to boost his magic and his strength, the wraith was more than powerful enough to cause us problems. That had been evident the first time around, and I doubted death would have changed anything.

As the scream's echoes faded, so did the undead creatures within the clearing. Only the dust remained, a swirling reminder of fury.

I released most of the wild magic back to the earth. Weakness washed through me, but I locked my knees and did my best to ignore the quivering in my limbs. I couldn't give in to the weary exhaustion just yet. There was still too much that needed to be done.

Besides, while we might have finally won a battle, the wraith was far from defeated, and he would make us pay hard for our win here today.

Belle's knees buckled. I lunged forward to grab her, then lowered her carefully to the ground. She sucked in a breath that shook her whole body and said, *Check our moms.*

I hesitated long enough to make sure she wasn't about to slip sideways or fall unconscious on me, then cautiously stepped over the still-standing protection circle that Belle and I had raised.

I might as well have stepped into another world.

One that assaulted my senses with dust and blood and pain.

Fuck.

"Mom? Ava?" I shouted.

"Over here."

It was Samuel who answered rather than either woman, and fear slipped through me. I ran toward the sound of his voice, the scent of blood sharpening in my nostrils with every step.

Three figures appeared in the gloom, two of them standing over a third. Mom.

"I'm fine. Truly, I am," she was saying. "I'm just winded. Nothing more."

That was a lie. I could smell blood on all three of them,

and it was definitely human rather than demon. But they were alive, and that in itself was an utter miracle.

Perhaps one due more to the wraith seeking to stop the banishment ceremony than kill those on the periphery.

"Is Belle okay?" Ava said

"She's fine. The ceremony just took a toll on her strength, and she's beat."

"Oh, good." Ava pushed several sweaty strands of hair out of her face, smearing blood across her cheek and forehead in the process. Her hand had been sliced open and was bleeding quite profusely. "What about Edward? And the others? I can't see them—"

"You won't until the dust settles more, but they're all fine. The demons never broke through our inner barrier."

"Is that what was glowing?" Samuel said. "Because it felt and looked like a whole lot more than a mere protection circle."

"Remember that conversation we're going to have over cake? Ask that question again then."

He rolled his eyes. "It's going to have to be a bloody big cake at this rate."

I smiled and drew another bottle of holy water from my pack. "You'd better use some of this on that cut on your cheek, otherwise you'll be left with a scar."

He glanced at the bottle but didn't take it. "Save it for your mom and Ava. They need it more than me. I'll go meet the team and the medics—I managed to call it in when the demons hit, so the team shouldn't be too far away now."

He walked out of the clearing, heading toward the path. It was only then that I noticed the wind had blown the salt ring away. No wonder the bastards had hit us so easily.

I offered the holy water to Ava, but she brushed it aside with a quick shake of her head, then headed through the fading curtain of dust, no doubt to check on her husband and daughter.

I knelt in front of Mom. "How's your back?"

"It's fine—"

"It's not. And there's no need to be stoic in a situation like this."

She half smiled. "Stoicism is my go-to reaction when the unusual happens. Hard to change a lifetime of habit."

Stoicism—and perhaps stubbornness—was something else many would say I'd inherited from her. I'd certainly been guilty of stating more than once that I was fine when I was anything but.

I pulled my knife from my pack, asked her to strip off her coat, and then carefully cut away the torn remnants of her sweater. Her entire back had been raked, and though the wound was relatively shallow, it was already festering. I carefully poured the holy water over the wounds. She hissed but resisted the colorful and rather appropriate swearing that usually left my lips in these situations.

"Why is it hurting now but not before?" she asked, clenching and unclenching her fists.

"Because these wounds were caused by a demon. Even with the holy water's healing properties, you may be left with scars."

She shrugged. "Did the banishment work?"

"Yes. The wraith wouldn't have attacked otherwise."

"And that surge of bright magic we all saw and felt?" Her gaze searched mine. "That was you, wasn't it? Or rather, the wild magic you now control."

I hesitated, but it was pointless lying. "Yes."

"How?"

"I'm linked to the reservation's wellspring. It was her power I called."

"But how, when it is so far away?"

"Not for the Earth. Not for the power that resides in her. It provided a channel—a superhighway, if you want—to reach me in an instant."

She was silent for several seconds. "This gene anomaly that we both carry—it was ignited in you by the wellspring that almost killed me, wasn't it?"

"Yes."

"Then why are you connected to the reservation's wellspring rather than the one that changed you?"

"I honestly don't know."

"But you do have suspicions."

I recorked the empty bottle and tucked it away. "We think the wild magic woke within me the night Clayton tried to rape me. That was the reason Dad was so determined to find me, you know—both he and Clayton saw the wild magic in the spell that killed Clayton's ability to get an erection."

"You father was never certain wild magic was responsible for the anomalous nature of that spell until he went to your café. Before then, he was merely helping a friend regain what he had lost." She carefully tugged her coat back on. "And it doesn't answer the question as to why you're now connected to the reservation's wellspring."

"The wellspring was unprotected when I arrived." I shrugged. "It wasn't an instant connection, but rather one that developed over time."

And use. But I wasn't about to add that.

"Which means your father, no matter how much he might wish, cannot make use of the gene in Juli's children. Not without risking their lives, even if he *was* able to locate a newly risen or unguarded wellspring at the right time."

"Which won't stop him from trying, Mom."

"Perhaps not, but *I* will. Until more is known about the reason for this gene adaption *and* the consequences the awakening of this power has in you—and whatever children you might have—I think it better to wait and watch."

On that, I wholeheartedly agreed. And it was a major relief that on this matter, at least, she was on my side rather than his. "Are you going to tell him what happened here?"

Her smile briefly teased the corners of her silvery eyes. "Have you any idea of the power you raised tonight? Half of Canberra would have felt the vibrations of it."

"Maybe, but they won't know the cause."

"Your father will, but he won't release the information without there being some benefit to himself or our family. Right now, there is none."

"Unless he uses it to force me into another marriage."

Or, at the very least, continued to send a never-ending stream of "suitable" suitors my way in the vague hope that I'd crack and marry one of them just to get him off my back.

She laughed softly. "I think the days of forced marriages are well and truly over. The days of your father forcing you to do anything certainly are. You have grown strong since you left us, Elizabeth, and I do not refer to either your magic or your psi skills."

Those damnable tears touched my eyes again. I blinked them away and glanced toward the dirt path at the sound of footsteps. "Samuel and his crew are almost here. It's probably best if you remain sitting and wait for the ambu—"

"I will do no such thing," she cut in sternly. "I am a part of this hunt, and I remain a part of it until this bastard is caught. I will not have you use the wound to sideline me."

I couldn't help but laugh. "You know, if Aiden was here right now, he'd be saying I'm definitely my mother's daughter."

"And he'd be right," she said. "Though it is not some-thing I noticed until recently, much to my undying regret."

There was absolutely nothing I could say to that. Not even a simple "It's not too late for us." Because, in all honesty, it might well be. There was a part of me that *did* want her in my life, but that would mean bringing Dad in as well, and that was something I absolutely did *not* want. No matter what punishment he received from the high council, it was never going to be enough to erase the hurt, the anger, and all those years of terrified running.

I could forgive Mom.

I could never—would never—forgive my dad.

I pushed to my feet, offered her a hand, then gently pulled her upright. "We should check on the others."

She nodded and moved, rather stiffly, toward the center of the clearing. Ava was sitting beside her daughter, one arm slung around her shoulders while Belle treated her cut palm.

The men remained inside the inner protection circle but were in the process of dismantling the pentagram. The cups remained untouched in the center. A demon had drunk from one, and it would need special treatment before anyone dared touch it.

Ashworth tucked the last of the candles away and then said, "We need to get somewhere safe, because our wraith will be seriously pissed, and he'll come after us with every-thing he's got."

"And what he hasn't got right now is a demon to give him a power boost," I said. "After that dust storm, and summoning what looked to be an entire cemetery, he's going to need recovery time—"

"And so will you," Eli said. "Especially after that light

283

show you put on. We're all well aware of the toll that'll take on you."

"I'm still standing, and I intend to remain so until this bastard is caught."

"And in that reply, I hear echoes of me." Mom lightly— briefly—caught my hand and squeezed it. "But trust me when I say that running on empty is never a good thing. And before you mention it, I am wounded physically not magically. There is a difference."

I knew that. Just as I knew I would undoubtedly crash. But not just yet. Perhaps it was the lingering high of all that wild magic that had coursed through me, but I actually felt almost normal, strength-wise.

Almost.

"Look," I said, "we have a very narrow window of weakness to track this bastard down. The wraith's demon gave us his last known address, and I think we need to go check it out."

"The laddie would already have sent his people there," Ashworth said. "It would be pointless."

"If one of his people is gifted with psychometry, I'd agree. But if not..."

Ashworth blew out a breath. "It's a risk."

"Right now, everything is a risk," I replied. "But I'm utterly certain of one thing—we can't sit back and let him continue to write all the rules."

Ashworth grunted and glanced around as Samuel, his people, and a couple of medics walked into the clearing. "I'll go talk to the laddie. You and Belle best deactivate your protection circle so the demon cup can be accessed and treated. Mrs. Marlowe, if you want to be a part of this team, you need to get those wounds treated."

She raised an eyebrow at the command in his tone but nevertheless headed for the medics.

I glanced at Belle.

On it, she said and pushed to her feet.

She didn't wobble, despite the fact I could still feel the weariness in her. Her recovery time had definitely improved in recent years.

Recent months, she corrected. *And it's not my recovery time as much as yours.*

Because normally I'd be so drained that I wouldn't have enough energy to share with her. That hadn't happened here today though—or at least, not yet—and I couldn't help but wonder why.

We deactivated our protection circle, picked up our stones, and then walked across the clearing to where Ashworth and Eli were still talking to Samuel. The wound on his cheek had obviously been treated, because there were a couple of butterfly bandages holding it together. While it wasn't as long as I'd initially thought, he'd nevertheless be left with a smallish scar.

Which would probably give his handsome features a more roguish look rather than detract from them in any way.

His gaze met mine. "I don't think this idea of yours is a good one."

I stopped and crossed my arms. "Have you anyone capable of psychometry on your team?"

"No."

"Then we have to try."

"Oh, I agree. I'm just stating I don't think the idea is a good one."

In that one statement, I caught echoes of Aiden, who so often went along with plans he disagreed with.

Because he trusts your judgement, same as Samuel, Belle said. *I do wonder who the idiot was that hurt this man, because he really would be a great catch.*

On that, we agree. Hell, had my heart not been taken, I might have toyed with the idea of seeing where a relationship might lead, despite the fact he'd been "preapproved" by my father.

"I'll grab the keys for two of the team's cars," he was saying. "Then we'll get underway. Just give me a few more minutes."

While we waited, we went over to explain what was happening to Ava, Edward, and Brian, then made our way up the hill to the parking area. Mom, Belle, and I climbed into the first car with Samuel while Ashworth and Eli were in the second with one of Samuel's men.

"Did your people find anything at the address the demon gave us?" I asked as Samuel reversed out of the parking area.

He shook his head. "No wraith, and no evidence that he'd even been there recently."

"What sort of evidence were they actually looking for, though? It's not like he'd leave the usual sort behind."

"We sent a Kang in. She couldn't sense any lingering dark energy, so either he wasn't there, or enough time had passed that his life force no longer stained the air."

While the Kangs didn't perform magic, per se, their ability to tap into the resonance of all living things and "see" both past and present events through the eyes of that energy probably made them one of the most formidable houses. I'd also seen Samuel track someone through the energy imprint their footsteps left in the soil.

"Is it possible the wraith disguised or somehow erased

the metaphysical signs of his presence?" Belle asked. "Or would she have sensed that as well?"

"She would have sensed the spell's output," Mom said before Samuel could. "Even if it did run along a different energy plane."

"If there'd been something to find there, we would have found it," Samuel confirmed. "This really *is* a fool's errand."

A smile tugged at my lips. "It wouldn't be the first time I've been involved in one of those."

"She's got one of her feelings," Belle said, in a weighty sort of tone that belied the amusement running through her thoughts. "And the wise do not ignore them, no matter how frustratingly poor they are with actual information."

"That's because it's so much more fun walking into an unknown situation completely devoid of any relevant information or warnings."

My tone was dry, and Samuel snorted softly. "You two really are crazy, aren't you?"

"There's not many who'd debate that question, be it here or at home," I said.

Silence fell. I closed my eyes, grabbing what rest I could, because I had a bad feeling there weren't going to be many other opportunities in the near future.

"We're here," Samuel said eventually.

I started and opened my eyes. We were in an area that appeared to be an unusual mix of commercial and housing, and the nearest buildings so closely resembled the one in which we'd lost Cat that old ghosts began to stir.

I shivered. Mom's hand slipped over mine and lightly squeezed. She didn't say anything. She didn't need to. She'd no doubt felt the ghosts too.

While Cat wasn't amongst them, it worried me that I hadn't heard or seen her for a while. I hoped it meant she was with Dad, because if things went south and he was taken, she might well be our only hope of finding him.

We pulled into a parking area opposite a small church and climbed out. The house we wanted sat behind the church complex, which was somewhat ironic considering wraiths couldn't handle anything holy. But maybe the fact it was the last place we would have searched was the exact reason he'd chosen it.

There were five official-looking vehicles sitting out the front of the house, and blue-and-white tape had been stretched across the driveway. A fierce-looking man stood behind it, his stance and expression foreboding. "Pass by at your peril" was definitely a vibe.

Samuel flashed his badge as we approached, and the big man lifted the tape to allow us entry. The house was a nondescript red brick, single story with a tiled roof. Its door had been forced open rather than magicked, meaning Samuel's team hadn't even taken the time to spell. Maybe they feared giving the wraith warning of their presence by doing so.

Another man guarded the door but stepped aside as Samuel approached. I followed him into the small hallway and, a heartbeat later, felt it.

Magic.

I stopped so abruptly that Belle crashed into me and sent me stumbling forward a couple of steps before I could catch my balance.

Samuel spun around. "What?"

"You didn't feel it?"

"Obviously not, given I have no idea what you're referring to."

"A spell just activated." I scanned the hallway but couldn't see or even feel anything untoward.

"It was obviously primed for your entry then." Samuel's tone was grim. "But how is that possible, given he hasn't been here for days if not weeks?"

"He could have left a trigger spell of some kind in *every* location he's stayed at," Ashworth said.

"Except the magic felt *fresh*, not old," I replied.

"Then we need find out what it triggered, and fast," Samuel said.

He'd barely finished that sentence when a woman shouted, "Boss, you'd better get in."

He immediately took off down the corridor. We followed him into a well-furnished living room. The magic I'd sensed was here in force, but it held no threat.

Instead, it had left a simple but bloody message on the far wall.

My blood ran cold.

I have your father, it said. *Come to me, or he dies. You have one hour.*

CHAPTER FOURTEEN

Mom immediately phoned my father, but the call rang on and on without answer. I briefly closed my eyes and tried to get hold of the fear clenching my gut.

Because my dreams had been filled with this exact scenario many times over the years. They'd known it would always come down to a battle between the dark sorcerer and me.

Except it wasn't just you and him last time, and it won't fucking be just you and him this time, Belle growled. *And don't for an instant think Ashworth and Eli are about to let you walk into this alone.*

He'll kill Dad the minute he senses anyone else.

He won't know I'm with you telepathically.

He might, given it's what helped defeat him last time.

Then we'll figure a way around it. We always do. Her mental tone was filled with a certainty I wished I could believe. *He underestimated us the first time, and I'm pretty damn sure he's doing the same thing again.*

Maybe he believes there's nothing we can do to stop him now.

He's a wraith, not a god.

One that's been playing in the demonic world for a very long time, remember.

And that alone could be his downfall.

How?

He's forgotten just how dangerous a cornered witch can be. And before you snort in disbelief, there's been a good array of demons over the last year who can attest to that.

It was meant to be comforting, but it really wasn't. Not when I remembered just how many times I'd come close to losing my life over that year.

Mom left a request for Dad to ring her ASAP, then hung up and glared at Samuel. "I thought he was under full guard in a secure bunker?"

While her expression and her voice were utterly controlled, her aura was so fierce and bright I was tempted to shield my eyes.

"He was. He *is*," Samuel replied. "Let's not jump to conclusions before we know what, if anything, has actually happened."

He dragged out his phone and made a call. Mom crossed her arms and waited, one booted foot tapping an angry tattoo that echoed out across the silent room.

While I was too far away to hear the other side of Samuel's conversation with whoever he'd called, it sounded an awful lot like Saska.

And she didn't sound happy.

"Cancel leave and call everyone in. I want them found ASAP," Samuel growled. "And send someone over to search Rodrika's house."

"Rodrika Marlowe?" Mom said, when Samuel hung up. "What's she got to do with anything?"

As far as I knew, there was no Rodrika related to us, so she was obviously from a different Marlowe line.

"Forty-five minutes ago, she walked into the secure bunker and removed your husband."

Forty-five minutes would have been around the time we'd finished banishing the wraith's second demon. Coincidence? I seriously doubted it.

"But how?" I asked. "Wasn't there an embargo placed on his removal?"

"Rodrika is a high councilor," Mom said, rubbing her arms. "No one working for the HIC would have barred her entry, especially if she had the right paperwork."

"And she did," Samuel said.

Mom nodded. "But why would she do such a thing? If a meeting had been called to change Lawrence's location, I would have been notified."

"Oh, I doubt this had anything to do with the council." Samuel's voice was grim. "Rodrika drove your husband to your compound, was there just on twenty minutes, and then left. We of course followed, by air and by car. All tags were intercepted."

"Was Saska injured? It was her voice I heard on the phone, wasn't it?"

He glanced at me and nodded. "Her team have a few bruises but are fine. But they shot Reggie with a silver splinter arrow, and he's been rushed to surgery before he loses the arm."

I'd never heard of a splinter arrow, but I had firsthand experience on just how painful silver lodged into skin could be, and I wasn't even a shifter. I hoped they got it out before he lost the arm and any ability to ever fly again.

"And the trackers placed on Lawrence?" Mom asked.

"Removed."

"Even the magical?"

"Yes." Samuel grimaced. "Rodrika was fully aware of all our precautions. She's undone every single one of them."

"But... why?" she repeated faintly. "Why would she do this?"

"I don't know." Samuel scraped a hand through his hair. "But we'll do our damned best to find them and answer that question."

"It's possible," Belle said quietly, "that our wraith had demons we weren't told about."

Ashworth frowned. "We were there, lass, performing the ceremony with you. You gave the demon a direct question, and it answered."

"Yes, but perhaps it was *too* direct. Maybe I should have asked how many other demons the wraith had blood agreements with rather than how many he had *with* him."

"Meaning Rodrika could be possessed?" Mom asked.

"We have to consider the possibility."

"It would certainly explain how he's managed to be two steps ahead." Eli's voice was grim. "He had a man—or rather, a woman—on the inside."

Mom's gaze came to mine. "But can you find him? Within the time frame?"

"If I can find something of his holding enough of a resonance connection, yes, but the wraith is aware of that skill—why else would he have said come to me and not give any sort of direction?" I hesitated. "It's probably why they went to your house—they know I have to go there, and they've laid a trap."

"But why would he—or the demon who controls Rodrika—bother?" Belle said. "He wants you to go to him, so why not give an address rather than play these games?"

"An address gives us time to plan a counterattack,"

Ashworth said. "This way, we're wasting precious time to find that location."

"And if his trap ensnares and weakens me," I said grimly, "all the better."

The wraith might want vengeance, but I'd beaten him once, and he wouldn't risk me doing it again. I doubted there'd be any coming back—no matter what the form—if death found him a second time.

Mom swore—something I'd never heard her do before. It said a whole lot about the tumultuous state of her mind right now.

"Then he's alone with the wraith and his creatures, and we have no hope of finding him without risking your life." She glanced at me. "I might be late coming to the party as a mother, but I do love you, Elizabeth. I cannot allow you to exchange your life for Lawrence's. Not when he has lived a full life and you have not."

A statement that made me feel all fuzzy and warm but also a little angry. It had taken so long—and too many deaths —for her to openly admit she loved me. I'd always known it, of course, but a child—hell, even an adult—liked to hear it said out loud every now and again.

But I guessed it was better late than never.

"Thing is, Dad's not alone. Cat's likely with him."

She stared at me for a few seconds, her eyes a little wider than usual, as if not daring to believe what she'd just heard. While that hint of incredulity was the only emotion she displayed, it was not the only emotion she showed. Her aura was a riot of disbelief and hope.

"Cat?" she whispered. "How is that even possible? Her soul was consumed—"

"It wasn't," I cut in gently. "The anomaly in our blood saved her."

"Then she is a *ghost*?"

"No. She's a spirit guide."

Mom sucked in a breath, then blindly reached behind her, found a chair, and all but collapsed into it.

"*Your* spirit guide?" she whispered.

I couldn't help smiling. "I think the general consensus in the spirit world is that I'm not a suitable candidate for a guide."

"*That* is a certainty," Belle said, amused.

Mom glanced at her. "Then why is she even contacting Elizabeth, let alone helping her? That's an extremely unusual situation, isn't it?"

"Cat was an extremely unusual woman, and that has transferred over to the spirit world," Belle replied. "According to my guides, her power gives her some flexibility in her interactions with our world, as does the fact that—despite her death thirteen years ago—she has not yet been assigned her witch."

Mom sucked in a quivering breath and released it slowly. Calm descended once again across her features. "Then we wait for Catherine to contact you?"

"I don't think we dare," I said, at the same time as Samuel. I flashed him a smile and added, "We leaving now?"

"Given we only have an hour, yes. Until we're sure you can track your father, it's impossible to make other plans."

"You'll still search for him in the meantime, of course," Mom said.

It wasn't a question but rather a statement, and Samuel's smile cooled. "Of course."

She nodded and pushed to her feet. Samuel led us back to the cars, and in very little time, we were heading back across Canberra to the Marlowe compound. Guards were still very much present, despite the fact neither Mom nor Dad were. Security opened the gates, and we followed the sweeping driveway around to the front of the building, then stopped. Belle's phone rang, the ringtone telling me it was Monty.

"Answer it, or he'll stress out," I said. "It's going to take me time to locate a link anyway."

She immediately did so. I climbed out, my gaze sweeping the building. I'd been born and raised here, but in some respects, it had never truly been the home of my heart, simply because I'd always felt like an outsider. It may have been nothing more than the imaginings of a child not getting the same attention as her siblings, but still...

It remained absolutely beautiful to look at—a Victorian-style double-brick residence of grand proportions—but the style and beauty were just a front. Its heart was barren and ugly.

I blinked.

That ugliness was *real*, not emotive.

I swallowed and said, "Ladies and gents, we have a problem."

"We do indeed." Ashworth stopped beside me and studied the house. "If I didn't know better, I'd say it's a transport void."

"Void spells are theoretical," Samuel said. "I've certainly never seen any evidence of their existence."

"Well, you have now," Eli said.

Mom frowned. "Rodrika would have the power to create a transport void, but I sincerely doubt she'd have the knowledge. All references are kept secure, and any attempt to access them is immediately reported." Her gaze swept the house. "Surely the twenty minutes they were here wouldn't have given them time to create such a thing."

"It's possible the demon managed to snare a naturally occurring one. They're rare, and generally too small for human use, but they can be adjusted." Amusement briefly flared in Ashworth's eyes. "It's been theorized such voids are the reason socks go into a washing machine as a pair and come out single."

I snorted. "If I find those socks when I go through this void, I'll let you know."

"You can't go through," Mom said. "You could quite literally end up anywhere in the world. These things can even cut through the rules of time and space."

"They didn't have the time to create a complex void, let alone one that allows backward travel," Ashworth said. "The latter is a dangerous and complex process that takes days, not minutes. And if things go wrong... well, let's just say there's a reason they're banned."

I glanced at him. "That suggests you've come across one before."

"I lost a friend to one." He grimaced. "You cannot alter the past without altering the trajectory of the present."

"The void doesn't encompass the entire house, though, so surely we can simply avoid the areas in which it sits," Mom said.

"We're on a countdown," I replied. "And that means we really can't waste too much time on a search that may well be fruitless."

"Then we try the garage," she said. "Lawrence keeps a selection of watches in a lockbox in the trunk of his car. There should be something there that holds his resonance, surely."

"It's worth a try," I said, and motioned her to lead the way.

"While you're doing that, I'll ring Black Lantern," Samuel said. "They've people who can dismantle the void."

"Can I suggest we don't do anything until we know for sure I can find something with Dad's resonance?" I countered. "It might end up being our only option to make the deadline."

Samuel hesitated and then nodded. "I'll still call it in, because the void will need to be dealt with even if we do use it."

I headed off after Mom. Though the house appeared to be two stories from the front, there were actually three, thanks to the radical slope of the land. It allowed a six-car garage and a large granny flat to be built underneath. Not that any of *my* grannies had ever stayed there. Not in my time here, anyway.

Mom rummaged through her purse, found the remote, and opened one of the doors. We strode past a variety of Jags and Porsches until we reached a rather ugly-looking black BMW. Once Mom had opened the trunk and the lock box, she stepped back and motioned me to proceed. There were seven watches inside, some of them brands I recognized, some I didn't. All of them looked expensive.

I flexed my fingers then reached for my psychometry and carefully ran a hand just above each watch. Mom watched me, her gaze heavy with expectation, a weight I could feel rather than see.

One watch held the faintest flicker, but the connection wasn't strong enough to follow. Disappointment stirred, but in truth I wasn't really surprised. It was inevitable we'd have to do this the hard way.

Or, in this case, the wraith's way.

My gaze rose to Mom's. I didn't need to say anything. She instantly knew.

"Well," she said softly. "That's it then."

"No, it's not. We'll head inside and see what I can find there."

"And if there's nothing?"

"Then we keep all things crossed Cat gets back to us with an address."

The words were barely out of my mouth when I felt her presence. The wash of relief was so fierce it threatened to buckle my knees.

You won't find anything inside holding Dad's resonance, she said. *Not without going into either his bedroom or study, and the void spell encompasses both.*

I guess that was unsurprising, but it was still fucking annoying. I scraped a hand through my hair and repeated what she'd said.

Mom's eyes widened. "She's here. Cat's *here.*"

Tell her that I love her, Cat said. *Tell her that I miss her. Tell her that we* will *save Dad from this monster.*

I repeated the message, and Mom blinked rapidly. "Dear God, this is... this is all too much. I don't... I can't..."

I hesitated, then wrapped an arm around her shoulders and gave her a fierce hug. She stiffened for just one second, then relaxed into my embrace. Her tears fell silently, dampening my jacket.

I looked over Mom's shoulder to my sister. She was so real and solid-looking, I just wanted to reach out and draw her into my embrace with Mom. She was the epitome of a powerful young witch just reaching her prime, except now it was as a spirit guide rather than a member of the High Witch Council. There was a bit of me that envied the witch that got her as a guide. She might not have life experience behind her, but her knowledge of spells and history had always been vast. More so than even Dad's.

I get the feeling, I said, *that the "we" you mentioned is just us two, not everyone else.*

We have to go through the void if you wish to save Dad. The wraith has chosen his location well—you could not get there in time from here.

Has he set traps at the other end?

Of course, but they will not work.

Why not?

Because they are set for you. They are not set for me.

It took a second to realize she meant to merge with me, and I swore softly. I trusted my sister, but there was nevertheless an innate fear that she'd find being in flesh once again a temptation hard to resist. I silently reached out to Belle and drew her into the conversation. Cat's personal connection to me and her status as a spirit guide might naturally exclude Belle—in the same way that I was excluded from any of Belle's conversations with her spirit guides—but this was too big a decision for me to make it alone. I needed Belle's input on this. There was too much at stake—not just for Dad, but for both her and me personally.

She was my familiar. My death would have serious implications for her.

Our connection deepened, and Belle came online, listening without commenting.

I couldn't take you over permanently, even if I wanted to, Cat was saying. *Your inner magic would not allow it.*

Meaning the wild magic, because my innate witch magic would be overwhelmed by hers in an instant.

Besides, do you think Belle, or her spirit guides, would allow such a thing? Amusement ran through Cat's mental tone. *I would be kicked out of your body and forever banned from the spirit world. That is a fate I would not wish on even my greatest enemy.*

Even the wraith?

He is a perversion of both flesh and spirit, and the fate that awaits if we do manage to kill him is far worse than mere banishment.

And if we don't?

Then our spirits will be consumed, and all that we are will forever be lost to the world.

It was said as simple fact, and a chill ran through me. It wasn't so much fear as an awareness that such a fate was far more likely than survival.

Mom sniffed and pulled away from my embrace. I handed her a tissue, but my attention remained on my sister.

Merging is dangerous. Bodies weren't designed to house two separate spirits, and it taxed mind, strength, and heart, sometimes to the point of death.

It is the only way, she said. *You cannot use your most lethal weapon, and your own magic isn't strong enough to counter his, no matter how much it has grown.*

"I'm sorry," Mom said. "It's unusual for my emotions to overwhelm my control."

"Mom, tears are understandable given this *isn't* a usual situation." And it was nice to know that beneath the facade she was as much an emotive mess as the rest of us. I couldn't say that to her, of course. Not only was it a little mean, but it would also hurt her, and I didn't want that. "But we still have an option. Let's get back to the others."

To Cat, I added, *Your magic couldn't counter the wraith's the first time round, so why would now be any different?*

The difference is he has no idea I am present and capable of magic and has set his spells solely for you. They will not counter or subdue my magic.

Except you'll be inhabiting my body, and his spells will

no doubt take any capacity for movement and spelling away the minute I step through that void. Having you along as a passenger won't change that.

Flesh and blood wise, yes, but your energy will be vastly different and will not be restricted. She paused. *In fact, it is vital to our survival that it isn't.*

Meaning I'll need to draw his attention and his magic before you can attack.

Yes. We must weaken him to have true victory.

It was never going to be easy to win this battle, but for fuck's sake... could we not, just this once, contain a supernatural entity without me having to be in the firing line?

I sighed and said, *Where has he stashed Dad?*

She gave me the street address, then added, *It's a minimum twenty-minute drive. Even using lights and sirens, you will not make it there in time now.*

I glanced at my watch and saw she was right. *Belle, given how much he appears to know about my psi talents, it's possible he'll activate some type of inhibitor the minute we're out of the void—will you be able to dismantle it?*

Before she could answer, Cat said, her tone surprised, *Belle was listening to our conversation?*

She's my familiar. There are few things that can void our connection.

This connection runs on a very different frequency though.

Doesn't matter.

Does that mean she can use her talents through you?

Yes, but—

Oh, this is excellent news. Cat's excitement was so fierce, it washed warmth through my body. *She can connect to Dad and break whatever hold the wraith has over him.*

If that hold was telepathic rather than magical, then she definitely could. But given that, as far as we knew, he'd been using magical rather than psi or even medical means to restrain his captives, I doubted that possibility would come into play.

I blew out a breath and returned my attention to my sister. *Cat, a deep connection with Belle while hosting your spirit may well push me past my limits.*

You have more strength than anyone I have ever met, dearest sister. This will not be your end.

Her certainty jarred against my own natural pessimism, and I wasn't sure which was the saner belief right now.

I briefly closed my eyes. We had no choice in this, even if a deep reluctance stirred. *We'd better do this now, before Ashworth and Eli get wind of our intentions.*

And before reluctance strengthened and I changed my mind.

I'll grab your mom and slow her down, Belle said. *You and Cat head inside.*

I'll need the keys.

Mom immediately reached into her handbag and tossed them to me. Her eyes were wide and a little furious, but she couldn't say or do anything because she was now in Belle's control.

"I'm sorry, Mom," I said. "But Cat and I have to do this alone. You and the others can meet us at the warehouse. Belle will give you the address."

One way or another, this whole thing would be over by the time they arrived.

I ran for the basement door and was a little surprised to discover the simple deadlock with an alarm spell overlay. But I guessed any would-be intruder first had to get through the multiple layers of protections woven around the house and garage doors. If they did, well, they were obviously more powerful than either of my parents, and additional measures here wouldn't have mattered.

I disconnected the alarm spell, then opened the door and ran up the stairs. The air was warm thanks to the underfloor heating, but the taint of foulness ran underneath it. I followed my nose through the kitchen, past the over-sized dining room, and through the guest lounge into the entrance hall. It was, like everything else in this damn place, vast and ornate, with a sweeping Y-shaped oak staircase dominating the center space. Thankfully, the front-door panels were frosted glass, so unless I turned on a light or tripped over something, none of the men standing outside would guess I was here.

I bolted up the stairs and went left, toward Mom and Dad's apartments and the unsettling pulse of evil. It grew stronger the closer I got to my father's study, and I had to clench my fingers to contain the sparks of wild magic wanting to dance across my fingertips.

The double oak door was closed, but magic crawled across its surface. Its source wasn't the void but rather a barrier spell, and it wasn't particularly strong despite the foul feel of the thing.

A distraction, Cat said. *The void lies immediately beyond. It will capture you the moment you step through the door.*

Which was why the void—whose presence had been so evident outside—was barely noticeable now when I was basically standing in front of it. He'd obviously hoped I'd place the deep pulsing of evil in the air at the feet of the barrier spell and rush into the study without taking additional precautions.

But rushing in was the reason I'd almost died the last time I'd confronted this bastard. I would not repeat the mistake, even though he obviously expected me to.

Underestimating me, as Belle and Cat had said.

Or perhaps overestimating your affection for your father came Belle's comment.

Probably. Where's Mom?

Just approaching the men. You need to get moving.

I flexed my fingers and then deepened the connection between Belle and me. Her being flooded mine, and while the connection wasn't as deep as the one we'd used to defeat the White Lady, it was close enough that there was very little separation between us. The little there was, however, gave us the ability to think and act separately if necessary while maintaining unity.

Your mother has reached the cars and my control on her ends, Belle said. *We need to go—now.*

I took one of those useless deep breaths that did little to calm my nerves and then said, *Right, Cat, in you come.*

I'd barely finished when her being flooded into mine, a force that was warm and familiar and yet so filled with power my being quivered in fear. My inner wild magic stirred, and a barrier rose unbidden, creating a safe zone around Belle and me. Cat had been right—she would never be able to claim my body as the White Lady had once tried to claim Belle's. My magic hadn't allowed it then, and it wouldn't allow it now.

As two became three, we swung off the backpack and retrieved the holy water and my silver knife, tucking the former into my coat pocket and the latter into the back of my jeans.

Then we tore the barrier spell apart, opened the door, and stepped inside.

Unleashing a maelstrom of magic that picked us up and swept us away.

CHAPTER FIFTEEN

W e tumbled through a blur of gray. There was no sound in this maelstrom other than the rapid tattoo of our own heart, and no smell beyond the stink of our own fear. We fell for what seemed forever, stretching time and patience, but just when we feared that we'd been wrong, that perhaps he'd intended nothing more than to doom us to this void forever, we were spat out onto a cold, hard surface.

We skidded for several feet on hands and knees, skinning our palms and tearing the knees out of our jeans. Pain washed through our body, but Belle caught the receptors and dialed them down.

Something we would undoubtedly need more of before this was over.

We didn't immediately move, instead using our sensory inputs to judge what lay around us. The air was ripe with the scent of refuse, suggesting this place was near a rubbish tip of some kind, but underneath that was an odd, vaguely musky odor we couldn't quite place. No flies buzzed, but that was unsurprising given the early hour of the morning.

Water dripped in the distance despite the fact it wasn't raining, and from somewhere closer came a soft moaning.

It took us several seconds to realize it wasn't the wind but rather our father.

We looked up. Darkness met our gaze, and for too many seconds, there was nothing to see. Our eyes quickly adjusted, and shapes appeared.

A row of broken packing boxes and stacked wooden pallets separated us from our father. A sea of refuse lay between us, some of it in bags, but most of it lying in slowly drifting waves. It made us wonder if perhaps this place had once been a recycling plant—

A footstep, behind us.

Our gaze snapped around. There was nothing and no one to see, only more shadows and the continuing sea of rubbish.

But our other senses told a very different story.

We could smell his foulness. Hear the soft whisper of his tattered cloak scraping the concrete. Feel the caress of the magic he'd yet to unleash.

He was on our left, moving around us.

We pushed upright. Just for an instant, the darkness swam, and our heart raced so fiercely we feared it might tear out of our chest. That such a small movement caused so much distress was a warning—we had to end this quickly, before the toll of being a vessel for three separate entities became too great on our body.

We moved forward. Magic stirred, snaking toward us.

Do not react, Cat warned.

We clenched our fingers and shoved them in our pocket. Our left hand met the coolness of glass, and we gripped it tightly. We were nowhere near close enough to throw the holy water that bottle contained, but holding it nevertheless shored up our courage.

Or perhaps it was only *my* courage that needed shoring.

The ribbon of power drew closer, skirting around us, tempting us to react. We ignored it and walked forward. It was a test, nothing more.

The wraith made no move to reveal himself. He simply kept pace from a distance, the scrape of his rags as soft and yet as annoying as nails down a blackboard.

Our foot hit a metal can, sending it bouncing across the concrete. The sharp noise echoed, and the moaning briefly stopped.

It was then that we heard it.

The soft skittering of dozens and dozens of tiny little feet.

Horror washed through me, through us.

Rats. There were rats in this place.

And they were behind the wall of boxes and pallets with our father.

We didn't want to know why. Didn't want to know what they were doing, even though a rusty, almost metallic scent now teased our nostrils.

Blood.

Blood, sweat, *and* raw flesh.

Flesh the rats were dining on...

Almost unbidden, our pace increased. In that instant, the snake attacked, wrapping around us, winding up our body, sinking its fangs into our neck. Foul coldness washed through our body as the venom-that-wasn't caught our limbs and froze them in place. We stopped, and panic surged, a brief wave that threatened to completely overwhelm us.

Then Cat's magic surged, countering the wraith's,

pushing it away from our limbs and our organs, forcing it into a thick knot of evil that was contained, if not erased.

We could move, but we didn't.

We simply stood there and waited for the bastard to reveal himself. To come closer.

The whispering of his rags stopped, but something flickered past our vision to our right. A shadow that wasn't.

A demon.

Perhaps the rats weren't feeding on our father but rather the woman who'd unwillingly betrayed him.

"I did not think you would be so easy to capture a second time."

The voice was harsh and gratingly loud, the words broken and a little incomplete.

We didn't reply.

He laughed. The sound made our ears ache. Behind the boxes and the pallets, the moaning started again.

It wasn't male. It was female.

Rodrika rather than our father.

Relief stirred, even as we clenched our fingers and fought back the urge to move, to react, to save. The wraith remained too far away to use either the holy water or the knife, and his demon now stood between us. Magic was not yet viable, as the minute we began to spell, his creature would be unleashed upon us.

To kill the wraith, we first had to kill said creature.

"You may speak, little witchling," came the wraith's raspy comment.

The knot of evil within stirred, reacting to verbal command even though it had no power over us.

"What have you done to my father?" we said, keeping our voice flat, without emotion.

"Nothing more than he deserves" came the harsh reply.

"Such a sanctimonious statement, considering you do nothing more than visit vengeance on a family that almost succeeded in destroying you."

There was a flicker of movement, a swish of dark ropes. A heartbeat later, our father screamed.

The wraith chuckled, and his creature stirred, its gaze sweeping us, hot and hungry.

We remained still. Time was running out, but there was nothing we could do. Rushing would kill us all.

"Do you not wonder how I intend to kill you?" the wraith asked.

"No, actually. I'm wondering why the fuck you're standing there talking about killing me rather than actually doing it. Could it be that you haven't the strength or the power? Could it be that without your other demons, you are nothing more than a raggy windbag?"

Anger surged, a force so strong we took an involuntary step back. Thankfully, he didn't appear to notice

"Oh, dear child, I do not need my demons to inflict pain on one such as you."

And with that, he hit us. Not physically. Magically. It knocked us off our feet and tossed us across the warehouse, until we smashed into the boxes and pallets with enough force to shatter. Splinters speared our flesh in multiple places, and pain rose, a battering wave that was once again dialed down by Belle. Talons scraped against concrete, and the sensation of evil grew so thick, we could barely breathe. We looked up, saw the twisted shadow arrowing toward us, and threw ourselves sideways.

One claw caught our coat, shredding it, cutting skin. We screamed but reached back, grabbed the knife, and twisted around. The demon lunged at us; we swept the blade from left to right, severing its snout. Blood gushed as its body hit us, the remains of its mouth tearing uselessly at our flesh. We lifted our knees and tossed it off us. As it flew over our head, we raised the knife and gutted it from neck to groin.

It crashed to the concrete and didn't move.

We gripped the bloodied blade tighter and pushed to our feet.

The wraith didn't attack. His rats did. They were a wave of furry fury that bit and tore at us, climbing our clothes, tangling their bodies in our hair, biting at our neck and our chin.

We knocked them away, but there was an unending wave of the bastards, all intent on eating us alive. Fury rose. Mine, not Cat's. It was unrestrained and uncontrollable, and it burned through every pore in my body. The rats leapt from us and skittered away.

The wraith laughed, the sound victorious. The black mass within stirred anew, and an odd sensation ran through our body.

The mass we'd contained but not erased was leeching—feeding—on that inner power.

This was what he had intended. What he had needed.

The wild magic.

And I'd just given him a direct line into the well that lay inside me.

But I was not alone, and his feeding frenzy had made him vulnerable.

We ran, with every ounce of speed we had, straight at the bastard. He didn't see us, didn't hear us. His eyes were closed, his expression one of rapture as he drained the wild energy from our veins, our body.

We opened the holy water, raised our arm, and flung it at his face. It burned through the protective shield around his body and splashed across skin that hung in rotting strips and eye sockets that were empty and soulless. He screamed, a high-pitched sound full of pain and fury.

He smashed one bony arm across our body, briefly knocking us back. We caught our balance but didn't close in.

It was then Cat took control. Her magic rose, a wave as strong and as powerful as anything I'd ever felt before. It tore apart the remnants of the wraith's protective barriers and pinned him in place, pulverizing his quick attempt to counter.

Footsteps, behind us.

Humans. Three of them, running straight at us from God knew where.

Belle's telepathy surged, and the footsteps stopped. But our brain felt as if it were on fire, and our body trembled. We needed to end this, quickly.

"As you lived in the shadows, wraith, so shall you die by them," Cat said, and began a secondary spell. One that felt old, dark, and extremely dangerous. But it wasn't so much magic as a demand, and it called to those who lived in shadows and nightmares.

Within seconds, they answered.

Creatures appeared, creatures that were malformed and diaphanous, moving cautiously at first and then with growing confidence as they scented the offering.

They surrounded the wraith, tore at him, eating his rags, his flesh, and his bones, while he writhed and screamed and fought uselessly against Cat's magic.

When there was little more left than spirit, they consumed that, each creature taking a tiny piece of him, ensuring that he could never be raised, never be whole. Ever again.

Then they left, leaving the only visible evidence of his presence an ugly smear of black on the concrete.

We collapsed onto our knees. Our head burned, and suddenly we couldn't get enough air into our lungs. Belle retreated, but kept enough contact to keep the pain at bay. We needed that. Badly.

We succeeded, Cat said softly. Wearily. *And now I must go.*

What about Dad?

He survives, though not without cost.

What cost?

You will see soon enough. Take care, little sister, and live well. I will see you in the afterlife.

She left, but not before warmth brushed my lips. A departing kiss from a sister I wouldn't see or hear from again.

I blinked back tears, then closed my eyes, fighting the fierce desire to just slide into the grip of unconsciousness. I couldn't let go just yet. I had to see my father. Had to under-stand Cat's cryptic comment.

I pushed slowly to my feet. Pain erupted in a dozen different places, but it was, for the moment, ignorable. I shoved the empty holy water bottle into my jacket pocket but kept grip of the bloody knife. The wraith was dead, which meant any spell he'd placed on or around my father should have died with him, but I wasn't about to take the chance.

I limped past the three men Belle still held immobile. Their gazes followed me, their expressions a mix of fear and confusion. Two of them were gripping knives, the third a rope. The wraith hadn't wanted me dead, but he obvi-ously had no concern about me being beaten up and bloody.

I skirted around the pile of pallets I hadn't destroyed and then stopped dead.

Rodrika lay ten feet away, her legs, hands, and mouth all duct taped. She'd been stripped, and there was what looked to be peanut butter smeared over her body. That was what the rats had been dining on... that and her flesh.

While she was conscious.

Bile rose, and this time would not be restrained. I staggered over to the pallets and lost everything I'd eaten over the last eight hours.

When there was nothing left but dry heaves, I wiped my mouth and then said, *Belle, are you able to dial down her pain sensors?*

Not without the risk of letting those three men free.

Order them to leave the building and not return, I said. *I really don't care about them right now.*

She did so, then deepened our connection and reached out to Rodrika. A heartbeat later, Rodrika's eyes closed.

She's unconscious, Belle said wearily. *It was easier to do.*

Thanks. How far away are you all?

A minute or so.

Don't come in with them. I'll reach out if I need anything.

Okay.

As our contact dropped, I turned, walked around Rodrika, and found my father. Like her, he was naked, but there was no peanut butter and no sign that the rats had taken even the smallest of nibbles. That, no doubt, was due to the pentagram that surrounded him. The dark candles still burned at the cardinal points, but I couldn't immediately see any indication of an active spell.

My father wasn't moving, and he wasn't awake. But neither was he dead. There was no sign of damage, no wounds, and no immediate indication of what had been done to him.

As the wail of sirens jumped into focus, I raked my gaze along the length of his body. Cat had said my father had paid a high price, but I had no idea...

Then I realized what was missing.

His aura—his *magical* aura. All witches had one. For the most part, they toned it down so as to not blind or overwhelm other witches, but this close, its thrum should have been evident.

Its absence could mean only one thing. The wraith had stolen the one thing my father prized above everything else.

His magic.

I walked up the steps to my family's home, my gaze lingering over the familiar facade.

I would never come back here. Ever.

Twenty-four hours had passed since we'd saved my father. He'd refused to go to the hospital—hadn't, in fact, even waited for the ambulance to arrive, but instead had insisted Mom drive him home.

We both knew why.

He wanted to limit knowledge of what, exactly, the wraith had stolen from him. The few specialists who *had* seen him—under threat of death if they so much as breathed information into the wrong ear—couldn't say whether his loss of magic would be temporary or permanent. Only time would tell.

I hadn't exactly wanted to go to the hospital myself, but mainly because I'd have to deal with the whole "could you be pregnant" thing before they treated my wounds and rat bites. And of course, I hadn't done the test. *Wouldn't* do the test, not until all the dust had settled, not just with my dad, but also the court case.

Thankfully, there was no indication that the wraith's leech link had done any damage to the overall pool of inner wild magic. Mom had carefully extracted it, given both me and Belle a royal dressing down for forcing our will on her, and had made us promise never to do something like that again.

Rodrika never recovered from her wounds, but at least in the end she had died without pain.

I pressed the doorbell and listened to the somber chime inside. After a few seconds, footsteps echoed. Mom rather than the staff. Apparently, Dad had sent most of them on holidays until he "recovered," though none of them were witches and wouldn't have known what exactly had been done to him.

Mom opened the door, her gaze quickly scanning me as she stepped back and waved me in. "You recovered quickly."

"I tend to these days." I shrugged off my coat, then walked over to the coat closet to hang it up—an automatic response left over from childhood. "How is he?"

She sighed. "Unpleasant. I really don't think it's wise for you to be confronting him right now."

"Mom, he can't hurt me. Not now, not ever again. Besides, there will *never* be a perfect time when it comes to that man."

She sighed again. "True enough. You remember the way?"

I smiled. "Yeah."

She hesitated. "Would you like a cup of tea before you go?"

"That would be lovely, thank you."

She smiled, touched my shoulder lightly, as if to wish me luck, then motioned me to continue.

I walked up the sweeping stairs and then down the hall to the study. The transport void had been dismantled, though an odd dark energy clung to the doorframe. It was obviously harmless, otherwise it would have been removed, but I nevertheless tugged my sleeve over my hand before I knocked on the door.

"Who is it?" came the sharp response.

"Elizabeth."

"I have no desire to speak to you—"

"Well, too bad, because you're going to, and you can't do anything about it."

The door was locked, but a quick spell fixed that. Dad was halfway to the door but stopped abruptly when I entered.

He didn't say anything. He just scowled, spun on his heels, and strode back behind the desk. He didn't sit, however. He simply pressed his hands against its edge and leaned forward a little. It was a pose meant to be intimidating—one that certainly *had* intimidated a younger me.

Not now. Not ever again.

"We have nothing to discuss," he said, his voice showing none of the bitter fury that burned around him. "Indeed, you should not even be here, given no decision has been handed down by the high council."

"You're very welcome to lodge an official complaint. I don't really care."

The anger deepened and, just for a moment, his knuckles went white. My father had never been one to resort to physical violence, but right now he was tempted.

I smiled benignly, part of me hoping that he *did* lash

out. It would be mighty satisfying to rebuff his punch and then send him flying.

But I wouldn't go down that road, as tempting as it was. Right now, I had the moral high ground, and I wanted to keep it.

"Are you here to gloat?" he asked urbanely. "Or to get a thank you? Because *that* will never happen. You might have saved my life, but I would rather have died than pay this price."

"Letting you die was certainly an option for me, and I'm sure Mom would have appreciated being handed total control over the family business. Sadly, she did not want you dead quite enough—though I daresay she'll get there quickly if you keep up the woe-is-me shit."

His gaze narrowed. "What do you want, Elizabeth?"

I pressed my fingers against the desk and leaned forward, imitating his stance and attitude. "I came here to give you a warning—once I leave this room, you are never to talk to me again. You are never to contact me again. You are not, in any way, to interfere or attempt to interfere in my life ever again."

"I am your father—"

"You were *never* my fucking father. I was never powerful enough, never smart enough, for you to show me any love or attention." I leaned closer. His scent filled my nostrils, thick with the anger and frustration that burned within him. What there *wasn't* was any sense of culpability. No indication that he in any way accepted he was wrong. "Well, guess what? That unwanted child, the child you illegally sold off to an old friend, turns out to be more powerful than either of your precious protégés. But you burned your bridges long ago, and your actions at both the café and in court have amplified the fact that the only thing you still care about is power."

"That is not true—"

I snorted. "Save the lies for those who might believe them."

"Bitterness does not become—"

"My bitterness has been well—"

"I am not interested in hearing anything else you have to say, Elizabeth. Get out of my study."

"Make me."

He half raised a hand, as if to spell me, then lowered it again.

I smiled. It was a very nasty smile. "You spent nearly sixteen years belittling me, telling me I was worthless, barely giving me the time of day. While I personally hope your magic never returns, I also hope you spend the intervening time experiencing *exactly* what being considered a 'lesser' witch is like in a town that values power above all else."

His gaze narrowed. "That sounds like a threat."

"There's nothing 'sounds like' about it. Come near me, come near anyone I care about, and all Canberra will know exactly what has happened to you."

With that, I pushed away from the desk and walked out.

And felt the weight of the last ten years finally lift from my shoulders.

EPILOGUE

I stared at the little stick in apprehension, waiting for the indicator to do its thing. The instructions on the box said it should only take a few minutes to get either a positive or negative result, but never in my life had "a few minutes" seemed more like fucking hours.

"Well?" Belle said.

She leaned against the bedroom's doorframe, her arms crossed, and her expression amused. Not by my possible pregnancy but rather the poor job Ashworth and Eli were doing concealing their presence further down the hallway. A herd of elephants would have paced quieter.

The council had finally brought down their verdict in the case—guilty, with instant removal from the high council and all his duties, for the period of one year. It was a verdict that had no meaning if he couldn't regain his magic. Even if his knowledge of magic and spells was unrivaled in Canberra, he couldn't be a councilor without any power of his own.

The wraith had given him a punishment far harsher than the council ever could or would.

And I still didn't feel sorry for the man.

Not one little bit.

I did feel sorry for Mom, because she was going to have to deal with the fallout. But I had no doubt she could cope. The family business would go on in leaps and bounds, probably more so now that there was a kinder hand fully guiding it. We'd spoken nearly every day on the phone, and our relationship had improved to the point where we'd already agreed on a date for her to come and stay with us for a week or so.

The paperwork for the agreement we'd made with Clayton's family still hadn't come through, but Anthony had said that, given I needed to sign them in the presence of a lawyer and a witness, he'd bring them down to me as soon as they did.

We were going home this afternoon, having already said goodbye to everyone who mattered. This was the last thing on our list.

Two lines appeared.

I closed my eyes, a weird mix of excitement, joy, and apprehension swirling through me.

I'd dreamed for so long now of my blonde-haired, blue-eyed little girl that I wanted nothing more than to bring her into this world, wrap her in my arms, and give her all the love and attention and encouragement that had been missing from my childhood.

The apprehension stirred from the fact that I had no idea if I'd be doing it alone.

"Hardly alone" came Belle's wry comment. "Not when she'll have not only me and Monty, but also the two self-assigned grandfathers and babysitters currently pacing the hall."

"It's positive?" came Ashworth's query.

"It is," I confirmed. "But no one can tell Aiden until I say so, and you definitely can't mention it to Monty. That man cannot keep a secret."

Footsteps echoed, and Belle stepped to one side, giving the two men room to enter. In two seconds flat I was wrapped in their arms and given the biggest bear hug ever.

"Okay, okay," I said, with a laugh. "Enough. We have a plane to catch, remember?"

Ashworth laughed, kissed the top of my head, and then grabbed my suitcase and headed out the door. Eli repeated the process with my handbag.

"I'm pregnant, not incapable," I called after them. "And you can't be doing this sort of shit once we get home."

"At least not when Aiden or Monty is near" came Ashworth's reply from down the hall.

I snorted, linked arms with Belle, and headed after them. "You heard from Monty?"

She rolled her eyes. "Yeah. The Ford is at the mechanics, the Mustang has some sort of drive shaft damage because he hit a pothole, so he's asked Ashworth if they can just drop us off at the café."

"I never understood why he insisted on driving us there anyway." I glanced at her, and my lips twitched. "Oh, that's right, the long kiss goodbye."

She nudged me but didn't deny it. I laughed and added, "Why the café?"

She shrugged. "He let slip something about a cake. I think he's planning a welcome home party."

"You haven't been gone that long."

"According to him, it's been centuries."

"For him, or his little swimmers?"

She grinned. "The latter, no doubt. The man definitely has an appetite."

Samuel and Saska were waiting out front. Apparently, they'd wanted to make sure we got to the airport safely. I was of the belief it was more to ensure we actually left.

As Saska had said when my statement was being taken, shit sure had gotten interesting since our arrival.

We'd said our goodbyes to Belle's parents last night. Belle hadn't wanted them at the airport today, because she didn't want to cope with the goodbyes and the tears that would invariably happen. Hers as much as theirs. They hadn't argued, which I did find a little surprising, but then, they'd already made plans to spend time with us over Christmas, which wasn't all that far away now.

It didn't take us long to get to the airport and through security, and in no time at all, we were on the way home.

It was a good hour and twenty drive from the airport to Castle Rock, but the closer we got to the reservation, the more my heart sang. I'd spent half my life looking for home and family. I had it now, and I was never going to lose it.

Ashworth pulled to a halt in front of the café and switched off the engine. "Mind if I use the loo? I don't think I'm going to make it home."

Belle raised an eyebrow but didn't comment. She just jumped out of the car and raced for the door, her suitcase forgotten in her eagerness to get inside and see her man.

She opened the door, stopped dead, and said, "What the fuck?"

I stopped behind her and peered past. The café had been decorated to the nth degree. There were streamers and balloons and flowers everywhere. But that wasn't all. Everyone we considered a friend was here. Belle's entire family was here, including her grandparents.

Aiden was there and, just for a moment, time seemed to

stop, and he was all I could see, all I could smell. All I wanted.

The desire to rush over and throw myself into his arms was so strong that I took a step forward.

Then common sense hit, and I stopped.

Too much remained unsaid between us. Until all that was sorted, I needed to be careful.

Then Monty stepped forward, devilment in his eyes and his grin wide.

"What the hell have you done?" Belle said, her voice a mix of amusement and love. "It hasn't even been two weeks. Hardly a reason to throw a party."

"On that, we agree, my dear witch."

"Then why go to such—"

She stopped abruptly, shock reverberating through her. Monty reached into his pocket, pulled out a small red velvet box, and dropped to one knee in front of her.

"Isabelle Nelinda Kent, I fell in love with you at school and have spent most of my life searching for an emotional connection that got anywhere near the depth of my feelings for you back then. Fate bought me to this reservation and the realization that you are the other half of my soul. If this near fortnight has proven anything, it's that I can't risk losing you again."

"Monty, I..." Belle's voice faded, but her joy was so fierce it was sun-bright.

I wasn't the only one with tears in my eyes.

"Isabelle Nelinda Kent," he repeated softly, "will you marry me?"

"Of course I'll fucking marry you," she said. "Now get off your knees and kiss me, you damn fool."

He laughed and obeyed.

The celebrations ran long into the night.

ALSO BY KERI ARTHUR

Blackbird Crowned (June 2021)

.

Kingdoms of Earth & Air

Unlit (May 2018)

Cursed (Nov 2018)

Burn (June 2019)

The Outcast series

City of Light (Jan 2016)

Winter Halo (Nov 2016)

The Black Tide (Dec 2017)

Souls of Fire series

Fireborn (July 2014)

Wicked Embers (July 2015)

Flameout (July 2016)

Ashes Reborn (Sept 2017)

Dark Angels series

Darkness Unbound (Sept 27th 2011)

Darkness Rising (Oct 26th 2011)

Darkness Devours (July 5th 2012)

Darkness Hunts (Nov 6th 2012)

Darkness Unmasked (June 4 2013)

Darkness Splintered (Nov 2013)

Darkness Falls (Dec 2014)

.

Circle of Death (July 2002/March 2014)

Circle of Desire (July 2003/April 2014)

Ripple Creek series

Beneath a Rising Moon (June 2003/July 2012)

Beneath a Darkening Moon (Dec 2004/Oct 2012)

Spook Squad series

Memory Zero (June 2004/26 Aug 2014)

Generation 18 (Sept 2004/30 Sept 2014)

Penumbra (Nov 2005/29 Oct 2014)

Stand Alone Novels

Who Needs Enemies (E-book only, Sept 1 2013)

Novella

Lifemate Connections (March 2007)

Anthology Short Stories

The Mammoth Book of Vampire Romance (2008)

Wolfbane and Mistletoe--2008

Hotter than Hell--2008

ABOUT THE AUTHOR

Keri Arthur, author of the New York Times bestselling Riley Jenson Guardian series, has now written more than fifty-five novels. She's won a Romance Writers of Australia RBY Award for Speculative Fiction, and six Australian Romance Readers Awards for Scifi, Fantasy or Futuristic Romance. The Lizzie Grace Series was also voted Favourite Continuing Series in the ARRA Awards. Keri's something of a wanna-be photographer, so when she's not at her computer writing the next book, she can be found somewhere in the Australian countryside taking random photos.

for more information:
www.keriarthur.com
keriarthurauthor@gmail.com

facebook.com/AuthorKeriArthur

twitter.com/kezarthur

instagram.com/kezarthur

CPSIA information can be obtained
at www.ICGtesting.com
Printed in the USA
BVHW031646280223
659404BV00004B/35

9 780645 303179